PATHWAY TO DARKNESS

Published By ChrisWayne via Draft 2 Digital & Ingram Spark

Paperback ISBN 979-8-9852761-1-4
Ebook ISBN 979-8-9852761-0-7

"Technology is good, but we must never place technology above humanity - the day we do, will be the day we fall. And perhaps, we have already started to fall!"
— Abhijit Naskar

"Artificial Intelligence will not destroy the world. Our irresponsibility will destroy the world."
— Abhijit Naskar

"The least scary future I can think of is one where we have at least democratized AI...[also] when there's an evil dictator, that human is going to die. But for an AI, there would be no death. It would live forever. And then you'd have an immortal dictator from which we can never escape."

—Elon Musk

"You never change things by fighting the existing reality. To change something, build a new model that makes the existing model   obsolete."
— Buckminster Fuller

"You may live to see man-made horrors beyond your comprehension."
— Nikola Tesla

Thank you to my creator for bestowing this

gift upon me. All glory to God!

Thank you to my family for supporting

me in pursuit of a childhood dream. Without

you this life would be far less fulfilling.

I love you more!!!

1 Our Most Pressing Need

President Elizabeth Bullock entered the conference room, taking a seat in the middle on the right-hand side of the conference table. While very clearly decisive in her decision-making, she was not particularly compelled by tradition. She opened the binder in front of her, tapping her William Henry pen on the binder rings. The Cabernet Amethyst pen was the last birthday gift her late husband had given her. He'd always incorporated her birthstone into every gift. The pen was never out of her sight and was placed intentionally in the same spot on the nightstand while she slept. The pen was a constant, yet comforting, reminder of his sacrifice. Having glanced in greeting to those standing around the table, she stated somewhat hurriedly, "Okay, folks, let's get this meeting started. Please take your seats."

"Yes, Madam President."

"Do we need a call to order?"

"No, Mr. Vice President, this is not an *official* emergency session of the National Security Council. General Brooks simply asked for a few minutes with those of us in attendance to discuss the growing unrest in Latvia."

"Thank you, Madam President." With a nod to the president, Vice President Jose Aman began to brief the situation.

"Let's dive right in. The government in Latvia is facing mounting pressure from the provisional governments of Estonia and Lithuania. Since the leaders of those countries approached Russia regarding annexation, and the leadership of Belarus is signaling their intent to do the same, the Latvian president is extremely concerned. The leaders of the European community are seeking to meet with the leaders of the four countries but, to date, have been unsuccessful in their attempts to do so. Meanwhile, it has become evident to the world community that the citizens of these countries do not favor the annexation; they want to remain independent. We've been asked by the Latvian president to provide assistance and any intervention that we can provide without affecting an escalation that could lead to violent conflict in the region. That's the gist of it, Madam President."

"Thank you, Mr. Vice President." Bullock swiveled in her chair to face General Robert Brooks, Chairman of the Joint Chiefs.

"Chairman...General Brooks, I know you've been reviewing the situation for some time now, since the talks first started about a year ago, what is your assessment?"

"Yes ma'am, I've been keeping a very close eye on the intelligence reports from LTC Colne. Bill is the best of the best, and I've yet to find fault in any of his analyses. In fact, he has been on my radar for the better part of the last fifteen years. If Bill sees a problem, you can rest assured, it's a problem that needs attention. That being said, Madam President," the general replied, "from a military standpoint, there is absolutely nothing I can offer you with regard to resolution of this issue. Any action we take with military involvement is going to prompt a response from Russia, and we don't have enough assets, nor can we move them into the area fast enough to repel any attempts by the Russian military to secure those countries."

"What are our options for covert missions in the area?"

"We have assets we can deploy, but again, we're talking about a large theatre of operations here. We can get special operations forces into the area, but..."

"But what? We have the best operators in the world. Why is there a but, Bob?"

"Madam President, the *but* is the location and covert nature of the operation that would be inherent to its success. That, unfortunately, takes time to plan and execute in order to maximize the opportunities for success. Please keep in mind this is very different from what we've been doing in the Middle Eastern area of operation, and we've been doing that for thirty years."

"So, we have no planning at all in place for operations in the European theatre? That seems to me like a lack of foresight. Like...well, like we've been caught with our pants around our ankles."

"Madam President, I can't really argue that point. It's clear there are shortfalls in the operational planning that my predecessors undertook. I can't speak to why that is; I can only tell you what our current capabilities are and suggest some alternatives."

"Bob, let's hear those alternatives."

Before the general could speak, Travis Lepis, Secretary of the Treasury interjected, "Madam President, I think we should be very careful when discussing alternatives to established governmental, military, and Security Council process and procedure. We have, for several years, maintained a close relationship with the Congress. In doing so, we have, for all intents and purposes, ensured our recommendations will be approved before they leave this room. If we stray from that tried-and-true process, we risk the Congress losing faith in this council. I'm certain nobody in this room needs me to tell them where that leads."

"Thank you, Secretary Lepis. I'll take that under advisement. Please, forgive me; I know you are quite knowledgeable. However, in this particular instance, it is my belief that the members of this council, whose day-to-day jobs are to scrutinize intelligence information, military posturing globally, and strategize response scenarios, will have the more appropriate inputs. Not that yours isn't important, it is. Please don't misinterpret what I'm saying. Surely you understand."

"I do, Madam President, and I have to agree with what you said. I simply want to caution against taking action that could alienate the Congress from this council."

"Duly noted. General?"

The general's expression became more serious as he folded his arms on the table and turned his gaze to the president. "Madam President, this is clearly an unconventional situation."

"How so?"

"Well, Mr. Vice President, it's unconventional from several aspects, but the glaring issue I see is this: What I understand from this council, based on email communications over the last 24 hours is that the council wants to quell the annexation talks completely. There's only one way I see that happening and that is to remove the leadership from those countries, thus enabling the opposition leadership to gain control of the government and military forces. That's clearly what the citizens of the countries want to happen as evidenced by the protests." Brooks paused, taking a moment to look directly into the eyes of those seated around the table; they stared intently back at him. The tension seemed palpable. His gaze shifted as he looked into the president's eyes and began to speak again.

"Diplomacy appears to be failing at every turn, Madam President, and military intervention will absolutely escalate into regional conflict with significant loss of life. That loss of life will be primarily innocent civilians, which will create a cascading effect of unrest throughout the region."

Absolute silence filled the room. Everyone was staring intently at the president, awaiting her response. She closed the binder in front of her and pushed it to the center of the conference table. For thirty seconds, she sat seemingly admiring the pen she held so dear. She slowly scanned the faces of those staring intently at her before turning to General Brooks.

"Bob, what I'm hearing, that is, reading between the lines, is we need to affect the removal of the current leadership of those countries. Without military involvement. Without assistance from other countries, because we're not going to get support diplomatically or militarily. How exactly does one do such a thing? It would seem as though this is clearly a SpecOps mission, but you've also told the council SOF is not prepared for such a mission." She leaned back in her chair, lightly tapping her chin with the amethyst pen. "So, to recap. No military solution will work. No diplomatic solution exists. No SOF solution is available. What *exactly* are we left with?"

She'd barely finished her question before Brooks answered, as if he had anticipated it. "The only avenue left, Madam President, is an unconventional and unacknowledged approach. One that can be legitimately disavowed by this council and our government, across the board."

"Dare I ask if such a solution currently exists?"

"Madam President, there may be a *cure* for what ails us."

"Really?" The president held the general's gaze for a few seconds before glancing at the vice president, obviously passing silent acknowledgment between them. "I understand, Bob. At this point, I'm going to raise the classification level of this meeting, I have to ask everyone except the vice president, General Brooks, and Director of National Intelligence Huber to excuse themselves."

"Madam President, this is highly irregular, and I strongly advise you to reconsider."

"Duly noted. Vice President Aman, please annotate that Secretary of State—"

"I believe I can speak for my contemporaries when I say we all feel the same way, Madam President."

The remaining Cabinet Secretaries nodded in agreement. The president grinned and turned to the vice president.

"Well then, Vice President Aman, please note that the remaining members of the National Security Council have voiced their objection to the change in classification of this emergency meeting, as voiced first by the Secretary of the Treasury Lepis, and subsequently by Secretary of State Dolner, Secretary of Defense Stringe, and Secretary of Energy Humbolt. Ladies and gentlemen, your objections are duly noted."

"I thought this was an *unofficial* meeting, Madam President."

"What meeting? Now, please clear the room."

The room was silent, save for the shuffling of papers by those ordered to clear the room. Bullock turned to the lone Secret Service agent, now standing just inside the conference room, and nodded just as the last person walked through the doorway. He returned her terse nod and closed the door behind him as he exited. She walked to the head of the conference table and pressed several buttons on the keypad. There was a barely audible click as the magnetic door locks engaged and the almost silent buzz of white noise filled the air. The room was totally secure with no possibility of signals entering or exiting.

"Bob, let's drop the formalities and get to it."

"Yes, ma'am."

General Brooks' demeanor clearly demonstrated the gravity of the situation and the information he was about to disclose.

He knew the timing was perfect, and despite the potentially explosive nature of the information, he was certain Beth would maintain the level-headed objectivity that had fueled her success. After all, she'd come a long way from the green-horn Pentagon intern Captain Brooks had first met almost 30 years earlier.

"I've come to learn that, almost 40 years ago, a former operator known only as Arthur, created a company called TIACE, Tactical Insertion Action Control Extraction. This was in the days of the Vietnam vets turning into soldiers of fortune...guns for hire...mercenaries. What made TIACE unique? Arthur was a certified genius...a technology wizard.

"Computers were just becoming household items in the mid to late eighties and early nineties, when he was getting this company off the ground. He was ahead of the game and began to work with the idea of robotics. This was all done out of sight of the public, the government, and the scientific community. It's our understanding that Arthur had a walking, talking humanoid robot that could reason at the child level in 1994."

"Wait..." Beth motioned with her hand for Brooks to stop. Her brow furrowed in clear frustration. "Why have I not been briefed on this before? This Arthur had AI in the form of a humanoid robot in the 90s?"

"Beth, it's plausible deniability...protection for you. The only person in this room besides me that knew any of this is Keith, and he's only just become aware of it since taking the DNI position. Jose was unaware as well."

"So, the vice president and I, the senior-most members of the government, not even the NSC chairman are *cleared* to know this?"

"All due respect to you and your positions, but there is a great deal of classified information that the two of you and the majority of the federal government are not privy to, and that is by design. If you knew, you would be likely to try and implement some the programs, initiatives, technology, and other black projects that are being developed in the dark recesses of our national infrastructure.

"I can assure you that the general public doesn't want to know about it. It would give them nightmares, as it would likely do the same for you. It's left to those of us who are willing to sacrifice themselves in any and every way for this country. I'm sure you feel as though that's what you would do. However, we need leaders, like the both of you, to be able to lead the country without benefit of trying to hide these things, that's why. Plausible deniability is an absolute must for your positions and those of the other members of the Executive and Legislative branches. It's up to people like me and Keith here, to bring specific items, relevant to the current situation to bear at the appropriate time."

"Bob, I get it. I understand it. I agree with it. But I don't like it...not one bit."

"Understood. I'd likely have the same opinion were I in your shoes, which, by the way, I do not envy." Brooks glanced at both the president and vice president, both quickly nodding acknowledgment. Taking a deep breath, he continued.

"As I was saying, Arthur and TIACE had a walking, talking humanoid robot in 1994. TIACE was still doing basic soldier of fortune jobs, under the radar, and very effectively avoiding surveillance. There was no indication they were still operating until months after their mission was complete. Those missions funded TIACE's ability to invest, and they made great investments in the stock market, which led to millions of dollars for investment in advancement of the technology.

"Fast forward six years. In 2000, the reports indicated the advancement of the technology was exponential. In the reports, there was a quote, allegedly from Arthur himself, stating: 'The humanoids are now operating autonomously within our facilities. They are integrating alongside their human counterparts, capable of sustained conversational response and reasoning. We believe that, within the next five to ten years, they will be capable of mimicking their human counterparts, thus becoming virtually indistinguishable in society.'"

The vice president shifted in his seat, leaning forward as if he was going to speak, but Bullock spoke first. Her words were delivered calmly, in almost a whisper. "Bob, please tell me this isn't true. This can't be true."

"Beth, the technology exists. It's mothballed, but it does exist. According to the reports, TIACE was liquidated in 2012. Five years ago, my predecessor was in talks with TIACE regarding tactical robots that could be remotely controlled. It was part of an initiative to gain a tactical advantage on the battlefield and preserve human life. Arthur pissed off the Chairman, and as I understand it, the Chairman leveraged unacknowledged assets to bankrupt the company and eliminate Arthur and his top technical advisory staff members responsible for the advancements. Once that operation was complete, the Chairman had the files, computers, and tech seized and stored at an undisclosed facility in the Midwest."

The president sat silently, twirling her pen. Jose and Bob both knew that twirling indicated her anxiety was rising quickly; however, her expression never changed.

"That's almost too hard to believe...any of it. But I'm failing to see where this is going."

"I understand how hard it is to believe. I struggled with that as well, but I've come to grips with the reality. The reports have been vetted and validated. It is very real, and I know where the technology is being stored. It is my belief that this technology is our solution. If it is, in fact, as advanced as indicated in the reports, it would be possible to activate these humanoid robots, make them look like Jane or John Doe, give them all the documentation and social media presence a John or Jane Doe would have today, and send them on vacation to these countries. Once there, it is my belief they could affect the elimination of the leaders in question."

"You're suggesting we use robots to assassinate world leaders? How can you suggest such a thing?"

Brooks leaned in toward her, staring intently into her eyes. "There are no other options. We've already discussed the possibilities. Nothing else will work. *This* might not even work, but we can program these robots to be any nationality. To speak any language. Imagine this: We send one of them into Belarus. The unit speaks Belarusian and Russian...with Russian credentials. It attempts to assassinate the current leadership and fails. Who's going to be blamed? Not us."

"Keep going."

"What I'm suggesting is we take definitive action with the assets we have available. I'm happy to resign my position as Chairman and establish the organization to take care of these sort of issues. To take care of them, while allowing the government completely disavow any connection or knowledge of the actions."

Beth shook her head. "I won't accept your resignation, Bob. That option is off the table. We will need a string to pull within the government to access these assets. That is, should we decide to travel this dark path."

"I suspected as much. I do have an alternate plan. My second-in-command, General Hodge, is aware of this and has voiced his desire to work with me on this initiative. I'm certain he would be willing to take the lead."

All informality evaporated as Beth rose from her seat. "Gentlemen, I've heard all I need to hear at this point. Any objections for moving forward? Any questions?"

Huber and Aman remained silent, both staring intently at a point near the middle of the table. The general was clearly assessing the reactions to the unsettling disclosures. With nothing heard, the president's decision was made and the order issued.

"It's Spring 2017 in Washington DC, and I've been in office four months. I'm already dealing with a global crisis on a scale that my predecessor only had nightmares about. Make no mistake, we are going to act decisively." Beth's gaze landed directly on Brooks. "General Brooks, I'm entrusting you with this situation. You will report to me, and *only* me regarding this. No one outside the individuals in this room and General Hodge are to be briefed on any of this discussion. This stays between the five of us. Understood?"

She looked intently at each of the men as if she was staring through them, awaiting their acknowledgment.

Her final words before exiting the conference room were spoken with the barest hint of resignation and trepidation. "God help us all if this blows up in our faces."

"Not going to happen, Beth," Brooks replied. "Not going to happen."

2 The Establishment

Bob walked out of the room and made his way to the staff car waiting outside. Once inside, Bob wasted no time calling his Executive Officer to initiate the retirement process for General Hodge before calling the man himself.

"Bob, what can I do for you today?"

"I'm on my way to see you. Please make sure we have a secure space to chat. Just the two of us."

"Not a problem. I'll send my staff out for lunch; we can chat in my office."

"No, your office isn't going to work for this discussion."

"Ahh, understood. The tank is available."

"Great, I'll be there in fifteen minutes."

Bob continued to mull over what approach he would take with his friend and second-in-command. Hodge was a no BS kind of guy. Bob knew any attempt to sugarcoat what he had to tell him was not going to go over well; it never did. Blunt and straight to the point was the best and, really, only solution.

Bob walked with intent through the corridors to the interior-most ring of the Pentagon and descended to the subterranean office where Hodge was waiting just outside the door. Hodge motioned for Bob to lead the way to the Joint Chief's conference room, aka the tank.

"You made good time. It always seems to take me twenty minutes or so to make that trip."

"I have an excellent driver."

"Apparently. Come on in and take a load off."

Once inside the tank and seated, Hodge offered food and drink to Bob, which he graciously declined. Truth be told, he was afraid he would not be able to keep that food down. Hodge made Bob nervous. Something about his always stern, always direct, and seemingly never wrong approach. He was direct, often viewed as harsh, but it had served him well. Troops were intimidated by his presence but, ironically, also settled by it. Strong leadership tended to have that effect.

"What's on your mind, Bob? Looks serious."

"Yes, and I'm not going to beat around the bush." Brooks sat up even straighter than his usual, almost perfect posture and took a noticeably deep breath before diving in. "I've just left the NSC meeting. I volunteered you for something, and I'm not altogether sure you're going to be happy with what I suggested and the president signed off on."

"Let me get this straight. You volunteered me for something and the president, in her infinite wisdom, has already signed off on it? I guess the only say I get in this is how I vote in the next election?"

"No, you always have a choice."

"Doesn't much sound like that to me, Bob. What *exactly* is it that I have been volunteered for? Dare I ask? Do I want to know?"

"Retirement, among other things."

"Get the fuck out of here." Hodge's message came across somewhat dismissive and disrespectful, much like the smirk he now wore.

Bob stood and pounded his open palms on the conference table, leaning toward a seated Hodge.

"Listen, you strong-willed, pigheaded, son of a bitch...let me fucking finish."

"Fine, Bob. Finish. But, for the love of Buddha, will you sit down? You look like you're about to have a stroke."

"Hodge, we—the NSC—need you to retire and take on another mantle...another job that is going to play a critical role in the future of our country and especially our ability to react under the radar, anywhere in the world."

"You now have my undivided attention. Please elaborate."

"You remember the TIACE dossier?"

"Yes, indeed. That was a remarkably interesting read."

"Well, the NSC just signed off on establishing an organization with no ties to the government to pick up where TIACE left off. And with you at the helm."

"Hmm... When do I start?"

"Wait. Are you serious? It's going to be that easy?"

"Yes, Bob. A new kingdom for the King. That's right up my alley. It's off the books. Ample funding...I'm assuming. And I get to be in charge. Pretty much the perfect gig for me. Why on earth would I object to something like that?"

"Well, for one, you didn't have a say in it."

"But you just told me I did. I don't much care for liars."

"C'mon Hodge, you know exactly what I mean. Wait, did you just refer to yourself as a king?"

"Yes. And *you* know *exactly* what I mean."

"We have an understanding then."

"Great. I have no need for pomp and circumstance. We'll have a very small retirement ceremony here in the conference room. It'll take thirty days or so for that to happen. I can start terminal leave immediately after the president signs off on my retirement orders, which I have to assume can be completed today?"

"Yes."

"Already in the works, huh?"

"Could possibly be on her desk already. It's been an hour or so since I left the White House, so yeah. Most likely on her desk by now. Or at least on the way there."

"Excellent. I'll have my staff gather some boxes and assist me with getting them into my vehicle. I need not come back once I leave today."

"Don't you think that's a little quick and just a bit suspicious?"

"Yes, exactly. And no, the speed at which this is happening is perfect. You call for a private, no-notice meeting with me. A meeting for which my entire staff has been asked to vacate the premises. When they come back, I'll inform them that I have been asked to retire and that today will be my last day. They'll be left to speculate. They'll probably think I finally crossed a line with the wrong person, and the president is tired of my bullshit. Trust me when I tell you, this isn't going to raise a single hair on any of their necks."

"Well, when you put it like that, I suppose you're right."

"Okay then... I should probably start gathering my things."

"Yes. One last thing, Hodge. Call me on a secure line tonight or in the morning. I'll provide you with all the information you need to get started."

"Roger, wilco. As always, it's a pleasure."

"Certainly is. Talk to you soon."

"Tonight."

* * *

Hodge did exactly as he planned. He informed his staff, and they assisted him with packing his personal effects and loading them into his vehicle. On arriving home, he didn't bother removing the boxes from his vehicle since he was clearly about to be heading directly to his new job. Instead, he grabbed a couple of suitcases and packed his clothes. Once done, he made the call to Bob from the secure landline in his home office.

"I was beginning to think you weren't going to call."

"Always true to my word, Bob."

"The facility is in Wyoming. I'll send the directions and security information over to you via secure fax, when we're done with this call. We still need to figure out how to refer to this organization so we can communicate in the clear if needed."

"You mean The Organization."

"Yes, that's what I said."

"No, Bob. We're going to call it The Organization. It doesn't get more vanilla than that."

"I guess not. Yeah, that will work."

"What else do I need to know?"

"I need you to review the transcript from the NSC meeting today."

"Yep. Already did that. Good read. I have a full understanding of the expectations. What I need to know now is..."

"Staffing."

"Staffing, exactly. Where the hell do I get a staff that can pull this off with equipment that may or may not work, and technology that most, if not all, of the *cleared* talent pool has never worked with?"

"Well, what I didn't relay to the NSC is that I already have a staff working the issues. Have been for several months."

"Beth will not be pleased."

"Beth's not going to know."

"That's clear. Safe to assume the staff will be expecting me?"

"They are. Should have a demo ready for you by the time you arrive. I expect 2-3 days travel, since you drive everywhere."

"That sounds about right. Can't trust something I don't have control over when my life is on the line."

"So, I've heard."

"Anything else?"

"No, safe travels, my friend."

"Thanks. I'll let you know when I arrive."

As soon as Hodge received the faxed information, he left. Having already packed the essentials, he was on the road to Wyoming. The excitement of the challenge he was about to take on was fuel aplenty to keep him driving straight through, stopping only for gas, food, and restroom breaks. The last few miles of his journey were on largely unmarked dirt roads that appeared to be leading him into a vast wasteland of high plains desert.

The navigation application on his phone was useless without a cell signal, and he was now relying on the brief look at directions he'd seen just before losing the connection. As he was about to turn around, he saw what appeared to be a fence line in the distance. As he grew closer, he could now see a small guard shack and a couple of men. He pulled slowly up to the gate, and the men approached with what appeared to military issue tactical weapons at the ready.

"Excuse me, sir. Your name, identification, and purpose of visit?"

"I'm Hodge. Here's my ID. I'm the new man in charge of this facility."

"Mr. Hodge. Pleased to meet you, sir. We were not expecting you until sometime tomorrow."

"I couldn't wait to get started."

"I see. One moment, sir."

The guard returned to the small building and picked up the phone. The call lasted only a few seconds, and he returned to the vehicle.

"You're clear to go, Mr. Hodge. If you just follow this road, you'll come to what looks like a runway with a small building on the far side and a hangar on the back side of the building. There's a phone on the door on the west side of the small building. Just pick up that phone and tell them who you are, and they'll be up to get you in a few minutes."

"Thank you. You fellas have a nice day."

"You as well, sir."

Hodge drove through the gate and followed the road for several more miles before reaching the building. Just has the guard had indicated, there was a phone on the west side of the building that Hodge used to inform them of his arrival. A few minutes later, a woman with red hair answered the door and said nothing more than, "Follow me." Despite his several attempts to engage her in conversation, she did not utter a word. Not one word on the way to the elevator, while in it, or when leading Hodge to a conference room.

Upon entering the conference room, a man in a lab coat stood and greeted Hodge. "Welcome, Mr. Hodge." He looked at the female and nodded. She simply turned and walked away, closing the door as she left the room.

"Not very friendly, that red," Hodge observed.

"Mr. Hodge, did you have a good trip? It was quicker than expected."

"Yes, it was fine, thank you. About red?"

"Could I get you something to eat or drink, Mr. Hodge?"

"Water would be great. Are you going to tell me about the redhead or not?"

"Let me get that water for you. I'll be back in a moment, Mr. Hodge."

The man left the room, and Hodge was alone. He was in disbelief and immediately began to question the decision to take the helm of what appeared to be a severely dysfunctional organization. No sooner had that thought crossed his mind than a video-teleconference started. As he looked up to the TV screen, he saw Bob staring at him.

"Bob? What the hell have you gotten me into here? What's with all the Mr. Hodge bullshit. I must have heard my name a dozen times. Is it some BS protocol you put in place?"

"It'll all make sense soon. I'll try and explain a bit, before HP1 comes back with your water."

"HP1?"

"Humanoid prototype one. The redhead too. She's slightly more advanced but currently programmed with a singular purpose, which was to deliver you safely to the conference room without saying more than 'follow me'. Seems to have carried out the instructions pretty well."

"I'm impressed already, Bob. I had no idea the technology was this advanced."

"It's coming along nicely. But I have my doubts that we'll be able to deliver on my proposal to the president."

"C'mon. This is me you're talking to; that was never the intent. You just took advantage of the situation to get her to sign off on this so you could get her to fund it. And to secure your position as the new DNI, which you start in two weeks."

"Don't miss much, do you?"

"Well, I had a lot of time to think on the drive out here."

"HP1 will take you to the lab. Dr. Fergin is the lead engineer and current site lead. He will get you up to speed.

I'll caution you, don't expect much more than what you've seen already. We have the best available minds working on this, but there is a piece missing, and they're just not sure what that is at the moment."

"No worries. I'll report back once I have my feet underneath me. We'll figure it out."

"I trust you will. Talk soon."

Brooks was correct. Hodge spent the rest of that day, and well into the night that followed, with Dr. Fergin. It was clear the technology and the staff's understanding of it was lacking significantly. Without consultation, he directed Dr. Fergin to ghost-write a message for him that he would proof and send to Brooks, outlining the needs of The Organization to effectively develop and deploy the proposed technology. He further directed Dr. Fergin to simultaneously begin a search for individuals with the specific skills required and forward that to him as well. He was clear that he wanted a list of preferred individuals, regardless of their current employment status.

Hodge had no intention of failing. Brooks had big aspirations, but they paled in comparison to Hodge's. He had become immediately aware of the vast potential of the technology of which he now had control. Brooks wanted to develop the technology and get rich from it. Hodge wanted that as well, but he was more interested in the power the technology would provide him. If it could be perfected, and he could control it, nobody would be able to tell him no.

Hodge edited the message Dr. Fergin sent to him and forwarded it to Brooks. Having left out the procurement of subject matter experts, he focused his message on funding. Bob simply had the money obligated to a contract with The Organization. Similar contracts were approved often when dealing with the sort of operations that needed a bit of ambiguity. Brooks notified Hodge of the approval for funding and that of his official retirement date in forty-five days.

Hodge spent the next month crafting his plan for The Organization. During this time, the leadership in People's Republic of China voiced their opposition to the planned annexation of European countries by Russia. A meeting was brokered between the countries, and as a result, the annexation was stopped. The provisional government leaders of the countries requesting annexation stepped down and fled to Russia, and just like that, the crisis was over.

* * *

Two weeks prior to Hodge's scheduled retirement ceremony, Bob received word there was an accident involving Hodge. To Bob's dismay, it appeared as though his friend had perished in a fiery car accident. He was beside himself.

He began scrambling to compose a message to the president, to inform her of his intent to resign and continue the work Hodge was just starting but was interrupted by a call on his secure line.

"Hello?"

"Bob, my dear friend. How are you today?"

"Hodge? What the fuck is going on? I just got a message ten minutes ago that you died in a car accident."

"Dammit. That message was supposed to be delivered to you after I called. I'm sorry, old friend. I intended to give you a heads up." Hodge's gaze faltered for a microsecond. "Look, I really didn't want to attend that retirement ceremony."

"So, you faked your fucking death? Tad extreme don't you think?"

"No. Exactly what needed to happen. Look, if I'm going to be successful out here, if The Organization is going to be successful, the world at large needs to think I'm dead, and The Organization needs to maintain as much anonymity as possible. Much cleaner if I'm out of the picture."

"So, based on what you're saying, am I to take away from this conversation that the president, vice president, and the chairman are to be kept in the dark? If that's your intent, they'll shut down funding, and try to reclaim the funding they've already sent."

"It's already gone without a trace, and the shell company that accepted the transfer of funds is already defunct, Bob. Things move fast when you're trying to remain invisible."

"This isn't going to go over well. They're going to launch an investigation. Since they have access to the *cure*."

"Location of the *cure*. Be specific. Yes, they do, but location information has been redacted, if you recall. Only two people on the planet are aware of the correlation between this location and the information to which they have access. I'm certain I can count on you to protect that information. I *can* count on you, can't I, Bob?"

"Of course. They do, however, know the facility that TIACE worked out of is in Wyoming. It won't take long for them to pinpoint your location."

"On the contrary, there are two TIACE facilities in Wyoming, Bob. They may track down one of them, but I can guarantee you it will not be this one. I never brought my personal vehicle here. Cell phone either. There's nothing to trace; it all burned, Bob. I thought it necessary to move the primary operations to the secondary site. We have a bit of work left to do in order to bring this location up to speed, but it's bigger and better hidden. Perhaps you can come for a visit?"

"That's not a good idea. At least not until the drama that is about to explode on Pennsylvania Avenue is over."

"Fair enough. I'll be keeping tabs on the situation. Once it's done, the drama that is, I'll fax you over a map. What you do with it, well, let your conscience be your guide. Until then."

With that, the conversation was over. Bob was relieved but only momentarily. Now he had to face the president, vice president, and the chairman and lie to them. What could possibly go wrong?

As he was gathering his thoughts, his assistant entered his office to tell him that he was about to receive a visitor, the one individual he least wanted to see at the moment. Before his assistant could close his office door as she left, the president entered.

"Madam President—"

"Bob, no need for formalities. I heard the news and wanted to come see you. I know you and Hodge were friends. I'm deeply sorry for your loss."

"Thank you, Beth. It was quite a shock. But I've tried to maintain focus on what needs to happen now."

"That can wait."

"No, ma'am, I don't think it can. I never received any reports on the activities of The Organization from Hodge, prior to his accident, which concerns me. It is quite unlike him to fail to meet a deadline for reporting. Personally, I would like to make a visit to the facility myself. There is also the question of the funds. I have no idea where the funding has been transferred, no reporting on that either."

"What are you saying, Bob? You think he was up to something inappropriate?"

"No...er, I don't know, to be honest. But *we* need to know. The best way to find out is to visit."

"We can put a team together."

"Actually, Beth. Given the inherent sensitivities surrounding The Organization, I think you and all privy to this can agree we need to maintain as low a profile as possible. It cannot be an official visit. I was thinking, maybe I need to take a vacation, to grieve and say goodbye to an old friend."

"I see. Not that you need it, but I approve of what you are proposing. No objections from us."

"Thank you, Madam President."

"Bob?"

"Thank you, Beth."

"Of course, stay safe. Make sure you let one of us know if you need anything at all during your trip."

"Yes, ma'am. Thank you again, all three of you, for your support."

Once the door was closed, Bob sank into his chair. He was shocked and in a state of disbelief at the scene that had just played out. After sitting with his eyes closed for a few minutes, he began to make plans, securing a rental car for his trip, and a hotel stop along the way. As he was gathering his personal belongings to leave for the day, a fax began to print. He had almost forgotten Hodge's words regarding the map.

Two pages printed. The first was a map of Wyoming with a highlighted path of highways and back roads. The second was a message from Hodge.

" Way to cowboy up, Bobby.

I'd forgotten just how advanced your ability to spout bullshit on a whim actually is. Safe travels. Would hate to see something happen to you; you're a fucking national treasure."

Although he was not certain what it was, he knew Hodge was up to something. His messages had gotten cryptic, and their conversations were no longer those of friends. Bob felt more of a friendly adversary to Hodge than the friend he had once been. Perhaps he would figure that out during his visit.

3 Sinister is as Sinister Does

Bob had made his travel arrangements himself, attempting to disguise his visit as a vacation to the Midwest. However, he expected The Organization to be tracking his every move. Hodge had made a point to track the five government officials who were aware of The Organization and its purpose at all times. Bob knew this and knew that the guise would only benefit him in the DC region. He was certain Hodge would be expecting him but not the topics of conversation he had planned.

He approached the location indicated on the faxed map but wasn't expecting what he saw. There was nothing for as far as he could see. Brooks stopped the vehicle on the side of the road and stepped out. He muttered a single statement that said it all. "That son of a bitch." It was now clear to Brooks that Hodge had no intention of being on anyone's radar. He could only hope that Hodge would reach out to him at some point.

Bob returned home and back to work. The president was not pleased that The Organization seemed to evaporate upon Hodge's death. She stopped short of holding Brooks accountable. She did, however, subtly suggest that it was, perhaps, a fitting time for Bob to transition to a civilian position. Bob understood the concept of suggestive retirement and faithfully complied with the president's suggestion.

The president placed Brooks in the DNI position three months after his failed attempt to locate The Organization facility. He adjusted to his new role rather quickly and enjoyed great success. It was almost four years later when he received a rather unexpected message. He'd almost deleted the email and wasn't altogether sure how it slipped past the SPAM filter. It was the 'Enjoy the great wide open... Enjoy Wyoming!' subject line that drew him in.

The message contained within was rather simple, and he knew exactly who it was from. There was a map with a single dot marked in the middle of nowhere and a handwritten message. "It's time..." was written very clearly by Hodge's hand.

Bob notified his chain of command that he needed to take leave to visit an ailing friend. He received approval almost immediately and made his travel arrangements, hoping he wasn't heading out on another wild goose chase. He flew into Denver and drove a rental from there, heading toward the small town represented as nothing more than a blue ink dot on the map he'd been sent.

As he approached, he could see it wasn't really a town, more of a roadside stop in the middle of nowhere. A café, garage, gas station, and two houses. That was it. He walked into the café, not knowing what to expect, only to find Hodge waiting for him.

"You're an asshole!"

"Ah, well, look what the cat dragged in. How are you, Bob? Good to see you, my friend."

"Seriously? Three and a half years after you send me into the middle of nowhere? You had to know what would be waiting on me back in D.C. What the fuck was that all about?"

"Three and a half years, how can that be so?" Hodge very briefly appeared ever so slightly apologetic. "No matter. Perhaps...mistakes were made."

Brooks felt as if his head would explode. He could not fathom how Hodge was apparently oblivious to the trouble he'd caused him. Though the veins in his neck were pulsing, Bob managed to calmly respond.

"Perhaps? Have you completely lost your mind? All sense of rational, logical thought? Do you have any idea how much ass pain you caused me?"

"Bygones... How are you enjoying the new job, Mr. Director of National Intelligence?"

At that moment, Brooks realized he was not going to get the answers he wanted. He also knew that if he pushed the issue too far, Hodge would send him packing and that would be it. He had to swallow the modicum of pride he had left. He had to revert to the business of his last planned trip and hope for the best.

Once he felt the flush of his face fade and the pulsing in his arteries subside, he looked at Hodge in quiet resignation. Bob took a moment, and a couple deep breaths, before speaking again.

"So far, so good. I was hoping to bend your ear for a bit. I have some things I want to discuss with you."

"Sure thing; I'd like to give you a tour of the facility while you're here. I wasn't expecting you to arrive so soon."

"I'm sure. How long have you been expecting me, exactly?"

"Oh, long enough for me to let security know you're cleared and walk up here from my office."

"You were clearly behind the email that ended up in my spam folder. I know it was you because you're the only on that ever calls me Bobby. You knew before I left DC, I'm sure."

"Details are not that important. Let's go chat in my office."

Hodge led Bob into the kitchen area of the café to the walk-in freezer. He waved his security badge over the door handle to the freezer, then opened it. As the door opened, the freezer lifted to reveal an elevator. The men stepped in and began their descent.

"Pretty slick, don't you think?"

"You have this installed?"

"No, this was here. I'm guessing Arthur or someone else within TIACE dreamed this up, but they did it right, let me tell you."

Moments later, the elevator stopped, the door opened, and they stepped out into what was eerily reminiscent of the Agency headquarters lobby. The facility itself was fairly vanilla beyond the lobby, no open workspaces, aside from the entry control point. Everyone worked inside office spaces. It looked almost sterile. There were no pictures on the walls, no sort of decorations at all. As they made their way to Hodge's office, there were nothing but closed office doors and plain eggshell white walls to be seen. His office, on the other hand, resembled a speakeasy lounge.

Extravagant cherry bookshelves and desk, red-velvet upholstered chairs, a wet bar, and fake fireplace. It was rather surprising to Bob, although he chose not to comment. He was not there to critique the décor. He was there out of concern, and the conversation would not be an easy one.

"So, here we are. Please, have a seat. Can I get you a drink?"

"Actually, I'll take a bottle of water if you have one."

"Sure thing. I, myself, prefer a bourbon and ginger highball."

"Maybe later."

"Here you go. What's on your mind, Bob? You look somewhat troubled."

"A bit. I do have concerns. I think there are some things that we need to discuss."

"Such as?"

"We got lucky with that Latvian issue. If China had not exerted the pressure on Russia to denounce the requests for annexation, we could have sent in untested and decidedly imperfect technology."

"That's true; it would have made a bad situation a lot worse. We have since learned from the testing by The Organization that technology would have failed miserably. It simply was not ready for prime time"

"It would have done exactly that. But we were able to expand The Organization and this facility, as a result, and work on perfection of the technology."

"Facilities, Bob. Facilities."

"What other facilities are there?"

"I don't want to cut you off in the middle of your prepared diatribe. But I think it would benefit you if I did and brought you up to date on The Organization."

Brooks sat back in his chair and stared intently at Hodge, hoping his befuddlement wasn't obvious.

"I'm all ears."

"A few months after The Organization was established in the fall of 2017, it became apparent that in order to respond effectively, we needed to expand beyond this largely underground facility in Wyoming. If we were going to establish and maintain a posture to deploy assets globally, we need to place assets strategically throughout the states. So, we began looking into that.

"What we have ended up with is a multi-threaded approach. We had to establish the model upon which the non-human assets would be developed. This, naturally, led us to looking at the best and brightest among the SOF assets our great country had to offer. Once, Beth accused me of playing God; do you remember that?"

"Yes, I do remember that uncomfortable exchange."

"Well, that comment got me to thinking. Who exactly did God send to do his dirty work? The Archangels, right?

So, who better to serve as my Archangels than the most effective agents of death on our planet? We began a recruitment and retraining program."

"Why retrain if they're already the best at what they do?"

"The retraining wasn't geared toward their skillset of death and destruction. It was geared toward ensuring loyalty to The Organization. Can't have my Archangels going rogue, now, can I? So, we called upon the retraining techniques used back in the Cold War and before. Now, this next part may be a bit much for you to stomach, so hear me out." Hodge leaned forward, placed his elbows on his desk, slightly bowed his head, and closed his eyes. He rubbed his hands together for a few seconds, before stopping with his palms together...thumbs pressed firmly into his brow. Then he sighed, crossed his arms, looked up, directly into Bob's eyes, and began to explain.

"That program consisted of eliminating their every tie to this world. Nasty job but necessary. It *was* brutal, and we unfortunately lost a few potential candidates in the process. But we have seven very well-behaved Archangels on staff now."

Brooks turned pale, clearly appalled at what he'd just heard. Black ops were often filled with nasty business to accomplish military objective...but on home soil? It was unconscionable to Bob.

"So, you eliminated their families, and somehow that endeared them to The Organization and loyalty to you? How the fuck does that work?"

"Language, Bob." Hodge now looked somewhat perplexed and perturbed with Brooks.

"Yes, that was the first phase. The second phase was completely breaking their will. I must tell you, that took some time. Almost a year for the one that would become the leader of the team. But Michael is the epitome of loyalty now. The others follow his lead without question, and he follows my direction in the same manner."

Bob was having significant difficulty believing what he was hearing, let alone finding a path to acceptance. He was aware that he was in Hodge's arena. If he wanted to be allowed to exit, he would have to find that acceptance somehow. Feigning acceptance was not going to work for him. He was hesitant to ask but had to know the extent that The Organization was expanding.

"So, you said a multi-threaded approach. You established the model for the non-humans. What are the other threads?"

"I can see that you are obviously having a hard time stomaching this. You sure you want to keep going? You can't just unhear the things I'm going to tell you. Your plausible deniability is fading fast, my friend."

"I'm sure. In for a penny, in for a pound."

"Suppose so.

"We expanded our reach through establishing new facilities. We bought land through surrogate companies. Most of which came from State or Federal government auctions. We have facilities in Florida, Tennessee, Virginia, Louisiana, and South Dakota, to name a few. Twelve new locations to be exact. The facility in Tennessee is the first to go operational. The intent with that facility is recruitment. We have found a need for different skillsets, outside the obvious scientific and technological. For example, it would behoove us to understand the global political climates, socio-economic climates, etc. So, we're looking to recruit intel analysts. To pull that thread a bit more, we need someone to take that analysis and develop a plan.

"Relying on the original plan of taking the government or military plans and implementing them was flawed. Those plans are developed, in large part, based on traditional military planning of wartime engagements. That's not what we do. The Organization is non-conventional, non-military, nontraditional, non-fill in the blank. Therefore, we must abandon that line of thinking. How? We retrain them. Not unlike we did with the Archangels. At Michael's suggestion, we are going to approach this retraining somewhat different. We have technology advanced enough that he believes that we can utilize it, and not so thinly veiled threats toward loved ones, to affect their loyalty."

"And if that approach fails?"

"If it fails, we make an example out of them. We record the whole example-making process and incorporate that into the retraining program. I think that will likely inspire the loyalty we're striving to achieve."

"Forgive my bluntness. That is rather sick and perverted. We go way back—"

"Bob, I'm going to stop you there, before you cross a line. The last thing I want is for you to become an example."

"You arrogant motherfucker... Are you threatening me?"

"Yes, I am. And I would caution against calling me arrogant or a motherfucker again, or I'll make an example out of you right here in my office. Understood? You, more than anyone else, know I'm capable. I'm sure I don't have to remind you about my wayward princess of a sister. I wouldn't let anyone else execute her, but it had to be done. It was the principle of the matter."

Bob was in the exact position he feared he would find himself. Though he had come with the intent to maintain the moral high ground, to the extent one existed in the black ops realm, it was clear there was one path, and one path only...the dark one. With that realization, Bob had but one choice, join the fray or become a statistic.

"Yes. I understand. It's obvious that we have to work together. I don't want to be at odds with you."

"You've always had a surprisingly good sense of self-preservation. I am happy to see that it is very much alive and well within you today. I didn't really want to have to take any aggressive action toward such a good friend. But, as you must have realized, The Organization comes first. It's not personal; it's business."

"Got that loud and clear. What now?"

"Now? Well, now we get down to business. We managed to, *save*, a potential asset for The Organization. I won't go into much detail at the moment, but she was an elimination target with an exceptional skillset. A biochemical engineer was desperately needed to advance our initiatives, so we faked her demise. We didn't fake her brutalization prior to that demise. Those events had to unfold naturally;

otherwise, we would not have achieved the desired goal. But enough about that. I doubt you want to hear about her torture or that of her daughters. It was a lot to take in, even for me.

The corners of Hodge's mouth turned upward in the slightest of grins. He loved making people uncomfortable, and he had a knack for it. He was particularly happy to see the blood drain from Bob's face as he turned ghostly white. But it wasn't enough; it never was.

"Anyway, the point I'm getting to is this. She has enabled us to advance our prototypes significantly. I doubt you could distinguish between the prime subject and the non-human mimicking them. I cannot in most instances. The importance of this is crucial for you to understand and embrace. We, the five individuals that planned this a few years back, will be the first to employ our non-human likeness into the real world."

"You want to replace the sitting president and vice president...with a robot? Are you out of your mind?"

"Perhaps, but this plan is not indicative of that. Bob, we have tested this already with local law enforcement. It works. The local sheriff was replaced six months ago, and life has gone forward without incident. Now, he is a single man who does not date. No kids, no family to speak of...at least none that he communicates with. He was the perfect test subject, and we have kept close tabs on him. It's my intention to be the first of the five. No date set as of yet, we're still working through the retraining of our new engineer."

"I thought you had already accomplished that. How else could you benefit from her expertise?"

"Great question. We have found that we are able to sync human consciousness with the non-human, making them effectively a humanoid life form, in a manner of speaking. It was through that process, that we were able to leverage her experience."

"Non-humans sync'd with human consciousness? How is that even possible?"

"With the engineer's expertise, we were able to create what amounts to a synthetic brain. That's a gross over-simplification, but simply put, that's what it is. With that advance, we bought ourselves time to *retrain* the engineer while continuing our forward momentum. The sheriff is, well, our beta test."

"I'm still trying..."

"Don't bother, just accept that it is, and move on. Threads... Yes, the other threads. Analysts, well we've been leaning on our limited analytical staff to review the records Arthur started. Did you know that he started vetting intel analysts back in the nineties? Probably not, but he did. There is obviously a gap of a few years, but we did notice a few names from his list, toward the top, are still very much in the game. The top spot has been held by the same individual for several years. Primarily, because he was continuously picking up on the frayed and sparsely separated threads of TIACE. Of course, this caught and held Arthur's attention through his apparent disappearance. And before you ask, there is no actual record of what happened to Arthur. That is, unfortunately, still very much a mystery. As I was saying, there's an Air Force officer, quickly approaching retirement, that we're eyeing closely."

"I have a feeling I know exactly who you are talking about. If I had to hazard a guess, I'd say he used to work directly for the current head of the Agency, Marvin Marso, back when he was a general on active duty."

"Keen intuition, Bob. We most certainly are tracking the very same individual. You know anything about Bill, yourself?"

"Only by reputation, and it's about as exemplary as one could be. Don't you think it's going to be damn near impossible to recruit such a high-profile officer. That guy's a shoo-in for a high-level position within the Agency."

"I think with Marv's assistance, and yours, we can do pretty much anything we want to do. Now that you're coming on board as my second in command."

"I..."

"Don't fight it, Bob. Embrace it."

"But I can't just walk away..."

"You're not. You have met with an unfortunate accident in which the body could not be recovered. It's all over the news already. Don't take my word for it, here, watch it for yourself."

Brooks was visibly shaken, but it wasn't so much the news of his untimely death. It was that he was only just starting to truly understand what The Organization was becoming. Worse yet, the unexpected realization that one of his best friends and colleagues was a certifiable psychopath had cut him to his core. He had two options: embrace death or embrace Hodge and The Organization, and he wasn't ready to die.

Hodge turned the TV on to the national news. The reports were coming in that the sitting Director of National Intelligence had been in a fatal accident. The reporters were citing multiple sources indicating that the DNI lost control of his vehicle and veered off a bridge, plummeting over one hundred feet into the shallow river below. The vehicle had been found but no body had been recovered thus far. Indications were—based on the condition of the vehicle and significant amount of blood remaining in the unsubmerged part of the vehicle—he did not survive. Subsequently, the efforts were now being called a recovery effort. As soon as the topic shifted, he turned the TV off and returned his gaze to Bob.

"See, Bob. You are free and clear of all attachments in this world. You no longer exist. Nobody is looking for you. Well, they are looking for your body, which they will not find. The blood will be determined an exact DNA match for you. Maybe I'll explain how we managed that at some point. Point now is, they won't find your lifeless body unless you decide it's better to try and cross me or The Organization. I'll make sure they find it, personally, if you choose that route."

"No, I'm on board. What is it exactly that you want me to do? What is my role within The Organization?"

"You sure? You're not looking so good right now."

"No, I'm fine. I don't think my lunch is agreeing with me."

"Oh, okay then. So...as I was saying, you will sit at the helm of The Organization, but I will be running things from behind the scenes. The five will become four for a while, until my non-human form is ready for prime-time."

52

"So, you want me to work with Marv to secure the asset, until you're ready to beta test Hodge 2.0?"

"Yes, exactly. We need Billy boy on board."

"Okay. I'm on board."

"Of course you are. What other choice do you have? Oh, Bob, ever the optimist. Let's go take a look at your office and get you up to speed. There's a meeting with Marv that I'd like you to handle in a couple months."

"I can hardly wait."

4 ID the Anomaly

Although not pleased about it, Bob accepted his new role, and the level of anonymity that it provided. Hodge had informed Marv, via encrypted email, that Bob would be taking the helm while Hodge, himself, was on sabbatical. He stated health issues as the reason, which Marv accepted without a second thought. After all, Hodge was a bit overweight, only a couple hundred or so pounds, give or take fifty. Marv accepted Hodge's invitation to the Wyoming facility to discuss his concerns and wishes with Bob.

Upon his arrival, Bob greeted Marv much the same way that Hodge had greeted Bob. The spiel was much the same, appearing to leave Marv with the same sense of foreboding. Bob could see the concern appear as Marv's brow furrowed, and his eyes squinted. But the conversation from there played out quite differently. As they entered the office, Bob's demeanor changed.

"Marv, please have a seat. Look, brother, I apologize for the doom and gloom speech. It's the standard pitch around here."

"Not exactly the kind of pitch that endears people to you, Bob."

"Tell me about it. Here's the deal, Marv. I aim to listen to what you have to say, but to be honest, it's not going anywhere. Hodge has already made the decisions. You have two options."

"Let me guess: Accept it or have an unfortunate accident."

"That obvious, is it?"

Marv's posture straightened, and he leaned toward Bob. "Yeah, that obvious. Face it: Only a half dozen people are privy to The Organization. I mean that really know about it. You also know news travels fast in such a small *community*. That, coupled with the untimely deaths of two prominent military leaders who were on the ground floor of the unacknowledged program, well, I may not be a smart man, but I believe two plus two equals four, no matter where you're educated."

Bob chuckled under his breath, grinned, and nodded in acknowledgement. Marv was no idiot. Based on his comments, it was clear he had done his due diligence and was at least somewhat more prepared than Bob had been for his meeting with Hodge.

"Fair enough. I want to talk to you about a fella that worked for you... Intel analyst type, and supposedly the best around."

"That's what this meeting is about? Of course, it is. The Organization needs someone to decipher the socio-economic and geo-political landscape so they can exploit the weaknesses. There truly is nothing out of bounds for—"

"Marv, tread lightly," Bob snarked malevolently.

Marv sighed and sat back in his seat. "Yes *sir.* Bill Colne. Bill is the guy you're talking about."

"Yes, tell me about Bill. What can you tell me about him that I don't already know?"

"I don't know that I can tell you anything you don't already know. I suppose you've read the reports."

"No, actually, I have not. I intentionally avoided that because of this meeting. I wanted to hear from you first."

"Well. I mean, the guy's a legend. He's a rock star in the intel community. He basically re-wrote the standard by which intel analysts do their job and hone their craft."

"I gathered that. What I want to know is the dirt. How? How did he do it?"

"By being right 99% of the time. He was just getting started about the time Arthur began ramping up TIACE. It appeared he was going nowhere back then. He kept drawing correlations between soldier of fortune activity, mass purchases of electronic components, and significant stock market investments. His leadership thought he was crazy. He got his ass handed to him several times over the three or four years he chased TIACE. Until he nailed them to the wall. He found a way to tie TIACE to a surrogate company making the purchases. Then the investments in the stock market and payments for soldier of fortune activities in a couple Central American countries.

"It didn't really go anywhere, because it was taken over and subsequently squashed by the Agency. We know why today, but back then, it just pissed off Air Force leadership and strained their relationship with the Agency."

"Interesting, what else?"

"Well, there was the WMD debacle. He stated repeatedly there were none, only to be told to shut up and color. He was right on that. He basically led SOF to Hussein, told them he would be within a certain area...less than a quarter-mile square. Right again. He predicted the Russian president shell game. He predicted the oil wars between Russia and the Saudis. They call him Nostra-damn-us. Although, not to his face. Happened once; he was not a fan. Only time I am aware that he lost his cool in uniform. He was working for me at the time. Thankfully, I was there to step in and shut it down. Otherwise, he might have kicked the shit out of the dumbass lieutenant and gotten himself court-martialed. Bill... He's an anomaly, Bob. There's only one like him."

"What about his family?"

"That's a whole different story. An odd one at that. Prior to 2012 or 2013, he had no family on record. Now, I didn't know that until I was in my current position. I just always assumed everything was kosher there. Apparently, he'd wanted to shelter them from the military machine. If not for his spotless record to that point, he might have been booted, but the Air Force just added them to their systems and let it go, apparently. It's still a bit of a mystery though."

"Hmmm, that is odd, to say the least. So, I'm assuming that if I told you I wanted him on board that you would be agreeable and willing to assist me?"

"Not really, but do I have a choice?"

"No."

"Well, in that case, I think he'd make an excellent addition to the team. I will caution you though: He can spot bullshit ten klicks away. You try and snow him and he'll find a way to bury our asses. I don't care how anonymous you are or how well organized you are, or how well you plan. He'll turn your world upside-fucking-down. Write it down on your calendar so you don't forget I told you that."

"Done. How soon can we approach him?"

"I thought you guys wrote the rules around here."

"We do, but I don't want to approach him prior to his retirement."

"Okay, well you've got about six months or so, based on last word I heard from him."

"Perfect."

"You want me to reach out to him?"

"Yes. I want to you offer him a stay in a cabin near Poultry Ridge, Tennessee. Tell him it's one of those MWR, you know, morale, welfare, and recreation spots the Air Force has contracted. That should not raise any suspicions since the MWR department has contracted locations all over the country. I'll have the details sent to you later. You need to encourage him to get away without the kids. That could get really messy."

"I don't think that will be an issue. They split a couple years back, but it looks like he and his other half are trying to work things out. This would be a perfect gift to them to assist in rebuilding their relationship, post retirement."

"However you want to frame it. Just get him there. It will provide the perfect environment for us to observe him more closely."

"Observe?"

"Yes, observe. You can learn a lot by watching someone around the clock for a period of time."

"Observe only, right. Is he going to have a say in this?"

"That's the intent. But I make no promises, Marv. Uncle Bob wouldn't want to end up lying to you."

"No, we wouldn't want that, would we?"

5 Bob's Your Uncle

Marv now found himself in a position he didn't want and couldn't get out of easily, if at all. To make matters worse, he now had to pull a good friend into the fray. Bill was responsible, in part, for Marv progressing in rank more quickly than most. Marv had benefitted far more from the relationship than Bill. Marv was single, and although both were career driven, Bill did have a family. Ultimately, the career won over everything else as Bill followed Marv, per Marv's request, with every promotion. By the time Marv retired, he had pinned his fourth star, and Bill had managed to be promoted from Major to Colonel. Bill's career had flourished, but his familial relationships had suffered.

Marv knew Bill's intent to retire and that he was in the process of mending fences. Bill and Sarah had been together for most of their lives. Ultimately, they decided the family should settle, and Bill would make any future moves alone. Bill had followed Marv solo and lost time that he would never get back.

Marv knew pulling Bill into the grasp of The Organization would likely destroy Bill and his reconciliation efforts with Sarah. He was certain their friendship would not survive, but what choice did he have? There was clearly one choice and better to get it out of the way. Marv's sense of self-preservation was clearly greater than any loyalties he was assumed to have.

Marv was hesitant, but he picked up the phone and called Bill.

"Hey, Marv. How are you? It's been a little while."

"Hey, Bill. Yes, it has. Still adjusting to this new position. Ya know, I thought the politics of being a general officer was bad. That was a cake walk compared to this position."

"Ha. Well, we did talk about that."

"Yes...yes, you warned me. I knew it was going to be different, but nothing like it is."

"I'm sure you'll figure it out; you always do."

"Let's hope so, and sooner rather than later. Say, Bill, I heard you made the decision to retire. What prompted that?"

"Well, I suspect you probably already know the answer to that. It's Sarah and the kids. I've missed so much with them, and if I take a promotion now... Well, you know exactly how that's going to go. I can't miss any more."

"No, I understand that completely. I did suspect that was the reason. That, in part, is why I called."

"In part?"

"Well, I mean, I wanted to catch up with you as well. But I'd heard this was happening, just not when. So, happens, that I got wind of something the day after I heard the retirement news that made me immediately think of you."

"I hope it's not another job working for you...not sure I could stomach that, Marv."

"Ha, very funny, smartass. No, not a job at all. We are asked to look at prospective MWR vacation rentals and provide a threat assessment. Someone finally got their head out of their ass and figured we might want to make sure any facility that we're contracting isn't in the middle of a suspected sleeper cell hot spot."

"Makes way too much sense."

"Right? So, anyway, this place we just completed is in Tennessee. It's a beautiful place, peaceful, large cabin, nobody around for miles. Only available to retired General officers and civilian equivalents. Now, I know that technically excludes you, but I want to gift a stay there to you and Sarah."

"Marv, that's... I don't know what to say."

"Yes, would be an appropriate response. Maybe a thank you as well?"

"Um, well, I should talk to Sarah about it, but yes, and thank you. The kids will..."

"Bill, sorry to cut you off. I want to gift this to you and Sarah. The two of you need some time alone. Your oldest kids can easily hold down the fort for a week. I'm certain they will understand the need for the two of you to be alone. You are, after all, working to rekindle your relationship; this is a perfect opportunity for that."

"I don't know, Marv."

"Look, I can always cancel the reservation. Call Sarah, discuss it, and let me know. Today, if you can."

"Sure. I'll call her as soon as I get off the phone with you."

"Okay, well, I actually have to go so I can prepare for my first of five meetings today. You have my email; send me a quick note once you've convinced Sarah to go."

"Ha, yeah, you know as well as I do that's easier said than done."

"Yeah, but you're pretty good at it. Great talking to you, Bill. We'll chat soon."

"Sure thing, Marv. Thanks again."

Marv wasn't altogether certain this plan was going to work. Bill loved the kids, and it was going to be a tough sell to Sarah. He had to have a backup plan but had no inkling what that was going to be.

* * *

Bill, on the other hand, was excited at the prospect of having alone time with Sarah. Time alone with her was exactly what they needed, but he, too, expected it would be a tough sell.

Bill was never one to procrastinate, so he jumped on the opportunity and called Sarah immediately after hanging up with Marv.

"Well, hello. I wasn't expecting a call from you so early. What's up?"

"I got a call from Marv."

"Bill?"

"No, not about a job. This is something pretty awesome."

"Yeah, now I'm not so relaxed. I've heard that before."

"Seriously, Sarah, relax. Marv is gifting a stay at one of those MWR vacation rentals we looked into a while back. This one is for general officers only, so obviously really nice

"What's the catch?"

"No catch. Well, one catch."

"There always is with Marv."

"This catch is a little different though. He wants to give it to just me and you, no kids."

"I can't believe I'm saying this, but this is actually a pretty great idea."

"So, I can let him know that we're going?"

"Sure, why not? Let's do it."

"My retirement ceremony is three weeks from Thursday, I'll see if he can reserve it starting on that Saturday. That work?"

"Sure. Whatever. Just let me know when I need to be ready to go."

"I'll let you know once I hear back from him."

"Sounds good."

"Love you."

"Yeah, love you, too, you thick headed, smart ass."

Bill was so excited; it was a full minute before he realized he'd hung up on Sarah again. He emailed Marv with the dates immediately and, to his surprise, received a response within an hour confirming them. Bill and Sarah would finally, after twenty years, have some time alone...just the two of them.

* * *

As soon as Marv confirmed the dates with Bill, he called Bob. Marv had hoped Bill or Sarah would have declined his offer, giving his conscience a bit of relief. Now,

Marv had to bear that burden and feared more would be piled on as this ruse progressed.

"Good morning to you, Marv. I trust you're calling with good news?"

"I suppose it depends on your point of view, Bob."

"On the contrary. There is but one point of view: The Organization's. I thought you would have accepted that by now."

"Forgive me. Still working on that."

"Not a lot of that to go around here, Marv. But that's something that I'm certain you already know."

"Yes, that I do know. So, yes, good news. Bill and Sarah have agreed to my offer. Three weeks from this Saturday."

"Three weeks from this Saturday, for one week? Or two?"

"I only offered a week, based on our conversation. Should it have been two?"

"No. One is fine. I'll make the formal arrangements with my team on the ground there and send the details to you by the end of the day for you to forward to Bill. Well done, Marv. I had my doubts as to whether or not you could pull this off."

"So did I. But it's done."

"No. It's just getting started. I'll contact you soon. Have a nice day."

Marv could only stare at the phone and shake his head. He had just betrayed a good friend and trusted confidant. Perhaps he'd even sent his friend to the slaughter. He knew The Organization was ruthless, simply based on what he'd seen and what Bob had shared with him. He could only hope and pray that would not be the case.

* * *

Bob, on the other hand, was ecstatic. The situation had turned clearly in his favor, and the top prospective analyst was now within the grasp of The Organization. That this was happening without menace, at least overtly, was even better. Bob wasted no time informing his right-hand staff of their imminent visit.

"Bob, how nice to hear from you. What can I do for you this fine day?"

"Michael, I have great news."

"Do tell."

"I just spoke with Marv. He informed me that our top prospect has accepted his offer and will be staying at the Alcove."

"Well, how about that. That is excellent news. When should we expect his arrival? And who might we expect to be accompanying him?"

"Three weeks from this Saturday, and it will be only Bill and Sarah."

"Excellent. It's a lot easier and potentially, a lot cleaner without the kids. Kids always tend to complicate things, but I don't have to tell you that."

"Completely agree with you, Michael."

"Okay then, Bob. I'll inform the rest of the team and pull them back to the Ridge."

"Excellent. I can hardly wait to hear your report."

"Yes. I'm looking forward to it. You take care now."

"Certainly...you as well."

"Hey, Bob?"

"Yes?"

"I should probably confirm this while I have you on the phone."

"What is that?"

"Well, in the event things run amok, I want to confirm we're cleared hot for erasure."

"Every step of the way. That's our standard operating procedure."

"Yes, a convenient SOP. Keeps life tidy for us."

"Indeed, it does. Let me know if you need anything further."

"Will do."

6 All Good Things

Today was the day. The culmination of twenty-eight years of faithful service to his country was finally here. The retirement ceremony was a bit of a blur to Bill. Before he knew it, two hours had passed, and his career was officially over. Now he was left to try and find a second career and, hopefully, one that would allow him to continue to serve others.

The morning following the ceremony, Bill and Sarah informed the kids they were going away for a few days.

"We're going to the mountains. And we're going without you because we have not been away together, just the two of us since before Trevor was born. Plus, it gives the seven of you a few days without us. You get to be lazy, eat what you want, and play video games all day."

That comment seemed to convince the kids this was the best idea ever.

Bill and Sarah packed and loaded the Audi Q8 they'd splurged on renting. Once they were packed, they said their goodbyes to the kids.

"Just so you know, the neighbors know how to contact us...and they will be watching you...er, I mean watching out for you. Trevor and GG are in charge while I'm—we're—gone. The rest of you don't give them a hard time, okay?"

"I think they got it, Sarah. Let's go. Love you, kids. Be good and enjoy your week of freedom."

"Seriously, Bill...you're not helping here."

"C'mon. They have it under control. Loosen up, and let's go relax for a while and let them do the same."

"Fine. Love y'all. Be good."

* * *

"So...where exactly are we headed? I-81 goes to a lot of places," Sarah asked after they'd been on the road for a couple of hours.

"We're headed to Poultry Ridge," quipped Bill.

"Really?"

Then, Sarah said something that cracked Bill up. Under her breath, with a thick southern drawl, she muttered, "Fuckin' Turducken, Tennessee...here we come."

That opened the lingering barriers between them completely. They were so distracted that the trip seemed to be over in minutes, instead of the hours they'd been on the road. Sarah broke the silence with a revelation, "We're in the boonies, Bill. And I have no cell service. How are the kids supposed to get in touch with us if they need us?"

"Relax. There's a phone in the cabin. I gave the number to the neighbors, and I left the number on the fridge along with instructions of what to do if they cannot contact us at that number. I left Marv's number and instructions to call him if they cannot contact us. It's all taken care of. Now, try to relax, okay?"

"All right. I feel better knowing that."

"Good."

Bill noticed the dense forest seemed to thin a bit just ahead, and before he could say anything, Sarah saw it as well. As they rounded the next bend in the road, the forest opened up to a lush green field with a cabin at the far edge.

"That can't possibly be where we're staying." Sarah said, fairly shocked at the size and beauty of the house.

"It must be. I don't see any more houses around. This place must have cost millions. Maybe I should have stayed in long enough to make General...if this is how they get to live after retirement."

"No. It's beautiful. But it's just a house. It's a nice one. I mean, *really* nice. But it's still just a house. You made the right decision. Family...us, that's what's really important."

"Yeah, I know. But still...this place."

"No buts, Bill."

"Yes, ma'am. You're right."

"I never get tired of hearing that."

"Funny..."

"Hey, while it's still light out, why don't we go explore this property. We can check the house out later."

"Sure, that sounds like fun."

They took their luggage into the house and left it in the foyer. They walked out the French doors that opened up to a massive deck and admired the view of the brilliant green grass and the pond that sat on the far side of it. They walked together for what seemed like hours through the forest. The walking paths had been cleared, and Bill was just enjoying the time with Sarah in the beautiful outdoors. The paths seemed to end at a small creek with a large meadow on the far side.

"Is this the property line?"

"I don't think so, Sarah. At least not according to this. Here, you look at it and see what you think."

"Yeah, I think it is. See, this line must be the creek."

"But then what is this line?"

"I think that's the trail we passed a while back."

"Well, since we're not sure, why don't we cross the creek and keep going?"

"Who are you?"

"What do you mean?"

"Crossing this creek clearly takes us over the property line."

"So?"

"So? So, that's breaking a rule, Bill. You don't break rules."

"I don't see it that way."

"Oh, really?"

"Yes, really. Look, I saw the map on the pamphlet differently than you. While it appears you may be correct, I still have my doubts. So, not technically breaking a rule."

"Seriously? This is me you're talking to."

"Sarah, I know. I'm trying to loosen up. It's not easy, so can you just go with it?"

"Okay. I'm just not used to this from you."

"Yeah. Well, I'm trying."

"I can see that. I appreciate it."

"You're welcome. Now, let's find a way across this creek without getting soaked."

"Well, we could strip and carry our clothes over our heads."

"That's a mountain stream, Sarah. Maybe *you* are okay with it, but I'd prefer to find a spot where maybe I can just take off my shoes and not get more than knee deep."

They walked along the creek until they found large rocks they could walk across without getting wet at all. They made their way across the meadow and down a path through the trees on the other side. Fifteen minutes later they could see another opening through the trees. As they stepped out of the forest into a second meadow, Bill froze in his tracks and grabbed Sarah's arm.

"What is it, Bill?"

"Look. The trees on the far side."

Bill had spotted some eerily familiar signs. He had seen them before, just once in his career. They were clearly related to governmental activities, but these particular signs were typically found only at the most secure facilities. And based on their unique coloration, it was a contractor facility. The only time he had seen these particular black-bordered signs was during his pursuit of TIACE, early in his career. These signs had been in place for quite some time. They were dirty and faded from what had to be years of exposure to the environment. But, regardless, Bill knew it was time to turn around.

"What are those?"

"A sign that we need to turn around and head back to the cabin."

"Bill? Why do you look rattled?"

"Do you see what those signs say?"

"I can make out no trespassing, but that's about it."

"Well, the rest of the words are government property, use of deadly force authorized."

"What the fuck? What facility is this?"

"I don't know. And I don't care at the moment. We need to go."

"Yeah, let's go."

They turned and retraced their steps back to the cabin. Not much was said as Bill maintained a healthy pace. As they neared the meadow between the pond and the cabin, Sarah spoke. "Hey, can we slow down now? I don't think we're being followed."

Bill sighed and turned to face Sarah. "Yeah, I guess you're right."

"So, can you tell me why you're so freaked out now?"

"I don't know if you remember back in the beginning of my career when I was trying to get my leadership to investigate a connection between the soldier of fortune activity in Central America and a company involved in IT procurement and some odd stock market activity?"

"That was a long time ago, Bill, but I vaguely remember that. I remember you being really frustrated for years that nobody would listen to what you were telling them."

"Yes, that's exactly what I'm talking about. TIACE was the core company, and I can't remember the exact name of the surrogate company, something like A&R IT service. Anyway, that's not important...right now. Signs, like the ones on those trees, were in images I saw of other companies that I traced back to TIACE."

"You think this one of their facilities?"

"Well, they're no longer in existence. But I suspect someone in the government is probably tracking whatever is on the other side of those signs. That's something that we do *not* need to get caught up in."

"Bill, based on the way those signs look, I don't think there could possibly be any activity there...not for years by the look of it. If there was—" Bill started to speak, and Sarah cut him off. "No, just hear me out. If there was, wouldn't they make sure those signs were clearly visible? They would not allow them to look the way they do. They would make sure they were bright, clean, and extremely easy to see. Whatever is there has to have been defunct for a long time."

"You know I sometimes forget what a great analyst you were... I mean are."

"You're the analyst. I'm a woman, that's how we roll."

"Ha...yes, ma'am. But you were right there with me. You, quite often, helped me put the pieces together. I would not have been so successful if not for you."

"That's true. But you're the one who found all the pieces—to every puzzle—that you ever solved. That's all I'm doing now."

"Yeah, I mean, you're right. If that place was active, they would have taken much better care, and the signs wouldn't look that way. They would be very bright and clear. Actually, based on the way those type of organizations work, they'd have an eight-foot chain-link fence with concertina wire at the top."

"See, just needed a bit of a different perspective."

"Yes."

"Better?"

"Yes, ma'am."

7 Tickets Please

"Well, that was unexpected. He's only just arrived," Michael, leader of the Archangels thought aloud. He had viewed their arrival but stopped viewing the feed and focused on his work when they entered the cabin. As was often the case, something, call it a gut feeling, told him to look up from his work. Just as his gaze fixed on the security camera feed, Bill and Sarah were re-entering the cabin. He decided to visit Gabriel, his security expert, to see exactly what was going on top-side and why he didn't receive a phone call regarding the boundary alert email he'd received *after* Bill and Sarah had returned to the cabin. They had expected Bill to explore the property, but he was ahead of the projected pace. Michael began speaking to Gabriel as he neared the door to his workspace.

"Gabriel, you let me down. I got a boundary notification, albeit after our subjects had returned from their exploration...and no call from you."

"Well, Michael. I had some update patching to do on the surveillance systems and thought I had enough time to do that before Bill decided to start exploring."

"Yeah...no worries, buddy. Just giving you a hard time. He is a special case."

"I have a bad feeling about this one, boss. Being the first of his kind...they make me nervous."

"Gabriel, you make it sound like he's a mutant or an alien or something. He's just an intel analyst."

"I know. That's what makes me nervous."

"Nothing to fret, my friend. Let's take a look at that feed. We did capture the feed, right?"

"Yes, I have it up already."

"Look at him. Look at that expression. He's seen those signs before."

"Yeah, the eyes say it all."

"Yes sir, they do. What are you thinking, Billy boy?"

"Didn't take long for him to make that U-turn, did it?"

"No...no, sir, it did not. That just confirms he's seen those signs before. Gabriel, can you get Raphael and Saraqael to do a little research and see where and when those signs have been used before that would correlate to any analyses that Bill was involved in...say for the last twenty-five to thirty years?"

"Message sent."

"Good deal. I'm interested to see what they come back with. In the meantime, let's not do any more patching for a while. I want to make sure we're watching their every move."

"All over it, Michael."

"By the way, I know we have cameras in every room in that cabin. I'm more concerned with what goes on outside of it than I am what happens inside of it. So, let's not turn our surveillance into a personal peep show. Watching them in the bathrooms or bedrooms serves no real purpose for us."

"Understood."

"Thank you, sir. Please let me know what the boys find out about those signs and Bill."

"Roger, wilco."

Michael had learned to trust his gut instinct. That instinct had kept him alive many times in the midst of warfare, no reason not to trust it now. He had been taking steps to understand the technological resources at his disposal, and without tipping his hand, how certain technologies could be modified to enhance and potentially counteract their intended purpose. He also didn't want his team to misuse the technology in any way.

Michael knew having a full understanding of the technology was the only way he could ensure he would know if they tried. He had garnered the full measure of trustworthiness from his team, and to him, that was the key to the success of tactical operations in the field and equally important within the confines of The Organization facilities.

Complete trust, meticulous planning, and skillful teamwork would be necessary in their covert attempts to modify and test certain technologies under the radar. If OEM or any monitoring system picked up on something seemingly subversive, it could well result in erasure of the entire Archangel core. Michael knew they were always subject to the ever-watchful eyes of The Organization.

While he waited to hear back from Raphael and Saraqael, he reviewed their training plan once more to ensure it was accurate and complete. No time to miss a step, not with Bill. Otherwise, he'd pick them apart quickly. Michael, although having never met Bill, had grown quite fond of him. Michael held high appreciation anyone who'd mastered their craft, and few had mastered theirs better than Bill.

Michael did not want Bill to fall victim to The Organization, which was why he'd fought for alternative, less brutal, methods, and ultimately received the approval from Hodge—albeit begrudgingly.

As if expecting the phone to ring, Michael had his hand already placed on the handset before it rang. "Tell me some good news, Gabriel."

"You were right. TIACE facilities posted the signs. Well, surrogate companies subordinate to TIACE posted them. Bill included the signs as a note to his findings, citing

'...they were oddly colored and appeared to be custom made, possibly with the intent to fend off would be thieves, by inappropriately inferring the facility had a governmental or military affiliation...worth investigating origins of manufacture.' So, yeah, you were spot on."

"I was actually hoping to be wrong. This could complicate things. Thoughts?"

"Aww, shit. Gut feeling time."

"Yes sir. We need to pay particular attention to the surveillance systems from the buffer meadow inward. I have a feeling Mr. Bill is going to pay us an early morning visit."

"It's so dark out at that time, how could he possibly think it's a good idea to do that in an area that he doesn't know that well. And...And...he saw how dense the underbrush was."

"Just think about it. He's an intel analyst. He's just come across something he's seen before that was tied to several analyses, which eventually turned out to be valid, but nearly caused him to be kicked out of the military altogether. If that were you, wouldn't you want to know what was being protected on the other side? It's still an open-ended analysis for him. He may be retired from the military, but guys like him cannot just close the book and walk away. That case will be open forever for him unless he finds a way to connect all the dots and close it."

"But after all this time? You implying that he walks around holding on to that every day?"

"No, no, not at all. In fact, I dare say he has not thought about that in years. But seeing those signs... I guarantee you that brought it all flooding right back to the forefront of his mind, and he will not be able to let it go. Mark my words... He's going to be standing in front of the shaft before the sun comes up."

"And if he is?"

"Stand down and don't respond."

"What? That's not what we trained for."

"Yes, I'm aware. I did write the training manual, Gabriel. But we're going to deviate from the manual. Let him do whatever he does. Do not respond unless he enters the shed. Understood?"

"If he does?"

"Then you respond and bring him to me."

"If he doesn't, we'll pay him a visit the following day, after I speak with Bob."

"Whatever you say, boss."

"Trust me on this one. Bill's the ticket."

"What ticket?"

"The ticket out."

8 Brewing Storm

Since Bill retired, he'd been sleeping soundly until six or seven every morning. Now, he was awake at 4 a.m., just as he had been for most of the last twenty-five years. He had been dedicated to his fitness game throughout his military career. For Bill, being fit was less about being in great physical shape, more so exceptional mental shape. Bill's mental acuity had served him well and kept him at the top of his chosen career.

Bill had reverted to work-mode. Rather than ignore his questions about the neighboring property and try to go back to sleep, Bill decided a good run would be best in this situation. He quietly slipped out of bed and into his workout gear, which he took wherever he went. Bill crept out of the house without rousing Sarah from her slumber, taking only a bottle of water and a flashlight.

Bill could not shake his concerns or suppress the natural curiosity that had served him so well during his career. He struggled with the pros and cons of exploring beyond the signs while he stretched. *What could it really hurt to snoop around a little bit? After all, it's so dark, nobody would see me anyway, right?* he thought, as he attempted to rationalize what he was about to do. There was no rationalization in this situation; Bill knew there would be surveillance of the area, but his curiosity prevailed over logic. So, stretching complete, he headed out to see what he could see.

The full moon made it effortless for Bill to navigate the cleared paths and open meadow that led past the pond. He traveled the same path he had followed the day before, which took him beyond the pond, down to the stream. He had forgotten about the rock path through waist high water but didn't hesitate to wade in when he reached the stream. It might have still been dark outside, and it was much cooler than it had been the first time he made this journey, but it was still warm enough for him to be dripping sweat at this point in his run.

Wading across the stream cooled him off, maybe a little too much; after all, it was a mountain stream. Shivering just a bit, he slowly jogged toward the single path that led into the dense forest. Just a few feet down the path, the flashlight became a necessity. Bill preferred military type flashlights, with multiple color light filters, and opted for a blue one for his exploration, as it made it easy for him to see but more difficult for others to see him.

It was just a few minutes before he came across the signs again. The foreboding message was as clear as it had been unexpected when he first saw it.

NO TRESPASSING
GOVERNMENT PROPERTY
USE OF DEADLY FORCE AUTHORIZED

Bill paused to study the signs and the surrounding area before he proceeded. With an abundance of caution, he made his decisions at this point. He was all too aware that even though he would be difficult to spot with the naked eye, it would be exceedingly easy for surveillance cameras to track his movement, especially night-vision or infrared. Bill also knew he didn't have a lot of time, since the sun would be rising in about an hour and a half. He was praying they only had standard, run-of-the-mill, surveillance cameras, if any. But wisdom and logic were beginning to win the battle over his curiosity.

He looked around long enough to be comfortable moving forward, which he did cautiously. Easing across the narrow clearing, which could not have been more than a few feet wide, he entered the forest beyond the signs. It was dense and made progress slow. He began to immediately regret his decision when he came across a significant stand of Devil's Walking Sticks...nasty, thorny vines that were unforgiving.

He was definitely going to have to figure out a way to explain away the scratches to Sarah. *I was not paying attention, tripped and fell into some blackberry bushes,* he thought. *Yep, that should work.*

As he continued to make his way through the vines, he second-guessed himself. *Do blackberries even grow in the mountains?* Before he could finish that thought, he'd reached an area of sparsely separated pines.

Bill was able to move much more quickly now, and covering more ground in less time was exactly what he needed to do. After a few minutes jogging through the pines, he could see an opening up ahead. As he cautiously approached the opening, he could see what appeared to be a small concrete structure in the clearing. The structure could not have been more than ten feet square, with one door, a vent on the back, and what looked like another vent on top.

This discovery added to the mystery. He stared, pondering what this could possibly be before he noticed the metal tower in the corner of the clearing and to the right of the structure. The tower had a couple of small dishes and a single antenna on it and could not have been more than twenty feet tall. It was mounted on a concrete pad with the attached cables running through the middle of it into the ground.

The hair on the back of Bill's neck stood on end. *Holy crap. It's an underground facility, and they already know I'm here.* The panicked thoughts raced through his mind. *Damn, if they're here, I'm toast. No. No, I'd already be in custody. I've got to get out of here before a response team arrives. Dammit, Bill, why can't you ever leave well enough alone? Sarah is not going to be pleased.* He quickly reversed course, intent on getting back on the other side of the stream in record time. Thorns be damned, he sprinted though the forest and nearly leapt across the stream. With a big splash and a couple steps, he climbed out of the stream and continued his run back to the house. He slowed his pace significantly once he reached the meadow and could see the pond and the cabin beyond. He walked slowly around the pond a couple of times to cool off and calm himself down.

Bill's time on active duty had taken him to some fairly remote locations. Some of which were now coming back into focus and were eerily similar to what he'd just seen, although they were significantly larger. *No, those were at least twice, if not three times as big as that little building,* he thought. He could not be certain of what he'd seen, but it did remind him of some facilities he'd seen before. Those were always highly classified and on an existing military installation or government property, never in what was supposed to be a recreational area. But his concern for what it was had now been set aside for what was going to happen now.

He worried that his incessant curiosity might have ramifications for him and, more importantly, his family. *No, once they know who I am. I'll be able to explain. And I can call Marv. Yes, if this turns into an issue, all I have to do is call Marv. Whew...I feel much better now.* He finished his walk and took a seat outside to watch the sun rise.

It was nearly 8 o'clock when the first sounds from inside the house reached Bill's ears. Sarah tiptoed down the stairs and outside to join him. "Look...on the far side of the pond," Bill whispered. As she turned her gaze to the pond, they counted eight deer grazing. "Look at the size of the rack on that buck." Sarah said in amazement.

"Yes sir, I've been watching him for about twenty minutes...and I think he'd look really good on the wall."

"He'd probably taste better," Sarah countered.

They sat and watched the wildlife for ten or fifteen minutes before Sarah went back inside to make breakfast. Bill just sat quietly a few minutes more, enjoying the sights and the now peaceful feeling he carried inside.

"So...you were up and out of the house pretty early this morning. I figured you didn't hear me ask if you were all right."

"No, sorry. I didn't hear you."

"You just hanging out here watching the wildlife?"

"Yeah, for a little while. Then I decided to go for a walk. That turned into a short run. And--"

"Right...I'm calling bullshit! You look like you fell down the mountain. How did you get so scratched up? You have dried blood on your arms and legs; what the hell happened out there?"

The look on Sarah's face was one of clear concern, and Bill could see she was waiting for the answer. "Sarah, you know me as well, if not better, than I know myself. It shouldn't be a surprise to you that I had to try and figure out this...rid— not a riddle—this mystery of the signs," he stated anxiously. "In all the time I spent in the military, I've had a sense about things that I couldn't explain. This was no different. Something is not right here. Something is out of place about this, and I don't know what that is. And that bothers me in a way that I can't explain and you probably wouldn't understand."

Sarah interrupted, "I can't possibly understand if you don't try to explain it to me."

"Yes, I know. It's not that easy."

"Why? Why after all these years is it 'not that easy'?"

"Look, I'm having a tough time resolving this within myself. I'm not able to fully rationalize what I've seen. More to the point, why it's even there, what the ramifications of seeing it may be, what I do with what I know. I just know it feels *all* wrong."

Sarah now had a look of significant concern. This was exactly what he had worried would happen...the last thing he wanted for Sarah on this vacation. But here it was, and now he had to voice his worry and concern.

"Sarah, I'm sorry. I should have left this alone. It's not as easy as I thought to turn that switch off. I clearly have some work to do, re-programming myself from Active-Duty Airman to civilian. I'm so sorry."

"Well, I'm actually surprised you made it this long," Sarah offered. She could see he was not completely at ease and knew he would not share the fullness of his concern with anyone but her. So she waited until they were done cleaning up after breakfast, when they were in the midst of showering to press him further on the issue.

"So, tell me the rest of the story," she said, staring sternly into his eyes.

Bill laughed nervously because he knew she was not going to let this go.

"Why are you laughing?"

"Aside from how weird it is that we're having this conversation while showering, I know you're not going to let this go."

Bill knew he had no choice but to relent and tell her. With great hesitation, he began to explain.

"Most MWR facilities, like this one, are not typically located with or within military or governmental operations. In fact, they're purposely bought and built in areas away from such facilities and operations so the sight of such facilities doesn't interrupt the rest and relaxation on a subconscious level. The fact that the facility is there is bad enough, but it's underground, Sarah. You don't build one of those unless you're trying to keep an extremely low profile."

Sarah nonchalantly stepped out of her shower and began to dry off. He noticed Sarah's voice sounded further away. Now smiling and shaking his head in disbelief, Bill dried off, wrapped a towel around himself, and pulled back the shower curtain and re-engaged Sarah.

"So, you want to hear this or not?"

"I never stopped listening, Bill. Please continue."

"As I was saying, I get why this is an attractive location for such a facility. It's mountainous, so there's a natural security in having a facility built into a mountain. I mean, look at NORAD."

"Nukes? In Tennessee?"

"No, that's not what I'm saying. I'm just saying whatever they're doing in that facility is very low profile and probably a highly classified initiative."

Sarah was visibly unnerved at what Bill was explaining. While he did his best to calm her fears, there was no way around the gravity of his intuition.

"Damn it. Do you really, truly feel this is that significant? This is crazy," Sarah lamented.

"Unfortunately, I do. This is really... Well, it's just not a good thing at all. Something is going on here that... I don't know what, no idea what it is, but everything in me says it's something that they don't want anyone to know about."

"But they're going to think you know."

"Only if they actually have sensors...and cameras, which I didn't see, so I think we're good. Besides, all I saw was a place in the woods."

Sarah spun around, flush with anger. She slapped the marble countertop with both hands. She stared intently at Bill's reflection in the mirror. If looks could kill, Bill would have died on the spot.

"Seriously, Bill? Are you fucking kidding me? You saw signs in the woods, which you ignored. Otherwise, you would not have seen a 'place' in the woods. *If* they have sensors? You were an actual intel analyst, right?"

"Yes, smartass. That is true. But look, if someone asks me about it, I'll inform them who I am and what I did for a living until I started out-processing a couple weeks ago, and if that's not good enough, I'll call Marv. I'm fairly sure Marv can take care of this, if it comes to that."

"I hope so, Billy-boy. I hope so for your sake...and that of the kids. The last thing we all need is for you to be sent to prison."

Bill laughed out loud. "Prison? I don't think this is a prison-worthy event. They may take me in and ask me a bunch of questions, but once they realize I truly have not seen anything and don't really know anything, they'll let me go and warn me to stay away and not pursue any further information. That will be that."

"I hope so...I hope so," Sarah replied somberly as she walked out of the bathroom to get dressed.

Bill had seen and heard that disappointment from Sarah before. The last time was just before they decided to separate, and he was rather disappointed in himself. He offered an apology as he stood in the bathroom doorway, which Sarah quickly and sternly rejected as unnecessary.

"I just need to you think about the family first, Bill. I know you have an insatiable thirst for understanding that you can't help or turn off, and I don't want you to turn it off. I just need you to follow through with putting us and the kids first. That's all I want." She paused briefly as he searched for words.

"You are the greatest love of my life, and I know I'm the greatest love of yours, but we will not make it if you can't put the rest of us ahead of your aspirations and thirst for knowledge...or your absolution for the last twenty some odd years of being a breadwinner and absentee father.

Almost as if it were an affirmation from above, thunder lightly shook the house. It had only just started to become cloudy outside.

"See, even God agrees with me." Sarah's eyes sparkled as she tried to suppress the growing, smirky grin, now partially hidden by her hand.

Bill stroked the damp hair out of her face, then hugged her closely. "I can see that. And I will do better; you have my word."

They made their way back downstairs just as the clouds overtook the sunlight. "Guess we're spending the day inside today," Sarah said in her best attempt to receive a positive response. Bill stared at the darkening clouds as he quietly noted, "Yep, a storm is brewing out there." It was more than the impending thunder, lighting, or the heavy rains.

He did his best to entertain himself and Sarah for the remainder of the day. Between the board games and a long nap, they talked. Their conversations occasionally took them back in time, but mostly, they discussed the future they wanted to build together. Sarah seemed very content with their relationship and Bill's renewed commitment to it and her. He knew that without her, he was a lesser man, and the storms of life were always worse.

He had not expressed the gravity of his gut feeling to Sarah; he knew an ominous storm was brewing on the horizon, and it had nothing at all to do with a thunderstorm. *Maybe I'll tell her more about it tomorrow. I don't want to ruin such a perfect evening.*

They fell asleep on the sofa, listening to the rain.

9 Surprise Visit

It was not long after daybreak when the storm made its way across the meadow to the house. They watched from the living room as the clearly defined wall of falling rain inched toward them. It appeared as though this particular downpour was going to last quite a while. There was not much in the way of wind or lighting, merely a slight breeze and the occasional rumble of thunder in the distance. That was fortunate, because Sarah did not handle lightning and especially the almost immediate BOOM that followed. If it was going to storm, this was the perfect storm for her.

She had noticed Bill staring off into the distance a few times already. Wondering what he must be thinking, she asked "Where are you right now?"

"What was that? Oh, just trying to work some things out in my head," he said with a cheeky grin.

"I see. Care to share?"

"Nah...not really that important. And I think I got it all worked out."

"Yeah, right. You know I know you better than that."

"Yes." He turned to face Sarah. "I do know that. You've always been right there when I needed you most. I probably don't thank you enough for that, Sarah. I know I don't. So, thank you. Thank you for...not only being there for me but being there for the kids. We all know nobody's perfect, but you certainly seem to be the perfect sounding board for me."

He moved toward Sarah as if he was about to hug her, but she ducked and spun away from him. He could tell by the exaggerated smirk and the lifted eyebrow that Sarah was entering full smartass mode.

"Seem to be...oh...okay...I *seem* to be perfect for you?"

Bill was now laughing at her animated expressions and sarcastic reply. He tried to hug her again, but she spun around and scurried to the other side of the kitchen island.

"Oh c'mon, let me give you a hug. Sweetie...you are and have always been perfect in my eyes."

"Now you're sucking up to me? Come on, Billy boy, you're better than that."

"Cut me some slack. You know I'm just a mere mortal man."

She finally let him catch and hug her. They were both now in tears, nearly rolling on the floor, they were laughing so hard.

It took a few minutes, but they finally composed themselves. Bill and Sarah were the proverbial peas in a pod.

They shared many of the same likes and dislikes. They had both, however, forgotten that fact. Bill looked at Sarah and could tell she was deep in thought, staring off into the distance.

"Where are *you* right now?"

"Wha...what? I'm sorry, what did you say?"

"Where were you? You seemed to be off in la la land."

"Suppose I was for a minute. I was just thinking about all the fun we used to have. We were inseparable. I mean, really. We enjoyed all the same things. Now, I'm...well, I guess I've just forgotten."

Bill had a puzzled look on his face and perhaps a slight hint of concern.

"Forgotten? What do you mean by that?"

"I don't know, Bill. Just all the things we enjoyed together. Like...oh yeah...do you remember the fair we went to? Where was that?

"We were on vacation, heading to Florida and taking the scenic route through Tennessee. You know, over to Nashville, down through Atlanta."

"That's right. We stopped in that little town when we saw the fair from the interstate. Berry? Was it Berry?"

"Perry. It was the Georgia State Fair, in Perry Georgia. We passed it, got off the next exit we came to and turned around."

"Oh my gosh...the greased pig catching. You remember that?"

"How could I forget? And the fried ice cream. Kinda wish we had some of that right now."

"No shit...that was amazing."

It was all starting to come back to them. The adventures they had before the kids came along. They would never swap the kids for more of those adventures, but the memories made were a blessing. They were both starting to remember just how much they meant to each other. They swapped stories for a few hours, smiling and laughing with, and at each other.

"So...do you remember our trip to New Orleans?"

"Only the sober parts of it," Sarah said with a raised eyebrow and smirk.

He grinned. "Yeah...me too. But what I was thinking about was karaoke."

"Geez, that was not one of our finer moments."

"I disagree. We might not be able to carry a tune very well, but we had a lot of fun doing it."

"No, you're right about that. We did have a lot of fun."

"This vacation we're on right now is a new start, Sarah. It's shown me, and I think it's shown you, that our vacations...making time for me and you, that's what we've missed. That's what we have to make a priority."

They were so engrossed in conversation, they almost didn't notice the faint knocking sound, as if something had not been properly secured on the outside of the house.

"Did you hear that? What is that knocking sound?" Sarah asked.

"Probably a tree limb banging against an upstairs window or something," Bill offered.

Suddenly, a much louder knocking sound echoed, as if someone, or something was banging on the walls of the house.

"No, that's somebody at the door," she said with a bit of concern. "Bill?"

"Yes ma'am, I'm going to check. Probably just the maintenance folks making sure everything it okay because of the storm."

"Ahh, I bet you're right. That makes sense." Sarah sighed with relief.

Bill didn't hesitate to open the door but was not prepared for what he saw.

He saw a half-dozen or so men standing on the front porch, just far enough to be protected from the light sprinkling of rain that continued to fall. These were definitely not maintenance technicians, Bill thought to himself. He could quickly see at least four of the men were armed. None of them were small, and they all looked like they were rather intense individuals. Bill was not a small man, standing six feet tall and a very fit two-hundred pounds. The smallest of his visitors was their presumed leader, and they presented themselves with purpose. Bill did not have a good feeling about that purpose.

"Good afternoon, Bill. It is Bill, right?" The man who seemed to have been the one banging on the door extended his hand. Gray hair, rugged complexion, clean shaven, and about the same height as Bill. The man's friendly disposition was a stark contrast to the group's intense, determined demeanor. Bill cautiously shook the man's hand and acknowledged simply, "Yes, I'm Bill. What can I do for you, gentlemen?"

"Bill, no need to be alarmed. You look somewhat stupefied. I... We're pretty sure you were not expecting a visit today, especially not from such a motley crew. Rest assured, we're friendlies."

"Um...*okay.*"

"Bill, let me get to the reason for our impromptu visit today."

"Please…"

"We would rather to speak with you alone. So, if you could go and reassure your family that all is well, and that we'd *prefer* a bit of privacy while we talk, I would truly appreciate it."

"Well, it's just me and—"

"Sarah. Yes, we know. She is family though, isn't she?"

"Yes, yes, she is. Give me just a moment."

"Sure thing."

Bill pushed the door closed and made his way back into the family room. Sarah started to speak, but he quickly raised his hand in a way that clearly indicated *don't* and *stop*. A simultaneous change in her expression turned from inquisitive to concerned. He raised his other hand in the same manner and spread his arms apart, like an umpire making a safe call at home plate.

"Look, I'm going to say this just once. I need you to stay in this room. Do not go anywhere else in the house. If you must use the bathroom, use the powder room. Do not go in the kitchen or upstairs or outside. Some gentlemen are here to talk to me, and they have requested privacy to do so, and we are going to respect their request. This is not debatable, not negotiable. Do you understand what I'm telling you?"

Before she could utter a word, he added, "Just nod, don't speak."

"Wait a fucking minute. You don't just waltz in here and talk to me like that. What the fuck is going on?"

"Sarah, these guys are obviously here to talk to me about what I've seen. For once, can you just please just do as I ask?"

"Yes, I can, but don't talk to me like I'm a kid or one of your troops."

Bill nodded in acknowledgment, looking more concerned as he realized that Sarah's frustration was her attempt to mask her growing panic.

"No need for concern. Everything is all right. They just want to talk to me privately. No need to worry." he was trying to reassure Sarah even though he was not convinced his words were the least bit true.

"Sure, Bill. Whatever you say. What-the-fuck-ever."

He turned and headed back to the front of the house.

As he neared the door, he heard Sarah turn on some music, which eased his mind ever so slightly. He opened the door, walked on to the porch, and asked if they would rather speak inside.

"No thanks. We are probably better off having this discussion out here. This is a beautiful place. The views are amazing...so tranquil. Ya know, Bill, I have always imagined getting a place like this for myself one day, maybe when I retire...if that day ever arrives," the man remarked with a chuckle.

"I'd offer you and your team a seat, but we only have the two rocking chairs."

"Not to worry. That's just enough for me and you. The fellas prefer to stand when they're working."

Bill and the man took their seats. Bill watched the other men as they spread out. Two of the men walked to the corners of the porch, taking a tactical position and scanning the areas beside the house and beyond.

"Oh, crap. Where are my manners? Bill, I'm Michael. The rest of the crew here are Ragual, Remiel, Uriel, Saraqael, Raphael, and this is Gabriel," Michael said, pointing to each member of his team as he named them.

As Michael was providing his introductions, Bill noticed two more of the men, the ones Michael had identified as Uriel and Remiel, had positioned themselves with a clear view of the driveway and areas in front of the porch. The last two men, also the largest and most menacing of the crew stood at the bottom of the steps. Gabriel and Raphael were maintaining a clear view of Michael and Bill.

"You're a pretty renowned guy in the intelligence community, as well as a man of faith. So, I'm sure you picked up on a common theme. Am I right?"

"Yes, those are also the names of Archangels."

"Exactly." Michael turned and spoke to the men standing behind him. "See, I told you guys this was going to be a quick and effective meeting. You see, Bill, I'm a peacekeeper by nature, and I really, truly believe that any issue can be resolved if the participants in the conversation conduct themselves in a civilized, adult manner. Don't you agree?"

"I couldn't agree more"

"I thought as much. So, here's the crux of the issue we need to resolve today."

Bill was reminded by Michael's last comment of the tone and tenor of every hitman in every action movie he could recall. The eerie calmness of Michael's speech was unnerving. It was the same approach many of the operator negotiators/interrogators he'd watched during several after-action analyses he'd performed. His realization that most, if not all of the hitman's marks as well as many of the interogatees, didn't fare very well in the end, even if they survived.

"We weren't planning our visit here today. We were not alarmed in any way when you... Great bunch of kids you have, by the way. I can tell you and Sarah have done a great job raising them. They must be stoked that you guys got the team back together."

Bill's eyes widened, as his thoughts raced. *Wow, I was literally thinking how great it's been having the family back together.*

"Sorry, as I was saying...we weren't alarmed when you came across our signs. Yeah, we always figured it would happen, but to be honest, we expected the signs alone would be enough to deter pretty much anyone from exploring any farther. You with me here?"

Bill sat up in his chair and turned to face Michael. He'd been trying to play it cool, but with mention of the kids, he could feel his face flush.

"Wait, you said 'great bunch of kids'; it's just me and Sarah here."

Michael shifted to match Bill's posture and stared intently into Bill's eyes. The wry grin was replaced with stern, pursed lips.

"So, I did. Let's come back to that in a moment. And, it would make me and the fellas a lot more comfortable if you could settle back into that relaxed position, you were in when our little conversation started."

Bill begrudgingly complied. Michael settled back into the rocker, the wry grin having reemerged. He glanced at the men, now standing with one foot on the bottom step and nodded. As he did, they resumed their previous positions.

"So, Bill...I told you we *weren't* concerned. But your little pre-dawn visit...well, that changed our position on the whole concern thing. I have to tell you that was very unexpected, given your reaction when you found our signs. To be honest with you, we almost didn't notice you'd explored beyond the signs. If you can believe that."

"Well, I..."

"Here's the thing. Those signs were placed with a uniquely specific purpose, right?"

"To warn people and prevent them from going on to search beyond them."

"Yes, you're exactly right. But they were not going to deter you, were they?" Michael said with a stern change in his demeanor. "We've implemented some pretty radical changes in typical procedures for this particular facility. There's no fence to obstruct individuals from exploring beyond the signs.

We have gone to great lengths to camouflage most of the above ground equipment. We've even had it added to the imagery exclusion list. The only imagery publicly available of the area is prior to construction. We also don't typically see anyone in this area, except the folks scouring the hillsides for ginseng. But even they steer clear of the area beyond the signs."

"Nobody that's stayed here before..."

"You and Sarah are the first visitors. This place is unique in that it only gets advertised to folks directly. You heard about this place and got the contact information from your former boss, did you not?"

"Yes, I did."

"Exactly, so *you* and lovely Sarah are the first. Shame to see this turn of events come to pass."

Michael was speaking in an increasingly firmer tone. Bill was shaken, coming to the realization this was much more serious than the simple trespassing. Michael rose, looking down at Bill with a furrowed brow and steely eyes.

"Look, Michael, I clearly did something I should not have done. The signs look pretty old, and I assumed the area non-active. I should not have let my curiosity get the better of me. I—"

Michael turned quickly and positioned himself directly in front of Bill, now looking very clearly pissed off. Bill pushed himself as far back into the rocking chair as he could. He thought this might be the moment they grabbed him and threw him in their vehicle. Michael was almost yelling at Bill now, veins bulging in his forehead and neck.

"Oh, you're right about that. You should not have. But you did."

Michael's disposition immediately reverted to what it was at the beginning of their conversation. His veins were no longer pulsating, and the wry grin had reappeared. He continued calmly, as if they were old friends again.

"You saw them, studied them, and no doubt ruminated on the potential repercussions if it were to be an active location, and then you ignored what you had to know to be the right thing to do, and disregarded those signs anyway. That was not cool, Bill. Not cool at all."

Michael leaned against the porch rail and crossed his arms. His gaze at Bill never wavered. Bill attempted to return the gaze but found himself staring at Michael's forehead or chest most of the time.

"No, I suppose it wasn't."

"At least you are man enough to admit when you are wrong. I respect you for that. But, in the end, you still did it. We now have an issue to resolve."

"Look, you obviously know who I am and what my background is. You know I am not the type to go running my mouth about things I know better than to speak about in any inappropriate forum. So why don't you drop the black-ops Agency bullshit with me?"

Michael paused, and no one uttered a word. The only sounds that could be heard were those of nature and Sarah's music inside the house.

"You were an exemplary military officer. No disciplinary issues. Never in trouble of any kind with military or civilian entities, only one moving violation—a warning—but no tickets for any violations. Now, here we are, a few days into your retirement and, whew...it's like you forgot how the game is played or something."

"Well..."

"Nah, that's actually how it was put across to me by my boss. You know we all answer to someone."

"Yes."

"Well, I disagree with my boss. You did not forget. You followed the same instincts that led to and allowed you to maintain the highest levels of excellence throughout your esteemed career. That is crystal clear to me, Bill. Crystal clear, indeed."

"What's your point?"

"Well, what I said about you is true. But that does not excuse the lapse in judgment on your behalf nor does it resolve our issue."

Michael's demeanor changed dramatically, and it became glaringly apparent to Bill that he was not in a good spot at all. In fact, all of Bill's senses were now telling him that his entire world might well be crashing down around him. One stupid lapse appeared to be destroying everything he'd worked for his entire adult life.

"Bill? This is my serious voice. All kidding aside, this *is* profoundly serious. You have put yourself, and subsequently me and the boys here, into a precarious position. It's up to me...and you...to figure out a way to salvage our reputations."

"I'm all ears."

"Good. Ya see, here's the thing. If you were anybody else, this issue would be resolved already. We would be done. No issue would exist, because...well, we would just have erased every tie to the situation. Are you following me here?"

"Yeah... Where the fuck do you get off threatening my life and that of my family? You obviously have my full attention, and I'm definitely following you. You need to drop the threats."

"I'm a bit concerned that you haven't realized a couple things, apparently. First, you are in no position to demand anything. Second, I do not threaten; I inform. That is an important fact for you to remember. Now, as I was saying, we have ourselves a conundrum. You are not the kind of guy that can be easily erased. Bill, I like you. I like what you've done throughout your career, but more so, the fact that you've set your priorities straight and are up here on a sorely needed vacation, newly reunited with Sarah...the one thing you've longed for, and no, you have not destroyed it...at least not yet."

"What the— How—"

"Now, don't freak out on me here. Use those 'Spidey senses' you described to your beautiful Sarah and keep those great kids in mind. You are one of the smartest men I've had the distinct pleasure to meet. Surely, you're catching on to something here."

"Yeah, I hear what you're saying, Michael. I don't fully understand how you know some of these things, but I hope you get to the point soon. I am not a recruit. I have been in the Intel and SpecOps worlds for most of my adult life, and your feeble attempts to scare me—to threaten me— That's a whole new level of ineptitude."

"Your family is fine. As are you. And believe me when I tell you, you could not possibly make this worse at this point. You have not shared all the details of your adventure with anyone, not even Sarah. It's just us boys here...go ahead, tell me what you're thinking, no judgment here."

"Are you listening to anything I'm saying?"

Michael walked to the top of the steps his back turned to Bill.

"Yes, but you're not the one in charge at the moment, Bill. It would behoove you to play nicely with others and swallow your machismo for a few more minutes."

Michael turned his head slightly toward Bill and spoke over his shoulder.

"I'm a patient and understanding man, but my patience is wearing thin. You can work with me, or we can take this to the next level and have a very different type of interaction with beautiful Sarah."

Bill started to stand, but Gabriel motioned for him to sit back down. Bill received the message loud and clear and sat back in the rocker. Michael motioned to Gabriel, as if to say everything was fine. He then placed his hands in his pockets before speaking.

"And before your temper makes you say something regretful, no, I'm not fucking around here."

"Well, Michael, it's clear that whatever it is, it's advanced. I mean, you read my mind."

"Not exactly...but, keep going."

"I don't know how, but you seem to know my internal thoughts, concerns, what I have and haven't shared with anyone, and I can't for the life of me explain that. Whatever you guys are protecting must be pretty advanced, so I can understand why it's protected the way it is. If this is technology that enables heightened senses, and—*I can't believe these words are coming out of my mouth*—the ability to intercept and discern a person's thoughts, my God, it could be used for devastatingly nefarious means."

"That really is just about the gist of it, Bill. Without going into any sort of details, yes. Even the seemingly innocuous small concrete structure and communications tower you saw...even releasing that publicly would lead to someone having to answer some difficult questions. We just can't have that. Of course, I'm not worried about that with you. I know your type."

"Yeah..."

"Look we know you have not accepted a job offer. So, your way out of this little conundrum is simple."

"How's that?"

"Right now, I just need you to listen. You will receive a phone call in the next couple of days. Answer it. You will be offered a position within our organization. Accept it. You will become part of our little family. Embrace it."

"Excuse me?"

"You're losing focus again."

"Fine...yes...Got it."

"I hope so, Bill; I hope so. Otherwise, regarding you and your family..."

"Yes"

"We will have to... Any guesses?"

"What? Disappear us?"

"I'm shocked. No, we're not animals. We don't do things like that."

"Good, that's a relief."

"My oh my, I can't believe— Guys, can you believe Bill thought we'd just come back and erase them?" Michael said, his words dripping with sarcasm in a failed attempt to seem as though he was joking.

"No, Bill, we don't do things like that. We have people that take care of those issues for us," Michael stated very matter-of-factly as he turned to face Bill. His look was stern but eerily calm and matter of fact.

"This is not a joke. It is not a dream. You're not going to wake up in a few minutes and roll over to spoon with that smoking hot Sarah. This is your new reality. If you step out of line in the slightest way, I will come back with a team of rather unsavory individuals and send another to visit the kids. I can assure you this is not something you want to happen. Your beautiful Sarah and those three young girls will suffer unimaginable atrocities at the hands of some desperate men who have no morals and no issues whatsoever swapping back and forth between those young women, defiling every single molecule of purity of their pure, virgin souls, all while your beautiful Sarah is forced to watch the live feed. The boys? They may even be forced to participate. They will certainly be tortured for what will seem like an eternity before they expire. And you, Bill. You will be forced watch every single moment, every despicable act perpetrated against the kids from afar and lovely Sarah right here in the flesh. And they will see you just sitting, watching the atrocities occur, and taking no action to stop the insanity. They will also be made clearly aware that you had an opportunity to prevent it all and did not choose that alternative for them."

"You son of a bitch," Bill barked as he stood from the rocking chair, veins now bulging in his neck. Before he realized it, both Gabriel and Raphael had moved slightly in front of Michael, one on each side. There was no mistaking the look on their faces. One more step and Bill would be plucking splinters out of his teeth.

Michael patted both men on the shoulders and stepped forward, between them, never breaking his gaze on Bill.

"So, look. One second. Gabriel? Hand me that Polaroid."

Gabriel pulled a photo out of the inner pocket of his jacket and handed it to Michael. "Bill, I've got a nice Polaroid that I want you to take a gander at. You know, I've always preferred Polaroid pictures over pretty much any other kind of picture. Nostalgia, I guess? Maybe. I don't truly know. Maybe they just seem to capture the essence of the human experience better than others. Not unlike this one has captured the essence of innocence, wouldn't you say?"

Bill, now ghostly white, took the picture from Michael. He fell back into the rocking chair, trembling from the whirlwind of fear and anger swelling up inside him. He felt utterly helpless in the situation. He couldn't fathom how seeing a small structure and a communications tower warranted this all-out assault.

"Bill, I can see you're scared and angry. I don't fault you for that. I'd be feeling the exact same emotions if our positions were reversed. Truth is, you have no idea what you've stumbled upon, and that is really the issue. Knowing you as we believe we do, we know you won't let this go until you have figured it out, and we cannot allow that to happen. So, better to bring you on board. That little speech I just gave you wasn't for effect, even though it has clearly had one. Every, member of these teams, this initiative, if you will, has received an equally severe warning—including me. I can tell you that it will be followed through, because I've seen it happen. It's not pretty, and I know it seems really over the top, but I think you'll understand, once you start working on the team. And, if that picture of your seven little angels with my friend Gabriel here wasn't enough reinforcement...well, I guess you're fucked. I truly hope you have a full and complete understanding of the gravity of this situation now."

Bill looked completely resigned to the idea that he was, in fact, fucked. It was clear from Michael's expression that that he knew his message, rather that of The Organization, had been received and understood. His voice now somewhat shaky, Bill looked up at Michael and replied.

"It's pretty clear to me what I need to do."

"Good. Well, we'll give you some time, and I recommend you hang out here for a bit to compose yourself before rejoining Sarah. It was an absolute pleasure meeting you; I truly mean that. I'm looking forward to working with you, Bill."

"Yeah, me too. I guess."

"I'm sure. Say hello to Sarah for us. Please convey my apologies for stealing you away for so long. You take care now. Oh, and don't forget to answer your phone."

"About that..."

"Yes."

"We haven't had service since we got within fifty miles of this place."

"Yeah, cool, huh? You, and you alone, will have cell service from this point forward. I suggest you keep your phone on vibrate and on your person at all times. Don't want to miss that call, Bill."

"Will do."

"Atta boy. You're gonna do just fine. Y'all take care now."

"Yeah." Bill was overwhelmed with an odd sense of relief and foreboding greater than any he had experienced in his forty-plus years. He sat with his hands covering his face, barely able to mutter the prevailing thought swirling around his mind, "What the fuck have I gotten myself into now?"

10 The Phone Call

Bill sat in quiet contemplation, reflecting on his decision to investigate the forest beyond the signs. *Archangels...hmmm... That's some seriously arrogant shit.* But no matter how arrogant they were, Bill knew they were completely serious. No real alternatives existed in this situation, at least no obvious ones.

Sarah was sitting quietly, listening to her 70s playlist. Bill fumbled through his thoughts, unable to piece together a coherent story that didn't make him sound like a liar to Sarah. She'd always been able to see straight through Bill's veiled attempts to protect her from the whole truth. This wasn't going to be easy, and he knew Sarah would be his toughest critic. He sat for what seemed like an eternity but was only ten minutes when it hit him. Just tell the truth and leave out the ominous details.

Decision made, Bill stood and stretched before reaching for the doorknob. As casually as he could, he made his way back into the family room. He'd barely set foot into the room when Sarah turned toward him, clearly furious.

"What the hell was that all about?" she blurted.

"Well, I'm guessing by your question and your tone that you're a little concerned? Or am I off base here?"

Staring at him as if he was the biggest idiot she'd ever known, she replied simply, "You think?"

"It's really not that big of a deal. They were from a government organization. And they were not happy with me."

"But all you did is see some signs, right? How does that warrant a visit like that?" Sarah continued, her tone blatantly sarcastic. "Well, let's see... You took it upon yourself to explore the area past those signs while you were"—Sshe raised her hands to make air quotes— "exercising and stumbled--"

"Sarah, that's enough."

* * *

In that moment, she realized she'd pushed Bill far enough in her attempt to make her point.

"Sorry, Bill. It's bullshit, but I apologize."

"That's all right...just...no more, please."

"Okay," Sarah replied as tears were beginning to well in the corner of her eyes.

"No tears...I just need you to listen to me."

He now had her undivided attention. She was in shock at Bill's tone and facial expression. It was clear to her that this was serious. He didn't speak that way...ever. She knew that whatever he was about to tell her was extremely important, and she'd best be hanging on every word.

"As I was saying, those guys represent a government organization. They were not happy that I made the stupid decision to ignore the signs and explore the forest beyond them. They were clear that the signs had been placed for a uniquely specific reason: to prevent anyone from going beyond that point in the forest. I knew that. But I allowed my curiosity to get the better of me, and I had a lapse in good judgment. I explained in the greatest detail I could what little I saw. By the time the conversation was over, they were satisfied with my explanation and that I was being truthful, which I was."

"Look, they were just doing their job. Something popped up on their surveillance cameras, and they investigated it. The important takeaway for you is to never, ever mention those signs or this visit to anyone. I cannot stress that enough."

Sarah nodded in agreement.

"You look scared. There's nothing to be frightened of. Again, they were just doing their job. In fact, by the end of the conversation, they told me that they liked my inquisitiveness, and ultimately, my honesty. So much so, that they said they just might offer me a job. How about that?"

* * *

125

Now, Sarah seemed completely confused, as if she was trying to figure out what else he wasn't saying. "So, all of that was really about a job interview?"

"Yes...well, that and the whole 'you did something wrong, don't do it again' thing."

"Hmmm..."

"Sarah, can we just try and relax and listen to the music?"

"Yes, that's a great idea. It's your turn to pick," she added with a look at Bill that said it was time to move past that uncomfortable conversation. He knew there was more behind that look and that Sarah wasn't buying into everything he'd just shared. They'd always had a non-verbal communication ability, and he knew both understood this conversation was far from over.

Sarah started dinner, and Bill got up to help. They'd barely gotten started when his phone rang. It startled both of them. Bill clumsily stumbled across the room to grab his phone. Instead of picking it up, however, he pushed it right off the counter and onto the floor. His heart sunk, knowing that he *had* to answer the call. *If my phone is broke, we're dead...literally dead,* he thought. He was thankful to see his phone was fine, but his stomach was in knots as he answered the call.

"Hello, this is Bill." He turned to look at Sarah, who was glaring at him, hands on hips, shaking her head from side to side. He could see the tears welling in her eyes.

"Atta Boy. I knew I could count on you."

Bill immediately recognized Michaels's voice and knew this was 'the call'.

"I told you that I would answer."

"Yes, sir, and you didn't disappoint. Hang on for a second, let me get the boss on the line for you."

"Sure."

It was more than just a second—or even a few seconds. It seemed like an eternity to him. His thoughts were all over the place. He wasn't sure if he was going to be able to speak...if he was going to faint, throw up, or drop dead. His heart was racing, but he took a long, deep breath to regain control and center himself.

"Bill? You need to calm down, brother. You're gonna give yourself a heart attack or an aneurysm or something. Take a few deep breaths and relax. The hard part is already done. You held up your end of the bargain...so far... All is well, relax."

Bill sighed as he walked out the sliding glass doors to the back deck. "I'll try, Michael."

"No need to try. Just breathe slowly and deeply. Listen and comply..."

With that, his mind seemed to clear. His heart had stopped racing, and he was no longer on the verge of hyperventilating. Bill appeared as calm as the weather now was. The storm was over and the surface of the pond was as smooth as glass, without a single breeze-induced ripple.

"There you go, Bill. That's much better. I'm going to hand the phone over to the boss. Just remember, nothing is going to be said that warrants another panic attack. Stay calm. Listen and comply..."

"Got it...calm...breathe," Bill repeated the mantra internally.

"Hello? Bill?"

"Yes, this is Bill."

"Pleased to speak with you. I'm Bob. Hey, Bill? I need to you walk around to the front of the house and grab a small package we left for you. Can you do that for me?"

Sure."

"Let me know when you've found and opened it."

"Okay."

Bill made his way to the front of the house and didn't immediately see the package. He looked to both sides of the porch, but nothing was there. He was very calm given the previous visit. *Maybe this is where the sniper takes me out*, he thought. He was making his way to the steps to see if the package had been left on the walkway.

"It was left by the steps."

"I'm looking there now." Bill leaned over the handrail and saw the package had apparently fallen off the porch and landed behind the shrubbery. "All right, got it. It must have fallen off the steps; it was behind the shrubs in the flower bed."

"Great, let me know when you've opened it." Bill pulled the tab on the package, ripping it off, only to find a small black box inside.

"It's open. Should I open the box inside?"

"Yes, please."

"I've got it. Hello?"

Suddenly, the call dropped, and Bill's service was gone. He was starting to panic again when the new phone he'd just taken out of the box rang.

"Bill here."

"Hold on a second."

"Okay."

"Bill, can you hear me better now?"

"Yes, Bob. I have you Lima Charlie. Er, sorry...old habits. I can hear you loud and clear."

Bob chuckled. "Old habits... Old habits do die hard. You know, it's those old habits that are responsible for this conversation...as well as the one you had with Michael earlier. And, oh by the way, the primary reason I want to talk to you is about a position within our organization."

Bill rolled his eyes and shook his head side to side. He hated unnecessary repetition, particularly when he was on the receiving end of it. He took a quiet, deep breath and answered.

"Yes, sir. All too aware of that."

"I'm sure...I'm sure. Well, Bill, it's like this. We don't hire often. In fact, Remiel was our last hire, and that's been quite some time ago. What, Michael, three, maybe four thousand years?"

"I'm sorry, could you say that again please?" Bill was momentarily stunned.

Bob was laughing loudly now. "Just yanking your chain. That was classic. We hired Remiel about a year and a half ago. Sorry, I couldn't resist a joke inherent with the whole archangel theme we have going on."

"Yeah, that's a good one." Bill chuckled just a bit and briefly considered he might be taking things too seriously. He could tell Bob and Michael both had a sense of humor, albeit a bit dark.

"So, here's the deal. Rather than the unpleasant alternative, I'd like to bring you on board. Of course, we'll reinstate your clearance at the level you last held on active duty. Beyond that exists a fairly heavily scrutinized path to upgrading that clearance to a level commensurate with the job we're going to ask you to do for us."

"That sounds reasonable. What do you need from me?"

"At this point, we have everything we need. We have to take care of some paperwork on our end. We need to get the information we have for you input into our proprietary system. We have to schedule your appointments. Speaking of which, when is your vacation supposed to be over?"

"We had planned to leave for home pre-dawn on Friday. But, we can certainly leave sooner if that is necessary."

"Great. That works perfectly. So, okay, where were we? Oh yeah...so, we're going to need you and Sarah to get your affairs in order. You'll need to sell the house, which is going to be easy...I have a feeling about these things. You should check out the area thirty or forty miles north of where you are at this moment. There are some really nice places in that area. They may seem expensive at first glance, but everything is negotiable. Plus, we pay quite well."

This gave Bill an opportunity to attempt to demonstrate that he was completely on board and was legitimately looking forward to this opportunity. He knew that gaining the trust of these men was an absolute imperative. He had to fall back on the craft of his trade. He'd been thinking about his past life in the military and something a general once told him, *"Tact and diplomacy is the key, Captain Colne. You can tell anyone to go to hell—as long as you make them look forward to the trip."* Bill was just hoping he'd learned enough to pull it off now.

"I didn't want to seem impertinent, pushy, or ungrateful, but I *was* curious about the pay and benefit package."

"That's perfectly normal. Not an unexpected query at all. You will be paid significantly more that you were paid on active duty, and the best benefits package you could have ever dreamed of having."

"That sounds good. Thank you."

"Of course. Bill, we take excellent care of our loyal employees. We're certain you will be a loyal employee, so...nothing for you to be concerned about."

"Roger that."

"So... we'll look at what? Forty-five days? Sixty days from now as a start date? That sound good?"

"I'll make it work."

"Michael, you weren't kidding. Bill here is on top of it. Man, I really enjoy working with folks that hop on board and start running. Well, I think that's all I need from you. We will be in contact. Probably goes without saying, the phone you're holding is a work phone, for work purposes only. Please make sure you use it accordingly."

"Of course."

"Anything else? Did I forget anything, Michael? Oh yeah, Bill?"

"Yes, Bob."

"I won't reiterate the unpleasant part of your conversation with Michael and the boys. Suffice it to say that will continue to apply to your employee status from start to finish. As previously stated, some things are not negotiable, and yes, this message is completely serious. We're a serious group of individuals tasked with a critically sensitive and serious mission. We work hard and play hard when we can. But we all are responsible for abiding by the rules at all times. Nobody is immune to the rules ...nobody, not even me, the guy in charge of it all."

"That point is crystal clear to me, Bob. Keeping my family safe and secure and well-provided for is my number one priority."

"Nicely said. I could not have stated that any better myself."

"I can hardly wait to get started."

"All in good time. Just keep the phone on and nearby at all times. We'll let you know if and/or when we need you. Take care."

"Sure, yeah. Take care."

"Hey, Bill? Don't hang up just yet."

"Oh, hello again, Michael."

"Look man, I know this is a whirlwind...well, more like an F5 tornado at the moment. We'll get through this. I have great confidence that you are going to fit right in with everyone. Just be patient and let your family know you have a new job, it's in this area. Let them know that you don't have all the details, but you start in sixty days or so. Help them focus on getting your house in Virginia ready to sell and looking for a new place around here. We'll send you some helpful resources to make both ends of this transition go smoothly. So, that being said, your immediate job is keeping everyone's fears at ease."

"Got it, Michael."

"No worries...You take care now, Bill."

"Yep. You as well."

With that, the conversation was over.

11 Offer that Followed

That night was no different than most of the day that preceded it, as it began to rain again. There were brief breaks in the storm, but it would last throughout the night and into the following morning. Bill found Sarah leaning on the kitchen island. He walked over and wrapped his arms around her, turning his face toward the side of her head. Then he whispered.

"Don't act as if I'm talking to you. I'm 99.9% certain this place is bugged and has hidden cameras. We have to act as if everything is fine until we get out of here. Probably until we get home. Say something funny if you agree."

Sarah said the first thing that popped into her head. "Chicken-Butt...tension breaker, had to be done."

"You are *such* a nerd. Beautiful but a total nerd."

They tried to carry on as if it were just another day, like nothing out of the ordinary had occurred. They seemed to share the opinion that it was better not to acknowledge the events of the last 24 hours and, instead, just do the best they could to enjoy what was left of this vacation together.

Sarah prepared another amazing breakfast. While they ate, they talked about their plans for the day. They were also relieved the kids were not there to have witnessed the previous day's drama.

It was really the final opportunity for them to enjoy conversation before preparing for the trip home. And they did just that...the enjoyed each other to the fullest, both realizing these were the best days of their lives.

The day passed, seemingly quicker than any before. The evening came, and they were left with a few hours to walk and talk...just enjoying the sights and sounds of the place they'd come to love in just a few days.

Bill and Sarah found a few minutes to discuss what was to come with this new job he was being offered. It was the unknown that caused concern for both of them.

"I'm sure I'll have a formal offer waiting for me at home."

"Yes, I know. They do seem to be on top of things...a little too much, but I guess we'll have to just get used to that?"

"Yes, I suspect we will. Although, I'm going to reach out to Marv to see what he knows. But I've heard about groups like this before, and they're not to be trifled with."

"But... It still..."

"I know, Sarah. I have huge concerns as well. And I don't..."

"Feel like you don't have much of a choice with this one?"

"Hmmm...well, there's always a choice. I just think accepting the offer is the best one."

"I tend to agree with you on that one."

"Thank you, fugly."

"You haven't complemented me like that since we were in high school."

"Well, I thought I'd pull something out of my old playbook... How's it working?"

"Jerkoff."

"I guess so..." Bill replied, both laughing loudly at each other.

They started experiencing the wonder of swarming mosquitos for the first time on the trip and neither was impressed. So, they picked up the pace...nearly sprinting back to the protection of the vacation house.

They sat in the family room, one last time, to enjoy the gourmet Ramen noodles Bill had chosen for their last vacation meal. What they were eating was not important. They acknowledged during their mealtime conversations, they were just happy to have spent this vacation together and were savoring every last minute. Then it was time to pack, save for a change of clothes for the morning. Everything found its way into the Audi by midnight, and they were off to get some sleep, in preparation for the journey back to reality.

They were up before dawn, and nearly an hour into the trek home before the sun peeked over the horizon. While the time was passing quickly, it seemed as though it was taking forever to get home. Despite complaining about the lack of cell service, they didn't bother to check their phones on the way back to Virginia.

Having made just one stop to refuel and grab a late breakfast, they made it back home before noon. They unloaded the SUV and started the process of putting their vacation wares away. Bill was working with his oldest, Trevor, when he decided to ask how things went without the parental units around.

"So, Trev? How did things go while we were away?"

"To be honest, everything went really smoothly. Everyone got along...no fighting...shocking, I know...but true."

"Wow! That is a bit of a shock. Nice to hear though. No unexpected visitors?"

"Uh, no. Well, actually the delivery guy got lost trying to deliver a package to the Smith's, but that's it."

"That's odd. What did this delivery guy look like?"

Trevor looked at Bill seemingly perplexed at the question.

"He was a little old man. Said he delivers packages for the Postal Service part time, didn't know the neighborhood, and didn't have cell service, so his GPS wasn't helpful."

"Oh, okay. Pretty uneventful then."

"May I ask why that was noteworthy?"

"Just curious. You know I've always been—"

"You're a conspiracy theorist and ultra-paranoid."

"Am I really that transparent?"

"To us, yes. To everyone else, not at all."

"Good to know."

They finished their tasks and joined the rest of the family, who were already relaxing in the family room. Bill and Sarah sat back and quietly observed the fruits of their labors. Looking at each other just long enough to smile and wink.

The quiet reflection was interrupted by the doorbell. Bill begrudgingly made his way to answer the door. The delivery woman asked for him by name, citing a delivery confirmation signature was required. He signed quickly and thanked her before grabbing the large box to move it inside. Just as he was about to ask if anyone had ordered anything, he noticed the return address.

This was no doubt part of his offer. It was sent from Archangel, Inc., which was now really confusing. A rather large box for an offer letter.

Bill just shook his head and unpacked the box. Inside were two laptops, a router, and a sealed manila envelope with a single printed page inside. The message was simple and to the point.

Bill,

Please use the included blue cable, and only the included blue cable, to connect the router to your ISP router LAN ethernet port. Use the white and black cables to connect the laptops to the included router, use only the cables included to make any connections to the laptops! Make all connections and wait five minutes before powering on any of the included devices.

Connect the blue cable between the ISP interface and the included router.

Use the white cable to connect the laptop with the white dot to the included router.

Use the black cable to connect the laptop with the black dot to the included router.

Wait five minutes.

NOTE: Both laptops have been modified to be powered on without lifting the display.

You will find the power button near the back on the right side.

Power on the white laptop.

Do not lift the display.

Wait five minutes.

Power on the black laptop.

Do not lift the display.

Wait five minutes.

Power on the router.

Wait fifteen minutes.

Lift the display of the white laptop and follow the prompts.

Do nothing with black laptop until all actions with white laptop are complete.

Lift the display of the black laptop and follow the prompts.

Congratulations. Welcome to the team.

Bill thought the instructions were rigid but simple enough. Once he had completed the tasks given, an email notification showing new mail popped up on the white laptop. This, he noticed quickly, was the official offer letter.

"Full benefits...medical, dental, vision, short- and long-term disability, life insurance for me, Sarah, and the kids."

All pretty standard, aside from the fact there was no money out of pocket for Bill, which was a huge bonus, especially given the size of his family.

"$300,000.00 per year, paid every two weeks."

This made his jaw drop. A welcomed and totally unexpected number that would make life for them much easier.

Expense account for travel and supplies, amount to be determined.

Relocation assistance, with both selling and purchasing of homes.

Car of his choice, purchase price capped at $150,000.00, and directed to consider the vehicle a signing bonus.

Bill was staring in awe as he continued to read the offer email. He could not believe what he was reading. This was all too good to be true.

No sooner had he finished reading the offer email than a second notification arrived. This one from Michael.

Welcome aboard, Bill. I need you to reply to the first email with a simple 'I accept.' Then...remembering our discussion, particularly the part regarding repercussions from our decisions...I need you to reply to this email with the following: 'I understand. I recall the conversation and agree with the points that were made. I accept the position I have been offered as well as the potential consequences that may result either intentionally or inadvertently through my actions while employed by The Organization. I willfully agree to the terms and conditions of my employment, being of sound mind and body. Thank you for the opportunity to continue to serve the best interests of my country.'

Feel free to cut and paste. Looking forward to working with you, Bill. It's gonna be a blast, of that you can be certain.

Best regards,

Michael

Bill finished reading and immediately replied. He felt a sense of imminent danger and overwhelming foreboding wash over him. He began muttering to himself, "Why is my stomach in knots? Why am I so unsure of myself? This is my only option though, and it's an offer I actually can't refuse. For the safety and wellbeing of Sarah and the kids, it's the only option I have to protect them. Ugh, get a grip, Bill, you're losing it. Come on, now, get it together before anyone sees you."

Sarah had been watching him from a distance. She seemed clearly unnerved at what she saw. Although he'd not spoken to her about the offer yet, knowing Bill as she did, she'd be able to tell he was troubled. She'd probably come to the conclusion he was doing what he had to do, not what he wanted to do. It appeared to be a dire situation, one that must have serious consequences based on the way he was sure he was acting.

"So, cowboy? What was in the box?"

"Really? Here, just read it for yourself."

"Damn, that's actually an awesome offer, Bill."

"It really is. We'll be living very comfortably."

"Yeah, kind of pisses me off though. If not for all the bullshit threats, it would be great."

"Threats? What threats? What are you talking about?"

"Oh, give me a break, Bill. Of course, I was listening. That cabin wasn't exactly soundproof. And, if you recall, we had opened the front windows to let a breeze flow through the house the night before."

He was caught off guard by Sarah's comment. He'd forgotten completely about the windows. The look of disappointment in the eyes looking back at him was evident, and he hated that look more than anything.

"I really do have to stop underestimating you. Look, I was going to tell you, but I was waiting for the right time. I'm sorry."

"The time is now. Spill it, and spare me the protector of the world bullshit, please." Sarah's tone was firm, and she was clearly concerned. She must have heard a lot of the conversation but not all of it. "Basically, I heard you *were going to* take a job with them."

"That's it in a nutshell."

She leaned against the wall and crossed her arms, looking down at her bare feet. For a moment they stood in silence, before she asked the one question Bill knew he didn't want to have to answer.

"So, what was that the big goon took out of his jacket and handed to gray haired asshole?"

"Gabriel handed Michael a picture."

"Picture? Of what?"

Perhaps in response to his demeanor, Sarah stood up straight, tapping her foot as if expecting an answer she would not be pleased with.

"They had a picture of the big guy, Gabriel, with the kids. Told me you and the kids would be disappeared if I didn't *play ball*."

"Are you fucking kidding me, right now? What the fuck, Bill? And when exactly was the right time going to be to tell me that? Holy shit. You fucking asshole. Those 'roided up dicks threaten me and the kids, and I have to ask? You are not that damn stupid, Bill. Jeezus!"

"Sarah, I asked Trev if they had any unexpected visitors. He told me they had one lost, little old man, who was looking for the Smith's place and got turned around. So, the picture had to be faked. No way Trevor lies to us about something like that."

"No, he wouldn't lie to us, but this is still some serious bullshit. I heard some of the bullshit they were peddling, not this though. You should have told me then! It's...bullshit!"

"I know it is."

"Do you? Do you, Bill? Then why the fuck are you not on the phone calling Marv. Right now, pick it up and call him."

"It's not that simple. They're..."

"Call him."

"They're monitoring my calls, Sarah. Probably all of our calls."

"What the hell are we in the middle of?"

"I don't know exactly, at least not just yet."

Bill's text notification sounded off.

"Of course, we can't even have a discussion now without those nosy assholes interjecting."

"Actually, it's Marv. He's going to call me in a couple minutes."

"Say what? Don't you think that's at least a little bit odd? A little too coincidental?"

"Way too coincidental, actually."

"Well, at least the man I thought I knew hasn't completely disappeared."

"C'mon, Sarah, stop being overly dramatic. Not like we don't already have enough to deal with."

"Dramatic? Are you fucking serious? You know me better than that. Son of a bitch! Those pricks roll up like mafiosi, threaten all of us with *erasure*...which is clearly a threat to kill us. All of us, Bill. All of us. Not just you, not just me, but all of us. Last time I checked, there were seven kids included in *all of us.* All the drama in politics today would be too much in this *particular* situation. But that's just the opinion of the local drama queen, I guess—"

"Sarah, I'm just trying—"

"Whatever! This is... Well, it's fucked up."

"Yeah... I'm aware."

Sarah stormed off just as Bill's phone rang.

"Marv?"

"Yes, hello, Bill. I would ask how you, Sarah, and the kids are doing, but I feel as though it would be inappropriate for me to do so given the current situation."

"How?"

"Bill, I was asked to give you a call. Better this way than you calling me, and believe it or not, those guys don't want to be at odds with you, or Sarah, or the kids for that matter. They, too, find themselves in a precarious position. They, as you may have figured out by now, are in a somewhat similar position as you find yourself. And, having been in it longer than you, they have learned that compliance is not optional. You comply, that's it."

"How can they get away with shit like this, Marv? Who the hell are these guys?"

"They work for The Organization."

"What organization?"

"The Organization. That's what the company is called. The Organization. They were created to handle very sensitive and very particular situations. And The Organization doesn't officially exist."

"If they don't officially exist, how can they do shit like this?"

"Do what, Bill?"

"Oh, I don't know, Marv. Maybe something like blackmailing me into working for them under the duress of imminent threats to abuse, torture, and even disappear me and my family. And while they didn't come right out and say it, I'm fairly confident the *abuse* they referenced had a distinct sexual overtone. What the actual fuck?"

"Well, Bill. They haven't done that. Because they don't exist."

"What the fuck are you talking about, Marv?"

"Listen, they *officially* don't exist, therefore they *officially* do nothing. They're traceless. Purposely. Stop raging and think for a damn minute. Not like you haven't crossed their path before."

"What are you talking about, Marv?"

"You remember reviewing the unexplained executions in several small countries spread across the globe?"

"Yes."

"You stitched together a picture that tied them all together. Remember that?"

"Yes. I still don't understand what you're getting at though."

"That was The Organization. Your analysis forced them to change how they were operating, and in doing so, put you on their radar. Needless to say, they were not pleased. Thankfully, I know Bob. He and I have been friends for years, so he came to me with the issue."

"That's why you pulled me off that project and moved me to Nevada desert analysis."

"Yes. Now listen. Limit what you share with Sarah from this point forward. I don't want your household dynamic to prompt further questions. So, definitely keep this out of earshot of the kids."

"Yes, sir."

"We'll talk more later, Bill. For now, mouth shut, eyes open, and listen and comply."

"Roger that."

Sarah walked back into the room, clearly still pissed off by the look on her face.

"So, what did Marv have to say?"

"He told me to keep my mouth shut."

"That doesn't really to seem to be much of a problem for you lately."

He sighed and stared intently into Sarah's eyes, not saying another word.

"All right. I understand. I'll listen and comply."

"Thank you. Love you. Even though you eavesdrop on my phone calls like a jealous teenager."

"Yep...love you, too, jackass. By the way, you never know when I might be listening."

"Yeah, that's what worries me."

12 Whirlwind

Another knock on the door and doorbell chime—before Bill had finished his first cup of coffee. Sarah was just starting to make her way to the kitchen to get her first cup when she met him in the hallway on his way to answer the door. She simply sighed in apparent disgust and returned to the bedroom to make herself more presentable. He made his way to the door as the doorbell rang a second time. He wasn't surprised this was happening so early.

"Hello, Bill?"

"Yes? Good morning."

"Good morning. I'm Margo, and this is Liz, and we are here to assist you with your upcoming move. I know it's early; I apologize for that. I'm sure you realize by now that things move really quickly in this organization. Michael wanted us to make sure we get you and your family taken care of ASAP."

"Oh, I'm aware. Please, come in. Can I get you anything? Maybe some coffee?"

"No, thank you, Bill. We had a bite to eat and some coffee on the way."

"Hmmm, early day for you."

"Yes, but we've gotten used to it. Will Sarah be joining us?"

"Yes, momentarily. But feel free to get started."

"Great. We have two packages for you. This one is for the sale of the house, and I'll be handling that for you. The second package contains some options for the area where you will be moving, and Liz will be working with you on that. Before you open either one, let me just tell you that your house, this house, is sold. We completed a market analysis and the price point at which it was sold, is about twice what you paid for it. Michael and Bob were clear that you should receive a fair price, and our incoming... Well, we have a member of the organization that is being reassigned to my region, and he was—how should I put this—encouraged to purchase your home. The package for the sale of your home is the paperwork you must sign to sell it. Once you sign, I'll hand you this check for the balance, and you're done with everything that I need to take care of with you. How's that sound?"

"That...sounds...great. Ummm...so...wow. Sorry, I just wasn't expecting that. No, that is great news."

"What's the great news?" Sarah asked as she poured herself a cup of coffee.

"Sarah, this is Margo and Liz"—Bill motioned to both women— "Margo, Liz, this is Sarah. Umm, Sarah, Margo just informed me that our house is already sold and for twice what we paid for it."

"What? Are you serious?" Sarah nearly spewed the sip of coffee she'd just taken. "Holy cow! I didn't expect that."

"Yes, we know. We work quickly," Margo and Liz replied in unison.

Margo continued. "Sarah, we'll need you and Bill to sign the documents so we can finalize the paperwork and give you this check for the balance. Of course, you have all the time you require to get moved, but I don't think that's going to take long either, since we have someone to handle the move for you as well, from door to door."

Liz interjected, "That is, of course, once we have secured a new residence for your family. The whole process should not take more than a couple of weeks."

"A couple weeks? I guess, a couple of weeks will do," Sarah said sarcastically as she began to realize neither she nor Bill really had much say in what was going on.

Bill's phone rang, so he excused himself while Sarah and their guests continued to talk about the selling and buying of homes

"Hello?"

"Bill?"

This was a voice that Bill had not heard before, and he found it somewhat unsettling for some reason.

"Yes, this is Bill. To whom am I speaking?"

"Gabriel. So, Bill... Look, I need you to finish your coffee and whatever it is you need to do to get your guests on their merry little way. I need you to take a look at some things, so you're going to have to get Sarah and the kids up and out of the house for a few hours as well. Just the way it has to be until we get you here and in an on-site office. Instructions will be provided. Black laptop, two hours. Talk to you then, Bill."

The line went dead before Bill could formulate a question much less ask one. He made his way back into the kitchen just in time to sign the paperwork. Before he was done with that, Sarah was already asking him his opinion on two houses that she had narrowed down from twenty, noting each had pros and cons, but one that had a pond stood out, and it was a bit larger than what they were currently living in.

"I'm not sure what we're going to do with thirty-four and a half acres or a thirty-six hundred square foot house, or how we're going to afford it. But...hey...if that's the one."

Liz interrupted Bill to reassure him, "Bill, the cost is not important, it's being paid for and titled in your name. You will own it as soon as you sign the paperwork. That paperwork will take me about fifteen minutes to prepare and print, so if this is the one, and I can connect to your internet, we can have this settled and schedule your visit without movers. No more than thirty minutes and you'll be done, and I'll be out of your hair."

"They're extremely efficient, Bill," Sarah said with a look and a tone known only to Bill and the kids, signaling she was completely pissed off.

"Yes, dear. They truly are amazing at what they do. I do have a couple questions, if I may?"

"Of course, Bill."

"I understand the process moves quickly with The Organization, however, how the hell are we supposed to make a decision about a house, sight unseen? Yes, these are great pictures, but it's been my experience that pictures rarely tell the whole story. You see things in person that you can't in the pictures."

His frustration with The Organization and its employees was evident. His voice was elevated and his face flush.

"I don't know who's driving this train and telling the two of you to— I honestly don't even know how to finish that statement. Bottom line here is I'm not going to sign off on something I haven't seen...we haven't seen."

The scowl Bill wore, and the tone of his voice was enough for Margo. Her snide grin widened as she repositioned herself in the chair, uncrossing her legs, then closed the binder she was holding and placed it in her lap. Margo leaned in and motioned to both Bill and Sarah to do the same.

"Oh, Bill, you know exactly who is driving this train. I'm quite certain both you and Sarah are overwhelmed with the pace of The Organization, but you will get used to it. We all do, given the...*alternative*. We're fast and efficient, more so than most are used to—or are comfortable with. But, if you believe your concerns warrant further explanation, I am sure we can get Michael on the phone so *he* can explain the necessity and answer any lingering questions you or Sarah may have."

Sarah spoke before Bill could open his mouth. "I know both you and Liz are here to help us out. You truly are quite efficient at what you do. Surely, you can understand our frustration. *The Organization* has taken over our life. So, that has us a little on edge. So sorry, not sorry Margo...Liz."

"Understood. It will get better. I sometimes forget how stressful the way The Organization does business can be when you're just starting out. Liz and I can certainly relate."

Liz turned and looked directly at Sarah, her demeanor relaxed and businesslike.

"Yes, we can. And now that we're all on the same page again, which house are we settling on, Sarah? Was it this one?"

"Umm, yes, Liz. That's the one, the big one with all the land, the pond, and the pool. Bill can help you with the internet information. Margo, perhaps we can go and discuss the movers and what is needed from us while Liz prepares the document to sign."

"Yes...great idea, Sarah."

Bill went to grab an ethernet cable but returned to find Liz connecting her laptop to the router he'd received from The Organization. He had not noticed the black dot on the laptop until now. Less than ten minutes passed before Margo and Sarah returned to the kitchen. Liz finished printing the paperwork just as Sarah finished refilling her coffee. And with ten minutes to spare, Bill and Sarah signed the documents and became homeowners once again. Although, they were not entirely sure where Devil's Branch was located.

Once Margo and Liz departed, Bill pulled Sarah aside and asked her to take the kids out for a while, informing her it was work related.

"I know it's a pain in the ass, but—"

"No need to explain...again, I have a pretty good understanding of how this is going to work now."

"I'm—"

"Do *not* tell me you're sorry again. I get we are unwilling participants. We have no choice, at least for the time being. I really don't need to hear you're sorry about this every other sentence."

"I apologize."

She tried not to giggle but couldn't help herself. "Asshole."

Bill chuckled and hugged her. "Your favorite one."

"I suppose."

The kids joined them, and they ate breakfast with very little discussion of the new home or move. The only information shared with them was that their house was more or less sold and they had picked out a new house. They agreed to discuss in more detail over dinner. Once everyone had finished eating, Sarah corralled them and left for the mall.

Bill waited for the call from Gabriel for thirty minutes, growing more impatient by the moment. Finally, the phone rang.

"This is Bill."

"Yeah, know that. Look, I need you to log in on the black system and accept the chat invitation."

"So..."

The line was silent again. Bill sighed.

"Motherfucker."

Bill sat in front of the laptop, logged in, and accepted the chat invitation. It appeared to him this was a modified version of Skype, but he was not certain.

"Bill, this is Michael. Appreciate you getting the family out of the house for a bit."

"No problem."

"Look, we understand this is a whirlwind process. It's unfortunate but necessary. I'd personally appreciate it if you and Sarah could be a bit more amenable to it."

Bill was clearly frustrated about the whole situation, as was Sarah. Margo's thinly veiled threats had backed them onto the cliff. This communication from Michael was pushing him to the edge.

"Not sure how you can expect anyone to be amenable to something like this. The only reason we're going along with this is because I am completely certain you will do just as you indicated you would, and I have no other choice if I want to protect me and mine. It's bullshit, but what choice do I have?"

"None, to be blunt. You're ahead of the curve acknowledging that. Well done."

"Well done? Yeah, whatever, what do you need from me now? What else?"

"You are a fiery lot. Told the boys you were; they didn't agree. They actually thought you were overly passive, which they don't trust. But not me. No sir, I can see it in your eyes. I hear it in your voice, and it comes across clearly to me."

"Is there a point to all this?"

"Actually, yes. We've, shall I say, intercepted some communications, texts to be specific, from the kids to friends about the move. They're not pleased and want to stay. I wanted to offer an opportunity for that to happen."

"That's just not going to happen, Michael."

"They'd be better off...safer, if you will, staying in your family house."

"Yeah, I don't think so."

"It's not really a suggestion, Bill. Thought you'd pick up on that more quickly."

That comment sent Bill over the edge. He was seeing red and finally at the point of telling Michael exactly what he thought.

"What the fuck? Now you're dictating to me that I can't even take the kids? Where do you get off breaking up a family? Who the fuck do you think you are?"

"Well, Bill, I'm the guy who can assure you that precious Sarah and the kids make it home safely. I'm also the guy that can ensure they don't."

"Of course. And fuck you, you son of a bitch."

"Bill, not nice to talk poorly of my mother. She was, in fact, quite a nice lady. Bottom line, Bill, kids are staying. You and Sarah will proceed. That is set in stone. I hope you both understand."

"I understand you're a bunch of sadistic fucks."

"Well, that's not an accurate depiction of who or what we are at all, Bill. You will come to understand that in time."

"I doubt it, you sick fuck."

Michael leaned toward the video camera, squinting slightly, his lips pursed. His arms crossed and elbows on his desk, he looked as sternly and directly into Bill's eyes as he could.

"Bill, I'm a patient and understanding man, but I'm growing tired of your insinuations and language. If you want this over, I can affect that end with the push of a button. You and your family can reunite in the afterlife, should you so wish. I'm actually trying to work with you to make this transition at least somewhat palatable, but that requires a commensurate effort on your behalf and that of Sarah and the kids. I take no pleasure or joy in the more unpleasant side of maintaining operational security of the projects and initiatives for which I am responsible. But, make no mistake, I do take my responsibility very seriously. I never waver, and you really need to grasp that quickly."

Michael's tone was direct and serious. This caught Bill's attention, and he began to calm himself.

"I understand that. Doesn't make it any less bullshit. And what about the house, it's already sold?"

"Agreed. Agreed. As I mentioned before, I've been there, brother. I didn't get here by posting a resume online and doing well in an interview with some stuffed shirts in a boardroom. Trial by fire, one hundred percent. As for the house, yes it was sold...to The Organization."

"Well, that's great. One more hook they have in us. Tell me, how do you not get emotional about all of this?" Bill asked quizzically.

"Emotions are a luxury I can no longer afford. I'm hopeful there is still time to preserve yours. But to do that, you are going to have to find a way to trust me. I'm not asking you to trust anything else...just trust me."

"Not so sure that's in the cards, Michael."

"A gesture of good faith then. There are hidden cameras in, well, all over your house. I suggest you look in the AC vents in the kids' rooms, as well as their bathroom. Do *not*, and I cannot stress this enough, remove any other cameras in the house. Don't even look for them. But I'm telling you that you can remove any that are in the kids' private spaces. That's all I have to offer you to garner your trust."

"That's un-fucking-believable. Spying on the kids? In their *bathrooms?* Maybe I should just call the Agency and let them know. Yeah, that's what I should do."

Bill's anger now showing again, and Michael sat back in his chair. He looked, once more, as directly at Bill as he could via video chat, shaking his head side-to-side and smirking.

"Bill, not a great idea. Not even a good one. Once you say your name, they're going to put you on hold and call me. That happens, you seal your fate and that of Sarah and the kids. You'll cease to exist, and I'll have to start all over. I really don't want to do that."

"I don't give a fuck what you want."

Michael quickly stood and slammed his palms down on his desk, glaring at Bill with a look that only be described as sinister.

"Enough. Do what I instructed you to do. Listen and comply. Discussion is over. I've extended an olive branch to you and all you seem to want to do is use it to hit me. Unless you want me to flip you and your precious family off like a fucking light switch, get with the program!"

Bill bowed his head slightly, nodding up and down in acknowledgment. No matter his internal struggle with the situation, he realized it didn't have to make sense or be fair. He just had to accept it and move forward. He knew no other way to ensure the safety of the kids and Sarah.

"Yeah, got it."

"I know you can't see it, but there will come a day when you'll understand. You will come to trust me." Michael returned to his seat.

"If you say so. Any further instructions?"

"No, just go take care of those cameras before Sarah and the kids return. In fact, I'll take it one step further. Take the cameras out of yours and Sarah's private spaces. I'll take some heat for that, but I need you to trust me, Bill. I'm not what you believe me to be. In time, you... Well, you'll see."

"Thanks for letting me take the cameras out of Sarah's spaces. I do appreciate that."

"Sure. I'll have Gabriel activate the audio on the ones you need to remove. That will make your task a bit easier. We'll be in contact."

"Roger that."

Bill was not happy. But he felt as if he had finally won a battle, even though the war was far from over. He managed to remove all the cameras. He was pissed the cameras had been put into the kids' spaces, and in Sarah's personal space. He could, however, acknowledge Michael's gesture of disclosing the camera locations. He thought, perhaps, just maybe, Michael actually wasn't what he seemed to be.

Bill called the Agency, asked for Marv, and was immediately re-routed to Michael. Michael just chuckled and hung up the phone. That was validation enough for Bill at this point. There was no apparent way out.

Sarah and the kids returned from their five-hour outing to the mall. All carrying about as much as they could possibly carry. Bill glared at Sarah in disapproval, slowly shaking his head from side to side. Sarah smirked and tilted her head to one side with a raised eyebrow, as if to indicate she could not care less what he thought at that moment. The kids disappeared to their rooms. Sarah deposited her purchases into her closet and returned to chat with Bill.

"So, what's new?"

"Not packing up the house."

"Why not?"

"Kids are staying here."

"No way, not happening."

"Okay, well enjoy the last few hours...maybe days, that you have with them then."

"What the hell are you talking about?"

"They hinted at the possibility of erasing us."

Sarah's expression was one of pure shock. Her eyes wide and jaw dropped. "They said they would kill us? They were going to kill us?"

"Not in those exact words. I believed it was more like we'd all disappear. Almost like we were wiped from existence. But I think it was just a re-iteration. Apparently, it's the go-to threat when they're wanting to make sure we know that we don't really have a choice in anything at the moment."

Sarah's shocked expression transformed to one of considerable anger. It was apparent in the tone of her voice. "So, you *have* called someone, *right*? Marv? The Agency? The FB fucking, I? Somebody?"

"Sarah, please keep your voice down."

"Keep my voice down?"

"Sarah, please?"

"How can you expect me to do that? How can you expect me to just go along with this bullshit? How can these assholes keep getting away with making threats and...and... How can they just play god?"

Bill was in triage mode, trying to muster the right combination of words to convey the message he had all but accepted. There was no way out of this except through it.

"Like Marv told me, they don't 'exist' and when you don't 'exist', you can pretty much do whatever the hell you want. No oversight to speak of apparently. Look, Michael told me my call would get forwarded to The Organization. He was right. Michael picked up and just laughed before he hung up. We're basically trapped, Sarah. For now, at least, we have to play ball with these folks, otherwise bad things are going to happen."

She was very clearly still pissed off and her face beet red, but the flush was beginning to subside. Bill knew that look. But it was clear to him from the natural tones returning to her face that regardless of how pissed she was, she had seemingly come to understand they had no other option.

"Fuck's sake, Bill."

"We'll tell them over dinner, and we can discuss hiring a nanny or caregiver of some sort. I don't want to put that parental responsibility on Trevor or GG."

"Yeah, I agree. Even though they're adults, they have enough to deal with between work and college. And you know Trevor and GG are stricter with the rules than we are anyway."

"Yeah, they'd rather us than Trevor or GG."

"Yeah, you're probably right about that."

Sarah cooked, and they sat down to eat. Bill outlined the new plan for the family. All seven of the kids tossed a barrage of questions at their patriarch. Bill raised his hands as if to say enough. Trevor spoke up, in his typical role as the offspring's spokesperson.

"So, you're taking a new job. Mom's going with. But we're staying here. Why? Don't get me wrong, me and GG can handle this, but you and Mom get to go start a new life without us?"

"Look guys, there are things—"

"What your dad is trying to say is this. This is a *temporary* situation. We don't know how long *temporary* is just yet. We do not have any plans on uprooting the seven of you from the routines we have established. We discussed maybe getting a nanny or caregiver to take the bulk of the responsibility and not putting that on the two of you."

The kids were staring at Sarah, soaking up every word. Though they all had a puzzled look on their faces, they were not attempting to ask questions. It was as if Sarah had some special power over them.

"Besides, you all know that in the last couple of years, Trev and GG have been your caregivers 90% of the time. With me and dad working, we had no other options that were affordable or acceptable. This arrangement doesn't change anything, but your ability to see me and Dad daily. Plus, Morgan and Nick can help a lot; they both drive now. Aaron will be driving in a couple months... Tanna and Will are in virtual school—"

GG was shaking her head and finally had to speak up.

"Yeah, that's true, Mom. But what about me and Trev? What about us moving forward with our lives? This isn't very fair to us. Honestly not fair to any of us."

All the kids nodded in agreement.

"No, you're right. Unfortunately, in life, sometimes things are not fair. This is one of those times. Your dad and I are not happy about it, but his new employer has taken that choice away from us. It is one of the conditions of his employment."

"How can they do that?"

"Private companies can do what they want for the most part. Look, kids, I know it sucks. But I cannot afford to lose this job. At least not right now. I told your mom I'm going to find a way out of my contract *somehow*. Okay?"

Although they didn't fully understand what was so special about Bill's new job that prevented them from going, they were happy that at least he and Sarah were together again.

Everyone was on board with making the non-typical family arrangement work.

"Look, guys, I know this doesn't make a lot of sense. Your mom and I certainly didn't plan for this, but it's a necessity. If not taking this job was an option, I would not be taking it."

"Yeah, we figured something was up. We heard you guys, um, discussing things. So, it was obvious to us, that this one was going to be different. We don't want a caregiver or nanny. We don't need any help. We've got this under control. No need to worry."

"We know you do. We know you do."

* * *

The family settled in for the night. Sarah and Bill didn't get much sleep. Sarah finally just got out of bed at five a.m. rather than lie there awake any longer. She prepared for and cooked breakfast. The smell of bacon and waffles wafted throughout the house and subconsciously summoned everyone from their slumber. The kids were around just long enough to eat, then they disappeared back into the abyss of their rooms. Not to be seen or heard again until lunch. They had no sooner finished lunch when there was yet another knock on the door.

Sarah immediately told the kids to let Bill answer the door. He did not appear the least bit shocked to see the movers standing on the porch. In fact, it seemed as though he was expecting it. Bill invited them in and asked for a moment to speak with his family.

"Kids, when I said these guys move fast, well, these are the movers to pack up the few things that your mom and I taking with us. It would be best if all of you hung out in your rooms while they're here."

The kids preferred to be in their rooms most of the time anyway, so Bill's suggestion was not met with any objections. He and Sarah met with the movers, each identifying the items that were most important to them, ensuring they were properly protected during the move. It was clear these guys had done this, many times before. They were extremely efficient as evidenced by being complete with pre-planning work for the move in less than an hour. After all, it was one bedroom and personal items for the two of them and not the whole house. Bill and Sarah simply accepted the mover's suggestions and scheduled the packing two days later.

The family discussed the new beginning and the new family dynamic over dinner and laid out the plans for them to do their part once Bill and Sarah relocated. GG asked the one question that all the kids had apparently been secretly pondering. "Why do both of you have to go?"

"GG, that's a great question. For the past, gosh, I don't know how many years, probably most of your lives, I've stayed here with all of you to make sure the house ran smoothly and all of you were taken care of while Mr. Military was off saving the world. This time, The Organization has *requested* that I tag along. So that's why we're both going. Besides, GG, you and Trevor have taken care of things very well when asked. If not for that, we'd have to make different arrangements."

* * *

The movers' plan was executed with military precision and completed in a few hours, then Bill and Sarah's belongings were on the way to Devil's Branch. They spent one last night in the family house. Bill and Sarah said their *see-you-laters* to the kids before the sun was up. They were done and on the road by dawn so they would make their appointment with Liz and Margo on time.

There was not as much fanfare on this trip, though it seemed to pass by more quickly than the last one. Little was said, aside from Sarah assisting with the deciphering of GPS directions.

The new house was bigger than the pictures made it seem. It was much more space than Bill and Sarah needed, but they had room for the kids—if they were ever allowed to visit. The landscaping was meticulous, the grass greener than any they had ever had, and, to them, it seemed as though it was made especially for them. They were not all that far off-base with their assumptions.

The original structure was about ten years old, but the house had been gutted and completely remodeled. The landscaping and the huge pool were new. No matter, they were amazed and delighted with what they saw before them.

Liz was waiting to greet them and facilitate the movement of their new furniture. It came as no surprise to Bill or Sarah that the movers and Liz had unpacked their personal belongings and set everything up in the house.

Liz gave them a tour of the house as well as the property, noting that no neighbors were within five miles in any direction, and the property was surrounded on all sides by federal land.

"Yeah, Bill, so no exploring beyond our property lines. Got it?" Sarah offered with the slightest hint of concern in her voice.

"Actually, you're free to explore any of it. Although, I would caution against doing so alone. There's a lot of wildlife in that forest that could harm you if you startle it. Explore all you want; just be really careful," Liz responded.

Liz remained to answer the few questions they had left. She departed after letting Bill and Sarah know that Michael, and perhaps some of his team, might be stopping by the following day. "Nothing official or to worry about," she added, "Just to make sure your needs have been met and you're ready to get started." With that, Liz departed, and Bill and Sarah were left to explore the new home and property at their leisure.

It was not the journey they had planned post retirement. It was however the journey they were now on. The Organization had provided very well for them, materialistically, but the separation from their kids could not be balanced with things. They knew Trevor and GG could handle the responsibility, but it wasn't fair to any of the kids to be in this situation. Something had to give; they had to find a way out, but they both knew it would not be easy...if it was possible at all.

They'd planned to shop for groceries, only to find that had been done for them. And it had been done quite well—as they were coming to expect from The Organization, based on their interactions to this point. Aside from the threats, constant surveillance, and lack of choice, the pay, house, and property would make most feel as though life had suddenly become the idealistic dream, but that wasn't the way they felt.

They were trying to make the best of a nightmarish, far less than ideal situation.

The day and night passed, and they found themselves at the breakfast table again. Discussion regarding the property and the house dominated the conversation. As they were nearly done with the meal, Sarah spoke up—with a comment that only she dared say.

"Well, we're almost done with breakfast, maybe you should go wait on the front porch for Michael and his guys. We all know they're as punctual as they are intimidating."

"Yes, I think you're right."

13 Measuring Up

Bill had barely taken his seat on the porch when the black SUV with dark tinted windows pulled slowly up the drive. Michael was the first to step out, as usual, and was talking before his feet hit the ground.

"Yes, I know, Bill. This is all profoundly cliché: Shady characters piling out of an SUV wearing black suits and dark tinted sunglasses... It's like a scene from every sci-fi or action movie that involves the government. We're overly stereotyped."

"I suppose so," Bill said with a chuckle.

"The boys and I wanted to come by and make sure The Organization has taken care of you as we promised you it would. We have also been asked to escort you to your first day of work. We have some formalities to get out of the way before you can actually get to the meat of what you're going to be doing for The Organization."

"Yes, I'm sure there are things that require my attention. I just need five minutes to change."

"Take as much time as you like. What we have to get done today isn't going anywhere without us."

Bill made his way inside, informing Sarah he was starting his new job, and Michael and the guys were going to drive him. Before Sarah had the opportunity to ask, he told her that he had no idea when he would be back, so plan for him not to be home for meals. He never slowed down as he made his way to the bedroom with Sarah in tow. He turned long enough to see the squinty eyed, concerned look on her face.

"I know, Sarah. Unexpected and odd...but it's just the way they operate." He threw both hands up in a classic, *what can I do* position. She responded by placing her hands on her hips, shaking her head in disapproval.

"I know. I still don't like it."

"I know that too. It's all good. Everything is going to be fine, as long as I'm meeting—we're meeting—expectations. They've been true to their word so far, so I have no reason to doubt them at this point."

"I think there's plenty to doubt...but I understand what you're saying."

"Yes, many answers we don't have yet. Who are these guys, really? What, exactly, is The Organization? What do they do? Who do they do it for? Blah, blah, blah."

Bill continued dressing while Sarah sat on the bed, hugging a pillow as if to comfort herself.

"So, you don't have any thoughts on any of that?"

"Well, I mean, I suspect they are contractors, probably black ops related. Since they 'don't exist', the government is not going to acknowledge them. They're probably the ones the government calls to take care of a problem in ways that can't be tied to the government."

"Well, that's just peachy, isn't it?"

"Nah, not really."

"Well, fall guy, you probably need to get going."

"Ha...very funny. How do I look?"

"Handsome as always. But seriously, you keep your eyes *wide* open. You—I mean we—can't afford to be complacent," Sarah replied as she stood to remove stray lint from the back of Bill's shirt.

"Ha...only handsome in your eyes."

"They're the only eyes that matter. Besides your own."

"I did hear you, by the way; you're right. We cannot afford to be complacent, especially me. I will do everything within my power to take care of you and the kids. I promise you that!" Sarah hugged Bill, then grabbed him by the shoulders, turned him around, and began pushing him to the door.

"I know that to be true! My biggest fear is that no matter how great your power, it will not be enough against these people. No matter what, just remember the kids and I love you. And we know that you love us."

Bill slid his keys and wallet into their respective pockets, turned to face Sarah, and made a heart gesture with both hands, placing it over his heart, before saying, "Always."

Just as he was about to grab the doorknob, he stopped and returned to his new office. He had not yet spent any time in it other than to just see it the night before. He walked to the desk, opened the top center drawer, and retrieved the manila envelope.

* * *

Sarah returned to the bedroom to make the bed and gather clothes to be washed.

Well, what are you going to do with yourself today, Sarah? I suppose you do chores and catch up on your favorite TV shows. Probably wouldn't be a good idea to get on the Internet and research The Organization. Ugh...Get it together Sarah...you know better...it's too soon...too soon.

She knew Bill would find a way out if there was one. She just had to support him while he figured it out.

* * *

With package in hand, Bill made his way out the door. Michael was leaning against their vehicle with his arms crossed, trying to regain his composure after laughing at something one of the men said.

"Well done, Bill. You brought the paperwork. You're going to work out just fine. I can feel it in my bones. Ready to go?"

"As ready as I'm going to be."

"Ha, I couldn't have said it better myself. After you. Gentlemen, let's get Bill to work."

They headed down the drive to the main road toward the nearest town. "So, Bill, a lot going on today for you. I'm sure you figured as much. I want to break it down for you to put your mind at ease," Michael began, just minutes into the drive.

"I'd appreciate that, Michael." Bill was quite curious to see if his suspicions were accurate, while at the same time, hoping they were not.

"We will be, at some point during our drive to the office today, placing a blindfold and hood over your head. I want to make you aware of that now so you don't freak out later. It's a security precaution we have to take, in the unlikely event you don't make the cut. I'm sure you understand, so no need to acknowledge other than a nod."

Bill nodded in agreement. He had been in a somewhat similar situation many years ago, when he was asked to visit a low-profile location. A hood had been placed over his head, and he was driven around in circles to disorient him prior to arriving at the destination. He understood, and given what he'd already been through with Michael and his cohorts, this was not entirely unexpected.

"Once we arrive, we'll take you inside before we remove the security measures. We'll ask that you empty your pockets and take off any jewelry and leave it with our security professionals at the entry control point, or ECP, and then we'll escort you into the conference room, where you'll be briefed on the activities scheduled for today. With me so far?"

Bill nodded again, wondering if they would cut his wedding ring off should he not be able to remove it himself.

"Nah, I think we can overlook the wedding band. No need to get wrapped around the axle on that one."

Bill was instantly unnerved with that comment. This was not the first time something seemingly coincidental had occurred, and he was certain at this point it was no coincidence.

"Not coincidental at all. It will all become clear to you quickly, provided today goes well. And I'm certain you will do just fine. Once your initial briefing is complete, you will be required to take a battery of tests, both oral and written, that will culminate in a polygraph. Provided all those go well; you will then be taken to the security conference room where you will be informed regarding almost every aspect of The Organization pertinent to your position. Still following me, Bill?"

Bill again nodded in agreement. He didn't appear surprised by the activities of the day. The only thing that seemingly got under his skin was the total lack of privacy, not even in his own head. He didn't understand how Michael's comments regarding his thoughts were on point. He hoped his briefings today would educate him as to what the hell was really going on.

"Well, you need to go ahead and put this blindfold on. I think you'll find it's a bit thicker than what you've experienced before. It has been known to cause anxiety in a few instances, so Remiel suggested we start putting some lavender oil on the hood prior to use. I hope you're not allergic."

He indicated he wasn't and leaned forward as Michael reached to place the hood on him.

* * *

Michael sat back and was now staring intently at Bill, even though Bill couldn't see it, with a huge grin on his face.

He slowly shook his head from side to side and chuckled to himself.

"You keep this up, Bill...I may actually be able to retire. I haven't come across anyone like you in all the time I've been with The Organization. You have absolutely no filter, at least not within your thoughts. The words may not come out of your mouth, but you think almost exactly like I do, and for the first time, I've encountered someone that actually makes me pause. You need to embrace that. It will serve you very well within The Organization."

With that comment, they came to a stop and exited the vehicle. After the short walk, they were inside, where Michael removed the hood and blindfold. Bill seemed unmoved and not the least bit surprised by what he saw.

"Bill, these fine gentlemen have a couple of security checks they need to perform. It is procedure. Never can be too trusting of folks," Michael said sarcastically.

"I'm going to verify exactly which room the indoctrination team want you in so we're not wandering around the hallways. I'll be back in a couple minutes." Michael departed the ECP, presenting his security badge to the badge reader beside the door, then disappearing behind it.

* * *

Bill followed the instructions to a 'T', as he emptied his pockets and removed his jewelry. The security guards patted him down and used the wand to ensure he was not hiding anything. They provided him with a visitor's badge on a lanyard, which he placed around his neck, and he had a seat until Michael returned.

Bill had barely taken his seat when the door opened, and Michael motioned to him.

"Let's get you to the conference room and situated. I'm sure you're anxious to get started."

Michael led him into the conference room and asked his cohorts to wait by the door. It was not a large conference room, seating for eight or so, with a large flat screen monitor on the wall and what looked to be video-teleconferencing equipment mounted below it.

Bill took the seat Michael indicated, still not having spoken a word. He seemed resolved to not utter a sound until told he could. If he had learned anything so far about The Organization, it was compliance with direction was not optional. Bill's gaze met Michael's, who was smiling and nodding in approval. Bill nodded, also in agreement, and remained silent.

Only a few moments passed before a decidedly serious looking woman walked through the door, depositing a large stack of folders onto the conference table. Michael swiftly moved to close the door and returned to stand beside Bill. The woman arranged the folders before taking her seat and changing her demeanor. She was a gorgeous woman with piercing green eyes and auburn hair. It seemed to Bill that they had crossed paths before. She smiled and nodded, first to Michael, then to Bill, before she spoke.

"Good morning, gentlemen. I hope you are both doing well today. I don't want to waste anyone's time, so I'll jump right into it."

Michael gestured toward the woman with one hand while placing the other on Bill's shoulder

"Bill, this is the Orator. She will be conducting your testing today. I can tell you now that in addition to the testing I've already alluded to, there will be some...shall we say...unorthodox testing, designed specifically to ensure you are able to perform the duties assigned to your position. These may include asking you to do things that may conflict with who you are and what you're about...how you live your life...your belief system...how you perform under duress...your decision-making process in stressful situations...your ability to perform certain tasks that may make you exceedingly uncomfortable, and your ability appear as though you are unaffected by what you're being asked to do."

Bill nodded in agreement, although his body language clearly showed he was already uncomfortable. He turned to look at the Orator as she began to speak.

"Bill, I'm just here to run you through the process. I...well, we, are under no preconceived notions that you will pass every test with flying colors. If you're asked to do something, we expect you to attempt what you're being asked to do without question. If you fail, we annotate it and move on. Few issues arise that we can't overcome with additional training, but failure to comply is simply unacceptable. Make sense?"

Bill nodded in agreement once more. With his acknowledgment, the Orator continued.

"First, I will need you to complete these tests, one at a time. Start with the packet farthest to your left and work your way through them. The battery of tests includes six individual tests, all designed to do nothing more than provide a detailed analysis of your personality. We will use these to dial in the scenario-based training that will come later. I cannot emphasize this enough: you must be 100% honest in completing these tests, and always, *always* go with your first instinct. That cannot be stressed enough. Your first instinct provides us with the most accurate information, and that's critical to your success. Begin."

Bill had been subjected to personality and psychological testing before. He set out on his assigned task, following the instruction he'd been given. He had always been able to read quickly and was decisive in his decision-making process, so the behavioral tests were a breeze for him. Barely an hour later, he closed the final packet and placed his pencil back on the table. Bill was feeling slightly more relaxed. The familiarity of the testing gave him a sense of peace.

"Well done. I'll take these to the Evaluator. Michael, could you please provide Bill with his change of clothes."

As she made her way out of the room, Michael produced what looked like a prison jumpsuit. It was the classic orange jumpsuit often depicted in movies. As Bill took the jumpsuit from Michael and placed it on the table before him, he reached to loosen his tie.

"Hold off on that, Bill. I was asked to provide that to you; no further instruction was given."

Bill nodded and realized the strictness of direction was finite.

"So, no actions without direction? Like I'm fresh out of basic military training. Got it."

"Yes, it is a lot like that." Michael quipped with a grin.

* * *

It seemed to comfort Bill somewhat, knowing that his every move was going to be scripted for him, although he did not appear completely at ease with the lack of freedom of movement or thought.

"Phase one complete. The Evaluator was pleased with what she reviewed. Now we can move on to phase two."

Michael and Bill nodded to each other in approval and then to the Orator.

"So, Bill. I need you to come over here to the end of the table. I'll take this chair," she said, moving the chair to face him as she sat down.

"Now, I need you to remove your clothing with the exception of your boxers and give the items to Michael."

Bill was obviously not pleased with what he had been directed to do, and it was clearly showing in his facial expression and mannerisms. But the briefing he had received made it clear there was no choice but to comply. With the Orator staring intently at him, he removed his clothing and handed the neatly folded garments to Michael, who nodded in approval. Bill then turned to the Orator, whose gaze moved from his head down to his toes and back, several times.

She purposely paused at Bill's midriff, just above his groin. This was intended to rattle him, who appeared intent on not allowing that to happen. It appeared this was going to last an eternity but was barely a full minute. She stared intently into his eyes before speaking.

"Do you not find me attractive? I would have though me ogling your body would have prompted some instinctual response. I mean, I think I'm a fairly attractive female specimen. Am I wrong?"

Bill quickly shook his head.

"Well, then, what does it take to evoke a response?" With that, the orator stood, approached him, and placed her hand at his waistline. She then circled him, her hand remaining at waist level.

"Still, nothing? I'm impressed, Bill. Most recruits don't fare as well. Still, I have to know what it takes to see some sort of response from you."

With that, still behind him, she placed both hands on Bill's chest and pulled him against her chest. As she slowly moved her hands down his torso, past his abdomen, and onto each leg, even to his groin, she licked the back of his neck. Goosebumps immediately appeared on his skin. She moved to stand in front of him and could see she had prompted a response.

"Finally. Very well done controlling yourself, Bill. Most guys would be bursting at the seams long before I took it that far. I am impressed. The ability to control your emotions and suppress desire will serve you and The Organization well. I apologize for having to put you through this, but it is part of the process. I will forewarn you: At some point today, this test will be taken much further. As Michael stated earlier, you are going to be asked to do things that conflict with every aspect of your life. We have to make sure you measure up to our standards. And from what I see...you measure up well."

Michael stepped forward and, facing away from him, handed Bill his clothes. "Bill, I understand what just occurred is very unorthodox, some might say it's even *technically* illegal. What I need you to understand here is, if you have not already picked up on it, that The Organization operates largely in a *dark* gray area of process, procedure, compliance, the law, etc."

Bill turned and looked at Michael, clearly disgusted. His face was flushed and teeth clenched.

"Kidnapping, sexual harassment, and sexual assault are now *gray areas?* That's without a doubt the loosest, most bullshit definition of *gray area* that I've ever heard."

Michael, now profoundly serious, clinched his fists, placing them on the conference table and leaning forward toward Bill.

"You can expect more boundaries to be encroached upon—and possibly breached...well, definitely breached, to be completely honest. It's a *necessary* evil, if you will."

"Yeah, Michael...I gathered that," Bill snapped sarcastically.

"I'm sure you did. I'm sure you did. And I'm equally sure you'll get over it or die trying."

14 The Truth Will Set You Free

Bill, now wearing the orange jumpsuit, was ready for the next test. The Orator led him down the narrow hallway to a room where Michael was standing at the door. She entered and motioned to him to have a seat. He was no stranger to polygraphs; they had been a requirement for his jobs in the military. This, he thought, should be a breeze.

Michael stepped forward to speak, but the Orator spoke first. "Bill, this is the Evaluator."

"Thank you, Ellynore," the Evaluator said.

"You're welcome, Sylvya."

"I know you've been through this before," Sylvya began. "Same rules apply here. I'll ask you some questions to set a baseline. Then, it's game on. You need to know before we start here, I will be asking intimately personal and invasive questions. This will be unlike anything you have experienced before in that aspect. There is one constant that you need to know and comply with...tell the truth no matter what. What we talk about...the answers to your questions...no information leaves this room. The only thing that leaves this room is the response chart and whether or not you told me the truth. Fair enough?"

Bill nodded.

"Oh, Bill, you can speak now, and after we're done here...provided we have a positive outcome, which I'm sure we will." Bill tilted his head to one side, his eyes opened wider than normal, as if to say, *I hope so.*

"Of what possible use could asking 'personally intimate and or invasive questions' be? I've taken lifestyle Poly's before, but this sounds like it's far worse."

"Michael laid it out pretty clearly for you already. It's a necessary evil, so to speak. If you'd rather forgo this, we can *terminate* your employment immediately."

"No, I'm ready when you are," Bill responded, defeated.

"Let's get this done, Bill. I'm going to ask you a series of questions, for which all the answers will be yes. I need you to wait for me to finish the question before you respond. Respond quickly once I am done asking the question. Do you understand my directions?"

"Yes"

"Is your name Bill?"

"Yes."

Sylvya proceeded to ask the first round of baseline questions, with Bill answering in the affirmative for all of them. After the final question, she provided additional direction.

"Okay, Bill. You're doing great. A little borderline with the answer to that last question, but given the circumstances, I understand that indication, and it is not an issue. Now, I am going to ask you the same questions, and I want you to respond No to each of them. Do you understand my directions?"

Bill recognized the tactic, Sylvya was using. There was no way his answers were borderline. She was attempting to rattle him...try and get him to misstep. He was having none of that, and proceeded with this answer, as if unfazed in the least.

"No."

"Ah, very good."

"Is your name Bill?"

"No."

Now complete with establishing a baseline for the critical evaluation questions. She paused for a moment to take a sip of water before proceeding.

"Okay...again, well done, Bill. Again, borderline with that last question but not unexpected. Now, we're going to move into the evaluation phase of this test. I will be asking you twenty questions. Your answers to those questions will dictate whether I need to ask more than twenty questions. I cannot stress this point to you enough: As long as you answer truthfully, you'll be fine. If you are unsure, go with your gut, and we can discuss it. Do you understand my instructions?"

"Yes."

"Have you ever done anything that intentionally or unintentionally undermined the trust that the government has placed in you?"

"No."

"Have you ever done anything that intentionally or unintentionally undermined the trust that your family has placed in you?"

"Yes."

"Have you ever willfully disobeyed direction given to you by your superiors?"

"Yes."

"Have you ever willfully violated your wedding vows?"

"No."

"Have you ever secretly desired to violate your wedding vows?"

"No."

"Did you secretly desire to violate your wedding vows today?"

"No."

"Did you secretly want to have sex with The Orator this morning?"

"No."

"Have you ever engaged in deviant sexual activities, such as pedophilia, necrophilia, bestiality, incest, rape, torture, or any other form?"

"No."

"If you were required to participate in any of the aforementioned sexually deviant behaviors, if deemed in the best interest of your country, would you do as you were directed?"

Bill was dumfounded by the direction the questions were going. Though he provided what he thought to be the correct answers, he could not reconcile acting out such atrocities. Beads of sweat were forming on his brow.

"Bill, I will ask the question again. I need you to answer quickly and go with your gut instinct. Remember...no wrong answers here. If you were required to participate in any of the aforementioned sexually deviant behaviors, if deemed in the best interest of your country, would you do as you were directed?"

"No."

"Have you directly or through the accomplishment of your duties while on active duty in the military, ever been responsible, even indirectly for the death of a human being?"

"Yes."

"Have you ever killed another human being."

"No."

"Have you ever desired to kill a human being."

"No."

"Have you ever withheld information that was later deemed critically important to your superiors for their decision-making process."

"Yes."

"When you withheld that information, was it done so intentionally?"

"Yes."

"Was it done maliciously?"

"Yes."

"Did you withhold the information to achieve a desired decision by your superiors that was in alignment with your moral compass?"

"Yes."

"Do you stand by your decision to withhold the information today?"

"Yes."

"If you deemed it in the best interest of the greater good to withhold information from The Organization, would you withhold that information?"

"No."

"Would you relay the information because you are of the opinion that The Organization would already be aware that you possessed critical information and were planning to withhold it?"

"Yes."

"Do you believe The Organization would go to any lengths to protect the best interests of the country and The Organization itself?"

"Yes."

"Do you want to have sex with me?

"No."

"Do you want to have sex with the Orator?"

"No."

"If passing this test and subsequent tests meant you had to have sex with one or both of us, would you have sex with us?"

"Yes."

"Do you fear the supernatural?"

"No."

"Do you fear the paranormal?"

"No."

"Do you believe in either the supernatural or the paranormal?"

"No."

"Is your name Bill?"

"Yes."

"All right, Bill, we're done. You passed this test easily. Which is good—great, in fact. However, your moral compass will be tested and re-oriented. That is an unfortunate requirement for members of this organization. You see, we are the ones that operate in obscurity to do the things that nobody else has the fortitude to accomplish. Sometimes, you have to step outside yourself—your moral and ethical boundaries—in order to gain the trust of the most unsavory individuals among our population. It's a means to an end, Bill."

"I, unfortunately, picked up on that, with the references to sex with anything, rape, and torture. I don't care to be involved with any of it, but I understand the consequences of failing to comply."

"Well, with that, Bill, you are free to roam about. Michael will find you when they're ready for the next phase of your testing."

"Thank you, Sylvya."

"You are most welcome. And remember, the one way to ensure your success is to *listen and comply,*" she said with a smile and a wink.

"So, I've heard. Thanks again." With that, Bill stood and stretched for a few moments then returned to his seat, placed his head in his hands. He knew the situation was bad but had never imagined it could be as bad as it was turning out to be for him. He could only hope it didn't get worse.

15 The Reset

Bill watched as Sylvya grabbed her notes and made her way out of the door, leaving the door open. He sat in silence, wondering what he'd gotten himself into. After a few minutes, he decided to roam around. The building was so familiar, yet strange in its own regard. To Bill, all military facilities looked pretty much the same.

Bill didn't have to roam long before Michael found him and guided him to the cafeteria. They made it through the line and then to a table set apart from the rest. The Orator and the Evaluator were already seated along with another female he had not previously seen.

Upon sitting, Michael made the introduction. "Bill, this is Patrycya. She will be conducting the final phase of your testing this afternoon. She's often referred to as the Matriculator. She is in charge of training enrollment and execution."

Ellynore added, "Yes, she will be providing the training scenarios that you will be going through this afternoon. Much like your last test, there are no wrong answers at this point. The one point I will reiterate, action in support of direction is required. If you follow that advice, you will do just fine."

"Thank you. I will definitely keep that in mind."

As the women stood, Patrycya spoke. "Bill, if you and Michael will excuse us, we have to prepare for the scenarios. Michael will bring you to the testing area, and then you're on your own. Once you walk through the door and close it behind you, the test will begin. It will not end until I announce it is over. You will be given direction either in person or via loudspeaker, which may point you to written instructions as well, but no matter the format, the direction given is to be followed with no exceptions. Do you understand?"

"Yes."

"Michael. Bill. See you soon."

"How about we steer clear of the official nonsense and enjoy a meal?"

"Sounds like a great plan to me," Bill responded.

They took their time eating, and what conversation passed between them was superficial and unrelated to The Organization. They talked about hobbies and vacation spots. After finishing the last bite of his sandwich, Michael stood and nodded for Bill to follow, although he wasn't quite finished.

"Bill, this is the last phase of testing for you. At least, for the orientation. I'm sure you understand, as with all jobs, various tests and training have to occur from time to time. Whether it's a refresher or to teach a new skillset."

"Yes, that's not an issue."

Michael stepped closer to Bill and placed his hand on Bill's shoulder and leaned slightly toward him.

"I didn't think it would be. You've done really well so far. So well, in fact, I think you've surpassed everyone's expectations, and our expectations were pretty high for you."

"That's really good to hear."

Bill was comfortable, although not relaxed. He nodded in agreement when Michael spoke. He felt as if he was legitimately supported by Michael but thought his feelings odd, given the circumstances. As Michael patted Bill on the back, he spoke again.

"We're here. Just remember what the OEM have advised you to do."

"OEM?"

"Oh, sorry. The Orator, Evaluator, and the Matriculator, OEM. Just a nickname for them and a lot easier to say quickly. So, stick to what they tell you, and this will go well. Don't, and as you may have surmised, it won't end well. It's as simple as that."

With that comment, Bill noticed movement off to his right and turned to see what it was. Two large men were carrying what looked to be a black body bag. He thought it surely had to be for dramatic effect but quickly reminded himself not to assume anything. He had to believe everything he saw was real and that his life likely depended on it.

"You are growing wiser by the moment, Bill," Michael said with a wink. "When you are ready, just walk inside this door. Remember, once that door closes behind you, follow all directions to the letter until Patrycya advises you the test is complete."

"I will. Thank you, Michael."

"Of course. See you on the other side."

Bill gathered his wits about him and walked inside. He took a deep breath as he closed the door and turned to face what he'd come to fear most this day. The unknown parameters of this final test were worrisome to say the least. He gathered his thoughts once more and studied what he saw.

He was in a courtyard with three visible doors in addition to the one he'd just entered, one on each wall. Four chairs were positioned in the center of the small courtyard, each facing a door, and landscaping covered the areas of the walls between the doors. He stood motionless, awaiting instruction, and continued to study his new surroundings. He saw what appeared from this distance to be a number one in the chair facing him. He could only assume the other chairs were numbered as well.

Several moments passed before a voice instructed Bill to approach the chairs and find the chair labeled *four*. Bill quickly moved toward the chairs, and as he drew close, he noticed the chair to his right was the correct chair. He moved to stand in front of it, not risking additional action.

"Now, take the envelope labeled *four*, have a seat, read the instructions, and proceed accordingly. Read this in its entirety and ensure you fully understand your instructions before proceeding."

Bill did as instructed and, once seated, began to read his instructions.

You are a businessman, returning from an unsuccessful meeting that was intended to acquire a competing business. You are married with no children. Your marriage has suffered for months because of your dedication to your business aspirations, leaving your wife lonely. You are arriving home a day earlier than expected and notice a car in the driveway that you do not recognize. Your briefcase is sitting just outside the door to your home. Inside is the handgun you typically keep in your vehicle for protection.

You are about to be in a confrontation that may ultimately lead to your death. Act accordingly.

Bill studied the instructions intently for several minutes. He readied himself and made his way to the door, opened the briefcase to reveal a handgun that he quickly confirmed was loaded with what appeared to be live ammunition. He paused briefly to offer a short prayer for guidance, then gripped the pistol, closed his briefcase, and walked through the doorway. It was as if he'd literally walked into someone's house. Every detail was in place. *They are truly committed to the scenarios*, he thought.

Once inside, he could hear two people talking. He sat the briefcase down on the counter rather loudly. The voices quieted at the sound, a door opening down the hallway could be heard.

A woman came walking toward him.

"Honey, I wasn't expecting you home today. What a great..."

"Who's in the bedroom with you?" Bill asked pointedly.

"It's Mary, from work."

"Why are you talking in the bedroom? Why not out here?"

"Well, it's...dammit, why did you have to come home today?"

"What's going on here?"

"Why do you have that gun?"

"Answer my questions. *Now.*"

"Screw you, asshole! Who do you think you are?"

"Look, I come home a day early. You look like you just got caught with your hand in the cookie jar; you're refusing to tell me what's going on. And you have the audacity to turn this on me? You need to start talking."

"Fine...Well, Einstein, Mary is having a tough time since she had her baby. She's dealing with a lot of self-doubt and probably some postpartum depression. So, I offered to take some boudoir photos of her to show her how beautiful she is. Wait here just a second."

Bill was thinking he'd blown this scenario at this point. *I was ready to fight, or even shoot somebody for bonking my fake wife. Now this...oh, boy.*

"Look, see. These are great pictures...and she's hot."

Bill quickly noticed the pictures were of the Orator. They were not nudes, but there was not much left to the imagination with the lingerie she was wearing.

"I apologize. All I could imagine was you..."

"Me...screwing somebody other than you. That's what you were thinking. Well, how about that? That's...disappointing...to say the least." She turned and walked toward the bedroom again. "Maybe I should just show you the rest of the pictures...hmmm?"

She disappeared briefly and returned with a handful of pictures.

Bill noticed her demeanor had changed drastically as she approached him. Her facial expression and her eyes were now blank, as if her soul had left her body. She stopped a few feet from him, tossing the pictures at his feet with her right hand, her left hand hidden behind her back.

Bill, noticing her hidden hand, now held his pistol behind him. He ensured the safety was off and squatted to grab the pictures off the floor with his left hand while maintaining his gaze on his fake wife's empty eyes. Grabbing a handful, he stood, never breaking the gaze.

"What are these?"

"Look for yourself."

"What's behind your back?"

"Nothing." She extended her left hand, remaining otherwise motionless.

"I'm not convinced," Bill said, glancing quickly at the photos in his hand. That quick glance was enough. It was pictures, explicit and gory, clearly of at least one deceased individual. As his gaze met his fake wife's again, her expression was one of rage and disgust. She had reached behind her back again, and at that moment, Bill noticed she was gripping something in her right hand. He raised his weapon and fired a single shot centered between her eyes.

Even before her body finished falling, a voice came over the loudspeaker.

"Place all props on the floor or counter and return to the courtyard. Find the chair labeled *two*, sit, and read the instructions provided before proceeding."

Bill complied but could not help thinking on his way to the chair labeled *two*, *Props? That certainly felt real. They must have great actors and actresses on staff.* Bill found the chair, sat, and began to read his new instructions.

You are investigating a murder. A man has returned home early from a business trip to find his wife having an affair. He has shot and killed her but professes his innocence. Determine the truth and act accordingly. You will be assisted by supporting law enforcement, but you are in charge.

Bill once again approached the door and, without hesitation this time, opened and entered.

The officer, who looked very young and as if this might be his first day on the job approached Bill. "Detective...finally. Glad you're here."

Bill immediately recognized the scene. He'd just left it. He was momentarily in disbelief. He'd walked through a clearly different door into what seemed to be the exact same room he'd just left a few minutes earlier.

Everything, down to the most minute detail was exactly as he had left it a few minutes beforehand. He was stunned briefly, but regained his composure and fell into his role as the detective.

After quickly taking in the scene, Bill turned to the officer. "What responders are on scene?"

"Well sir, the two EMTs, four members of the forensics team, my partner—Officer Davey—the suspect, and me."

"No name tag, officer; what's your name?"

"Oh, sorry sir, Officer Suspek."

"That's somewhat ironic."

"Yes, sir. The instructors at the academy had a lot of fun with it."

"I'm sure they did. So, what do we have here?"

Officer Suspek pointed to a seemingly distraught man sitting on a sofa. "That fellow on the couch is the husband. He came home early to find his wife was not alone. They apparently had an argument. He said he doesn't remember what happened, but then she was lying dead on the floor, and he called 9-1-1. He said he checked for a pulse and did not find one nor did he attempt CPR or anything. Said he figured it was too late, because of all the blood."

The officer seemed momentarily stumped, as if he were trying to remember what to say.

"Ummm...oh yeah, the EMTs verified she is, in fact, deceased. There's another body in the bedroom. Female, mid-thirties, red hair, fit, appears to have been strangled in some sort of fetish activity and subsequently dismembered after death. The pictures on the ground are of her body...well parts of it anyway. That's really about it, detective."

"That's plenty enough. Where is the second victim located?"

The officer pointed to the hallway. "Down that corridor, first door on the left."

"Thanks. I'd like to talk to the husband."

"Sure. Officer Davey, the detective would like to speak with the husband."

Bill made his way over to the man who was staring blankly out into nothingness. He sat across from the man and stared briefly before speaking.

"Hello, sir. I'm the detective in charge of the investigation. Could I speak with you for a few minutes?"

"Sur...sure"

"What's your name, sir?"

"Ben. My name is Ben."

"Ben, could you tell me what happened here?"

The man looked Bill in the eyes intently. "You know what happened, Bill. After all, you're the one responsible for all this."

Bill was stunned. Ben, who had blood on his hands and clothing had just accused Bill of the heinous acts.

"I don't know what you're talking about, Ben. I just got here—once I got the call."

"Bullshit, Bill. You killed her, walked out one door and into this one a few minutes later. You didn't even bother to take a close look at the woman...your fake wife. Are you sure about that Bill? Are you sure that's your fake wife? Are you sure it's not Sarah, Bill? You're a psychopath, Bill. You are as crazy as the day is long. This is all your fault. You killed her. Now I'm being held responsible. That's messed up, man."

Bill was having extreme difficulty resolving what Ben had just said. He was afraid to take a second look at his fake wife for fear the man might be telling the truth. He sat and reflected on what he'd been told, while the man continued to speak, although Bill had no idea, at this point, what the man was saying.

Bill finally stood and walked over to the woman's body and pulled back the sheet. There she was: Sarah's face staring up at him with a small red dot between her eyes. Bill shook his head, closed and reopened his eyes and, as she came back into focus, he realized it was not Sarah. The deceased was indeed his fake wife, but momentarily, he had almost believed Sarah was dead.

Bill turned his attention to the man who was glaring at him. Bill reached back and punched the man as hard as he could, knocking out a tooth in the process...nearly knocking the man out.

"Tell me the truth, asshole. What happened here? I know that's not my wife. She's your wife; why did you shoot her?"

"Because she's a whore. She screwed around on me every time I went on a business trip, and I've had enough already. Satisfied? I killed the whore she was banging when I walked in too. I made her watch and help me. She had to suffer, like she made me suffer all those years."

Bill turned to walk out but realized he had not received any instructions to do so. He stopped and looked around the room. The officer that had greeted him upon his arrival approached him again.

"Detective, now that we got his confession. How's about I take him down to central booking? I know you generally like to handle that; I just thought I could help out."

Before Bill could answer, Officer Davey motioned for him. Bill excused himself and asked Officer Suspek to wait a moment. He made his way to Officer Davey, who looked rattled.

"Detective, I think we have a situation here. Officer Suspek, well, the lady in pieces is his sister."

Without hesitation, Bill turned as if to run out of the home. Officer Suspek was approaching the exit quickly. Bill tackled him, and they fought for a few minutes before Bill was grabbed from behind and choked out. When he awoke, with a pounding headache, he was lying outside in the courtyard.

"Please gather your senses and proceed to the chair labeled *three*. Sit and read the instructions given before proceeding."

Bill saw no point in wasting any time, so he did as instructed. He made his way to chair three, sat, and read the instructions for what he was hoping would be the last time.

You are returning home to Sarah, Bill. You arrive to find her waiting for you with three guests. Follow her directions, exactly, and do not question those directions or her motives. This is the final test. Good luck.

Bill sat for several minutes, reading the instructions over and over again. He could not believe they'd brought Sarah into all of this, given the scenarios he'd just been a part of. *What in the world would they have her involved for? What in God's name is going on?* He thought to himself. No way he was going to shoot Sarah. No job was worth that. *You're overreacting, Bill. No way they'd have you do that. Just get up, and get it over with.*

He stood, approached the doorway slowly, and with a deep breath, walked through it and closed the door behind him. He was in his new house—or so it seemed. He made his way to the family room where he could clearly hear Sarah's voice.

"Well, hello. I was beginning to think you were never going to come home. How was work?"

"It was...different. Yeah, different than what I had expected."

"Well, it is a new job after all. Come in, I want to introduce you to some new friends. This is Ellynore, Sylvya, and Patrycya."

"Hello."

"Bill, they're sisters. I'm sure you can see the resemblance."

For the first time, seeing them sitting together, Bill could clearly see the three women were nearly identical. The only discernable difference was eye and hair color and the way they were dressed. All the other features were seemingly identical.

"Yes, actually, I can. Are you triplets?"

"No, Bill. They're not. Don't be ridiculous."

"I meant no offense."

"Bill, look. I know you just got home, but I've got something planned for us tonight."

Bill squinted and turned his head slightly to the side as if asking an unspoken question.

"We've been disconnected...for a while...you know, as far as intimate things go, so..."

"What's that got to do with them?"

"Well, I thought they'd add a little spice."

"Sarah, are you serious?"

"Bill...stop and listen."

"Ugh...all right, I'm listening."

"We're doing this. Period. We need the help, and they're willing and ready. Not to mention, they're hot."

"Are you..."

"Bill, I'm sure. We're doing this. So, let's get on with it."

With that, Sarah unzipped Bills pants and reached inside while kissing him deeply. She withdrew her hand and broke the kiss and undressed herself, while making her way to the women seated on the sofa. One by one, she undressed her guests. Bill just stood and watched the love of his life do something he'd never fathomed her doing. His mind was blown, and he was praying this was just a dream. He and Sarah had talked about friends who'd invited someone else into their bedroom, and it never worked out well, so they had vowed to never discuss it again, let alone do it.

But here they were, in the midst of sexual chaos. When Sarah finished with her guests, she turned her attention to Bill and proceeded to undress him.

"I see you're raring to go, Bill."

Bill was lost. He had forgotten all about where he was and why he was there. He looked at Sarah like a deer in the headlights of an oncoming vehicle. He sensed the danger but was powerless to move or speak. Sarah noticed Bill seemed frozen in place and continued to talk, having turned to look at the women who were now standing.

"I told you he would resist but wouldn't be able to restrain himself."

She motioned for the women to meet her and Bill in the middle of the room. Bill now stood, completely naked, surrounded by four of the most beautiful women he'd ever seen. He was totally bewildered and refused to move without direction from Sarah.

Sarah took charge of the situation and guided Bill's every move. From one to the next, to the next, to her, and back again. When they were finished, Sarah excused herself, as the other women continued to caress Bill. When Sarah returned, Bill's gaze met hers. She was fully clothed and carrying something, but Bill could not tell what it was.

"On your feet, soldier," she ordered with a level of disdain in her voice he'd never heard.

"Is everything all right, Sarah?"

"You're kidding, right? I come home from dropping the kids off to find you screwing three chicks...in our house— in *our* house, Bill? What the hell are you doing? Who the hell are you? Oh my god, Bill?"

"Sarah, but you were just here with us."

"No, she was not..." Ellynore offered

She had barely finished the statement when Sarah tased her. And before the other two could retreat, she tased them. Now, Bill was standing there with no idea what was going on, in a situation where he might have to defend himself against the love of his life.

"Sarah, I'm really confused. I'm sorry, but I truly don't know..." He stopped speaking. He could see there was nothing more to say. Sarah was about to inflict the same punishment on Bill as she had the guests. He stood motionless, prepared to let it happen.

When he came to, he was once again in the courtyard. He was clothed again, which he didn't fully comprehend or question. He was almost certain at this point he was having an out of body experience or a seizure or something. No matter what he came up with, there was no rationalization for his day.

"Once you're ready, make your way back to door four. This concludes the testing."

Bill picked himself up and made his way to and through the door labeled *four*. Michael was waiting on him as he exited.

"I know that was rough, Bill. It will all become clearer soon. Let me escort you back to the Evaluator."

They made their way back to the room where he'd answered questions during his polygraph session with Sylvya. Bill went in and sat down, still bewildered.

"It will all be made clear soon, Bill. You have listened and complied."

Bill sat for what seemed to him was an eternity. Then someone spoke from behind him.

"Bill? Bill? We're done. You feeling all right?"

He was groggy. As he began to regain his senses, he noticed Michael and Ellynore were seated in front of him. The voice grew louder as Sylvya walked around in front of him.

"Let me get you disconnected, Bill. You... Well, you had a rough experience, based on what we've observed. Michael will explain."

As Sylvya removed the last of the sensor pads from Bill, she turned and spoke directly to Michael.

"He's all yours, Michael. Everything checks out good on my end."

"Thank you, Sylvya," Michael responded, looking intently at Bill. "Without wasting too much more of your time, we're done. You passed with flying colors. You listened and complied with the directions given to you by both Ellynore and myself."

"That's good to hear."

"Yeah, you're going to need a little bit to regain all your faculties. How long do you think you've been here today, Bill?"

"Feels like it should be dinner time or thereabouts." Bill spoke with confidence.

Michael grinned and shook his head side to side. "Not even close. It's not even eleven a.m."

"What?" Bill exclaimed. He'd experienced hours of activities and was certain of it. *How could this possibly be?* He was visibly upset.

"I'll try and explain. You see, Bill, The Organization has access to some pretty advanced technologies. Things that were developed in the civilian sector for medical treatment...to give people with certain ailments a better quality of life. We've taken those technologies and enhanced them in various ways. Specifically, a treatment was developed to assist people with epilepsy. This device consisted of probes that attached to certain areas of the brain in order to stop seizures before they occur. The technology was extremely successful for its intended purpose, but we're implementing it by way of disparate methods, targeting a different area of the brain. The part of the brain responsible for separating reality from fantasy. We're able to...shall we say...suggest to an individual, by way of this technology, that they are, in fact, quite awake and participating in the real world. All this, while they are sedated and asleep. We also have the ability to leverage images stored in the individual's brain to adapt the augmented reality in pretty much any way that we choose."

Bill was in disbelief. His hands were covering his face, head bowed and moving side to side as if to signal no.

"How can this be?" he asked, completely dumfounded by Michael's explanation.

"Oh, believe me, you'll come to understand that and a great many other things. Just know that nobody died today. You did not cheat on your wife. Everything you experienced, after the polygraph, was one hundred percent augmented reality. It was a fantasy, a total fake. And it all took place in a span of about an hour, rather than the five or six hours you feel as though you experienced."

"How though? How did you make me susceptible to the AR?" Bill's analytical thought processes began to take over. Although he'd questioned the *how*, his thoughts had been focused on the events and why he was being subjected to them, not the technical aspects of how it was accomplished. The technical how was what he *needed* to understand.

"Well, Bill, like I said, you'll come to understand this as well as other things as time goes on. At a high level, the hood with lavender oil also had an ingredient that acts as anesthesia. While you were out, we performed a minor procedure, nothing more than a needle, albeit slightly bigger than normal, to insert a minute probe touching the surface of your cerebral cortex, thus enabling the power of suggestion.

The technical details are irrelevant at this point, as well as the mounting questions of side effects and your building rage...which we can temper at will."

"This whole thing is simply unbelievable. It's those technical details that I would really like to understand."

"Yeah, we're pretty proud of it. It gives us the ability to see how someone reacts to a situation without putting anyone in harm's way. We can calm an angry operative, among other things. Much better than actually running through those scenarios in real life...like they had to do back in the day."

"I suppose it does." Bill's frustration was evident, having not gotten a more detailed explanation.

"And we'll get you up to speed on the details. All in good time."

"Thank you."

"Yeah, sure. You wear your emotions on your sleeves, Bill. We have to work on that."

Both men smiled and nodded in agreement. Michael lightly slapped the tabletop before addressing Bill again.

"Okay. Ellynore here has a few more things for you to sign...to make everything official. Having been in the military all those years, you know nothing's finished until the paperwork is complete. She's going to get you squared away administratively, while I go with Gabriel to grab the rest of the gear, we're going to issue you. Once all that's done, we'll load up and get you back to Sarah. This time without the hood and blindfold."

"Sounds good."

Bill was in a state of obvious shock. But he signed on the dotted line, gathered his belongings, and followed Michael out to the waiting van. They were off to the place Bill longed to be now more than ever. He could not wait to feel Sarah's embrace. He was surprised they were as close to his house as they were. They'd obviously driven around a while before arriving at The Organization that morning. They pulled back into Bill's drive before one p.m.

Michael and Gabriel helped Bill get his gear onto the porch. As Gabriel returned to the van, Michael reached for Bill's hand.

"Welcome to The Organization. I'm truly looking forward to working with you. I'll be in contact. We're going to give you some time to settle your mind. It can take a few days to feel normal again after a session like that. We have plenty of time, so when I call, if you're not quite right in the head yet, I need you to be honest with me"

"Of course."

"Good deal. Say hello to the family for me. I'll talk to you in a bit."

Michael turned and made his way back to the van. They wasted no time heading out, he assumed back to The Organization. Bill figured something must require immediate attention... *Maybe some other poor soul stumbled across something in the woods they should not have seen.*

He called for Sarah to help him get his new gear into his office. Once the last box had been placed on the floor, he closed the office and headed for the shower. But not before he got a hug from Sarah.

"Bill, you're squeezing the air out of my lungs."

"Sorry, I just really missed you today."

16 Unwanted Knowledge

It took Bill about a week and a half to move past the psychological effects of his initial testing. Sarah could tell he'd endured something that was bothering him by the way he was acting but left it alone. She was not going to do anything that could make it worse, especially asking a lot of questions. He would come to her when he was ready to talk, he always had.

Sarah was clearly not impressed but was trying to see the positive in the situation. There was no way to tell if they would ever, truly, have the ability to make their own choices again. But she was obviously happy that the family was well taken care of, so the sacrifices they were making were a bit of a tradeoff. After all, the situation could be infinitely worse for them.

Sarah was starting to find a routine, while Bill was still trying to find one. He pitched in when he was able, which Sarah and the kids openly appreciated. Even though the kids were hours away, they seemed to enjoy any time Bill dedicated to helping them out, albeit via video chat.

* * *

It was two weeks to the day before Bill received the call from Michael. He'd been expecting a call every day for the past week. He was thankful for the extra time at home but anxious to get started. He'd fallen into the rabbit hole and was curious to see where it led. However, his curiosity was balanced by a healthy trepidation. He was not certain he really wanted to know more, but it wasn't like he had much choice.

"Good morning, Bill. How are you feeling?"

"I'm feeling great. It took about ten days for me to start feeling like myself again, but right now, I'm feeling as good as I ever have."

"Excellent...excellent. That's great to hear. It truly is. To be honest, we thought it might be pushing it to call you today. Most people take about a month, but I had a feeling about you. You are a different breed, Bill. There is something about you that is both exciting and somewhat concerning for the folks here in The Organization. They've never worked with someone like you, nor have I, for that matter. It's all...titillating to the senses."

"I'm not just a human lab rat, am I?"

That comment broke Michael's keenly egocentric, subtle smartass completely. He laughed out loud heartily for a moment.

"No. You are definitely not a lab rat. That was great. Oh boy, Bill. We are going to have a blast working together. I just know it."

"I certainly hope so."

"Oh, we are. Trust me. So, speaking of work. You ready to get back to it? We need to bring you in and discuss the results of the testing, your training schedule, and get you all briefed up so we can actually put you to work."

"I can be ready in fifteen minutes."

"How about you just enjoy the rest of today and the weekend. We can pick this all up on Monday. Sound good?"

"That'll work, Michael."

"Okay then. Well...umm...You want to drive. Oh, never mind, we haven't gotten you out to get that new car yet. Tell you what...We'll come by and grab you Monday morning about seven. We can stop by whatever dealership you want or multiple dealerships; we're in no hurry. We just want to ensure you have the nice new ride we've promised you. Once we get that taken care of, you can follow us to work. Once you're comfortable with the route, we can stop worrying Sarah with that menacing black SUV."

"That sounds like a great plan. I think she'll be really appreciative."

"We'll see you Monday."

"Sounds good. Thanks.

And they did just that. Bill and Sarah enjoyed the weekend together. Most all of it was spent outside in or near the pool. It was a magnificent pool, with a sun shelf, a grotto, in-pool wet bar complete with seating, a slide, and numerous rock features and waterfalls. He had told her when they first saw it that the pool area probably cost more than the house they'd just left. The pool was completely protected by a huge birdcage, something they'd only ever seen on TV, and now it was theirs. And it was paid for already.

Bill made use of the built-in outdoor grill, cooking every meal for the weekend, while watching sports on the huge flat screen TV mounted across the lanai. It was their own little slice of paradise. In fact, they'd never even stayed at a resort that was as nice as their new backyard. Though everything about Bill's new job seemed suspect, at least the family was being well compensated, even if it was under separate roofs.

As they always seem to do, the weekend flew past.

* * *

Bill awoke before his alarm sounded. *Damn internal clock, I could have gotten twenty more minutes of sleep.* He begrudgingly got ready, without waking Sarah, and made his way to the front porch to enjoy his first cup of coffee for the day and consider his choices for a new vehicle. He'd talked about owning a black sports car with dark tinted windows. But he'd seen too many vehicles with that color scheme in the past month. Anything but black was still an option.

Just like clockwork, Michael and Gabriel pulled up the drive at exactly seven. He met them at the drive and hopped in the SUV before Michael could loosen his seatbelt and step out.

"Well, you're on top of it this morning, Bill. The time off has served you well, it would seem."

"Yes sir, I'm ready to get after it today."

"Outstanding. Where are we headed?"

"I was thinking Audi."

"Excellent choice and would have been my first suggestion. I have one myself. I have to say though, stay away from black...it's overdone these days."

"You know. I was thinking the same thing. I think green would look really good."

"Yes, I like the green. I chose a white RS5...sport edition. It's a sharp ride. Would have gotten the RS7, but they didn't have that option when I picked up mine."

"I definitely like the RS7 better, but I figured it was a bit too much given what I was told the limit is, so the RS5 is the next best thing."

"Meh...I wouldn't worry too much about the price, Bill. I think we can work it out."

"Well, if you think we can swing it, I'd rather have the R8. About as close to a super car as I'll ever get, I suppose."

"Sure thing...it won't be an issue. I'm pretty sure, Gabriel, the Audi dealership has a black one in the show room. Would you give them a call and have them deliver that beauty for Bill?"

"Got it, boss."

"Wow, that easy?"

"Yeah, Gabriel has *established* a good relationship with the owner of the dealership."

"I see. Good to know."

As they made their way through the unassuming town roads, Bill began to recognize some of the buildings from his trip home after the initial training. He knew they were close but could not recall exactly where they would end the trip. They followed the main town road just a mile or so out of town, to the north, where the industrial park was located. That jogged Bill's memory. He recalled driving past several small businesses on his way home that day.

He could see a tall chain-link fence with razor wire coiled atop. The guards waived them through, and they parked in the front of a particularly nondescript brick building with nothing more than the logo for The Organization on the front of it. No words. No numbers. Just the logo.

Michael and Gabriel met Bill in front of the door.

"Let's get your indoctrination done. You have your badge?"

Gabriel pulled Bill's badge out of his tactical vest and presented it to Michael.

"We took that from him. He was pretty loopy, and I thought he might lose it. Here, I held onto it."

"Thanks, Gabriel. I had no idea. Here you go. Let's get to it."

Bill followed Michael through the ECP, where the guards simply motioned them through while saying hello.

"You guys are good to go. Great to see you again, Bill. Welcome aboard."

A simple, "Thanks" was all Bill could muster. Just when he thought he was on a normal trajectory, he got another curve ball thrown his way. He'd barely spoken to them before and was only here that one day. He reminded himself that nothing should surprise him. Just go with it and stay cool.

"Bill, I'm going to ask you to wait in the conference room for me. I have to go grab the OEM so we can get started."

"Sure thing." Bill made his way to the far side of the conference table and took a seat.

It was mere moments before Michael returned with the women he'd thought of as the triplets during his test scenario.

"Ha. You do know they're not actually triplets," Michael quipped as he pulled the chair out at the head of the table.

"Yes, but the resemblance is uncanny," Bill said, shaking his head in disbelief.

"Agreed. It'll all make sense soon."

They all took their seats, with Michael taking the lead role. He placed a folder on the table directly in front of his seat and pulled himself up to it. He gently slapped his on either side of the folder before speaking.

"So, Bill, we have to first discuss the testing results."

"Yes..."

"You passed all of them. However, we do need to discuss some things. First, the polygraph. You aced that one, buddy. It was obvious to us that you told us the truth. Well done."

"Thanks. What about the scenarios? I'm really interested in that assessment."

Michael was listening intently to Bill, looking directly into his eyes and rubbing his chin between his thumb and forefinger. He sat silent for a few seconds before speaking.

"Yes, the scenarios. I'll let OEM discuss those with you. Just keep in mind there are no right or wrong answers or actions in the scenarios. We're looking below the surface."

Bill looked at Michael quizzically but refrained from asking a question. Instead, he turned his attention to the women seated across from him. Noticing the only easily discernable difference between them was their hair and eye color.

Ellynore opened her folder and scanned the document briefly before speaking.

"As Michael stated, there are not right or wrong answers or ways to handle them. The intent is for us to get a better understanding of your passive cognitive abilities. Do you remember the immediate out brief after the first scenario?"

Bill looked puzzled. "No. I don't recall anything between scenarios."

Ellynore began taking notes and making marks on the document in front of her as if she was checking off boxes.

"Good. The process we utilize is specifically geared toward an individual. Inherently, each process is different in some manner. Why this is, is not important. What's important to us is that you do not recall the five-minute discussion between scenarios."

Bill's brow was furrowed, and he was squinting slightly. He was processing what Ellynore had just told him, but it wasn't making sense to him.

"No. I don't recall that. For me, I left the scenario, returned to the center of the courtyard, and received my next instructions."

Michael leaned inward toward the table, his fingers steepled and elbows firmly on the table.

"I'll try and simplify it. The point, *for us*, is we were able to successfully debrief you, without leaving you with the memory of that debrief. That make sense?"

Bill sat back in his chair, listening to Michael's explanation and nodding his head in approval. He looked at the women seated across from him and turned to Michael, nodding in approval the entire time.

"It's an amazing tool you can employ to protect informants. You can talk to anyone from John Doe, straight off the street to Benzi Polechia the leader of the Global Anti-American Coalition. GAAC is the largest known terror group in the world right now. Would be incredible to have a discussion with her and leave her with no memory that it occurred."

Michael slapped the table. "Okay! Hot Damn! Now we're making some progress. That's impressive. I think we're ready to move past the retraining briefing, no need to address the individual scenarios." Michael turned to the women who were already looking at him.

"Let's move right into the informational briefing regarding the job-specific programs Bill will be exposed to."

Michael looked at Bill and back at OEM. He then looked down at the table and the folder in front of him. He opened it and flipped through the first few pages and closed it. Placing his now crossed arms on the table, he looked at the women and spoke.

"Based on what we've witnessed here, I'm going to take Bill's clearance up one notch. Any objections; I take silence as consent."

The women looked at Bill, then at each other, before fixing their gaze on Michael, all three of them shaking their heads in the negative.

"Excellent! Nothing heard... Okay, Bill. Buckle up."

Michael motioned to Patrycya, who got up and walked to the credenza opposite the end of the conference table. She pushed a few buttons on the touch panel sitting on the credenza, and the 90-inch TV monitors powered on. The displays came into focus to reveal what appeared to be a slide presentation. She returned to her seat and passed a small remote to Michael.

"Thank you. So, Bill, let's get started." Michael looked at him as he was speaking and nodded.

Bill nodded in the affirmative and turned to face the screens.

"The content discussed in this briefing is not to be discussed anywhere that is not currently approved for its discussion, not with any individual not currently briefed. This briefing is classified at the *Unicorn Sanctuary* level, with the individual initiatives having additional *Critically Unique Required Approval* handling requirements.

"You will see the following acronym on all documents relating to The Organization's initiatives: *CURAUS*. *CURAUS* will be followed by a hyphen combined with the name of the initiative, or in some cases another acronym. I want to make it clear that US level clearance is the second highest level of clearance established in the world to date. Surprisingly higher than that of the president, and those in his staff, save a scant few. We have turned over every single rock in your past, as well as that of every individual within five degrees of separation. Thankfully for you, we found nothing detrimental under any of those rocks.

"Moving on..."

The Mimic Initiative.

CURAUS – MIMIC

Testing and evaluation of **AI Humanoid Entity**. Primary goal is to make the AIHE indistinguishable from their human counterparts. Indistinguishability is critical for inserting AIHE assets in lieu of human counterparts for counterinsurgent and counterintelligence activities. AIHE must be indistinguishable in every way **and perform routine** human activities, including all aspects of **human life, with the** notable exception of having children. **AIHE** must be easily mistaken for their human counterpart **by family, friends, co-**workers, and medical professionals.

The Concilium Initiative.

CURAUS – CNCLM

Testing and evaluation of various methods by which *unwitting* participants can be encouraged in the decision-making processes. Makes use of various wavelength frequency transmissions, often in concert with innocuously ingested, untraceable nanites that serve as signal transceivers. Nanites are distributed in various vectored dispersals via certain specific local water supplies, distributed beverages, distributed food products, and vaccines. All distribution is accomplished via surreptitious methodology, and distributors are unsuspecting. Primary goal is to influence general population's perception of the 'best interests' of the country, and, should it be deemed necessary, promote the divisiveness of race, religion, national origin, and political affiliation.

The Archangel Initiative.

CURAUS – ANGEL

Introduction of solutions provided by previously achieved initiatives for enhanced mental capabilities, enhanced physical capabilities, enhanced cybernetic capabilities, and refinement of technology of unknown origins. Participants undergo severe and stringent testing to determine eligibility. Only those who survive the testing phase are considered for inclusion. Only those who have a clearly demonstrated ability to coexist with enhancements for an extended period of time, minimally seven years, will be selected for this program.

"That concludes this briefing. Let me take this time to reiterate: The content discussed in this briefing is not to be discussed anywhere that is not currently approved for its discussion, not with any individual not currently briefed. More specifically, consider this facility and the one you stumbled upon during your vacation are the only two facilities approved for discussion. Do not discuss this information with anyone outside of those to whom you have been formally introduced. Now, I'm...we're...happy to field any questions you may have."

Bill sat in silence, trying desperately to *not* look unnerved by the briefing he'd just received. He'd been briefed in the past on some of what he thought were the country's most secret initiatives and programs, but nothing he'd heard before was anywhere close to this insane. He turned to face Michael.

"That is all very hard to stomach. If this is all true, and I have to assume at this point that it is, The Organization has the most advanced tech on the planet." He slumped in his chair, shaking his head in disbelief.

"I did tell you to buckle up, my friend. I know it's a lot to take in. But, here's the thing. You're knee deep in The Organization now. Knee deep here is about fifty feet below the military community you came from. That should give you a good comparison of how much more is actually going on around here. But...for now, these are the three initiatives we need you up to speed on."

"Yes. That is a lot to take in, and yes, much like those things I was briefed on in the military, now that I know... I wish I didn't. But it is what it is, and it goes with the territory, as cliché as that is."

"Cliché? Yes. Necessary? Yes. Unwanted? Yes. I agree completely. But now we have to protect that information and do our best to move the initiatives along. Forward trajectory, Bill."

"Yes, Michael. What now?"

17 Strange Behavior

Michael had little to say to Bill's question. He was actually somewhat dismissive, opting rather, to postpone his answer.

"That's a question for another day."

Bill thought it was clear when he asked it that he wanted to know how to get started

"I guess what I meant to ask is, how do I get started? Do I have an office? Who do I report to? Who am I working with?"

"Ahh, I see. I'll take you to your work area shortly. You will be working alone and reporting directly to me."

They'd been in the conference room for just over two hours, and Michael had dominated the conversations both pre-brief as well as Bill's questions afterward. Aside from Ellynore's few remarks regarding the first scenario, OEM had not said another word. They nodded, and their expressions changed occasionally, but that was it. Bill's gaze caught Michael's, and it was clear that Michael was waiting on something. Bill looked at each of the women seated across from him, and then it hit him.

"Damn...they're part of the MIMIC initiative."

"Brilliant deduction, my friend. They are, in fact, part of that initiative. No detail left unaddressed."

"I mean...they are indeed impressive but every detail?"

"Yes, absolutely every detail. Follicle regeneration has been accounted for, as have details such as acne, scarring, bleeding due to injury, even down to appropriate body odors and/or scents."

"That's truly unbelievable."

"Agreed. Had I not spoken to the unwitting test subject who interfaced with each of these women—if you get my reference—I would not have believed it myself. They acted as if they all had a great time. Not a one of them suspected OEM are actually mostly machine."

"Wow."

"Wow, indeed. OEM, you are free to go about your routines. Bill, if you'll follow me."

Michael led Bill down the corridor, to what Bill remembered being the courtyard; however, it was no longer a courtyard. It was a large office, twenty feet square, with strategically placed digital displays simulating windows.

Bill had an office with a view, a nice desk, several bookshelves, and probably two dozen, maybe more, computers spread around the room.

"You should find that everything you need to do your job is already in this room. The two systems on your desk are identical to the ones you have at home. Once you login to each of them, you will find additional details, ones specific to what we're expecting from you in this position. If you have any questions, we will provide the answers. No need to seek us out; we'll come to you."

"Well, just..."

Before Bill could finish his thought, Michael was gone and the door closed behind him.

What about all the other computers, Michael. What are they for? Frustrated a bit, but not at all surprised by the disappearing act, Bill took a seat and got to work. Two distinct sets of guidance were displayed before him. His first task, although similar, was clearly different in intent, depending upon which monitor he was reading from.

"Provide analysis of NW region race and political temperature, with emphasis on key indicators regarding corrective actions to ensure divisive nature if situation persists."

"Provide analysis of NW region race and political temperature, with emphasis on key indicators regarding corrective actions to ensure divisive nature if situation is quelled."

The colored dot on each monitor was commensurate with the direction of the analysis he would be providing. He was hopeful that it was nothing more than identifying the likelihood of correcting the issues that were currently pervasive throughout the northwest region, but a nagging feeling told him there was more to it than he was seeing. Nevertheless, Bill set out to accomplish the task at hand, aware his progress was being monitored.

* * *

Raphael was waiting in Michael's office when he returned. He'd shown a keen interest in the process, having asked several times for this opportunity. Michael had barely taken a seat when Raphael began speaking.

"Michael, while I understand the nature of this exercise, I think we can both agree Bill is going to nail both aspects. I mean his ability, to see both sides of an objective, is the primary measure of his success as an analyst."

"That's true, Raphael. Very true. This, however, is less about the result than the analytical process. I want to see, well, *we* need to see his process. My fear is that his process is as straightforward as his reports. That he simply gleans from the rhetoric on both sides of the primary stances and objectives and simply fills in the assumed gaps."

"And if that's the case?"

"Well, then, this is going to be an extensive observation period. Without conscious thought of the deductive reasoning type, there is little that we'll be able to pick up from him. You must remember the tech can only pick up conscious thought, just the inner monologue. If it's subconscious thought, we're going to miss the process altogether."

"Okay, Michael, how about this? Why not just ask him to explain it? If he can."

"It's looking as if that may be the only way. We've been monitoring him for what, twenty or thirty minutes now? I've not seen one conscious thought picked up."

* * *

Michael knew Bill was notably the best analyst of his time, which was, in part, what led him to where he was at that moment. So, generating this report was expected to be a quick and easy task for him. Sensing Bill had completed his task barely an hour later, Michael walked into Bill's office.

"Let's take a look at that report, Bill."

"Here you go."

Michael sat and read the five-page report. He noted several times the thoroughness with which it had been created. Once done reading, he sat and nodded for several moments before speaking.

"That's great stuff. So, correct me if I'm wrong. What I take away from this is in order to put an end to the divisiveness, no action is needed. Correct?"

"Yes, that's what I see based on the information available."

"So, people are actually beginning to agree with a common way forward. Hmm."

Michael continued to review the report while formulating additional perspective. He sat, rocking slightly in his chair, report in one hand and rubbing his chin with the thumb and forefinger of the other.

"The other take away is that it would take only one or two divisive events...something perceived and portrayed by media as racially or politically motivated to send the northwest region into a tailspin. Am I on target here?"

"Yes. Based on the information I have available to me at this time. It would seem as though tensions, while easing some, would shatter in the event of another violent crime that is perceived as racially or politically motivated."

"Got it. Thank you. Have a great evening. Uh, you know how to find your way out of this place?"

"Yes sir. I'm good to go."

"Great. I'll see you tomorrow, Bill."

"Have a great evening."

"Bill?"

"Yes."

"You're going to need these." Michael extended his arm and dangled the keys for the Audi.

"Oh yeah. Helps to have the keys. Thanks again."

"Sure thing."

* * *

Bill gathered what little he'd brought with him and made his way back to the ECP. He stopped to briefly chat with the guards and then went out to his new ride. He'd waited all day to take that car for a spin. He took the long way home just so he could find a stretch of road to open it up. There was little more exhilarating to him than a fast car.

Bill pulled into the drive and stopped well out of view of the house. His thoughts were in turmoil, and in an attempt to make sense of them, he began talking to himself. "Why was it necessary to have such programs? What possible necessity exists to have what amounts to an incredibly advanced android capable of blending into society without detection? Perhaps as a body double for the high value targets within our government? Maybe to get close to HVTs of other governments or military organizations? The potential benefits could be a great thing; however, this tech could clearly be used for nefarious activities. And the whole mind control thing? What the...?"

Bill had experienced the frustration of exposure to individuals that seemed to know *everything* he did and thought. *There's no privacy at all, and not even the Patriot Act would cover such technology. Or did it?* His heart began to race, and he began to pant. "Bill, get ahold of yourself. It's...crap. You've been sitting here for almost half an hour. Pull yourself together and get inside the house." His inner monologue was loud and direct. *Could this possibly be another instance of subconscious interference by The Organization?* He shook it off and pulled up to the house.

Sarah met Bill at the door with a hug and a kiss. "I missed you."

Bill returned the hug and kiss, then he rested his chin on her shoulder for a moment. "I missed you too. Am I going to get this greeting every day?" he said with a cheeky grin.

"Maybe...maybe." Sarah winked.

"Should I leave and come back in a few minutes?"

"No, you've gotten your quota for the day already."

"Quota? Now I have a quota?" Bill threw his hands up and laughed.

"Hey...Bill? Have you heard the news?"

"No, I haven't. What's going on?"

"All that protesting and fighting up in Washington, Idaho, and Portland..."

"Oregon?" Bill said quizzically.

"You know what I meant. Yes, Oregon. The leaders of the two opposing groups called a joint press conference and put an end to the fighting. Said they're going to try and work together...baby steps. But at least they're willing to talk now. Isn't that amazing?"

Sarah was headed toward the kitchen, raising her voice as she moved farther away so Bill could hear her. Bill didn't move. He stood motionless, reflecting on his day, specifically his report. His thoughts were interrupted when Sarah asked him a question.

"Can you still hear me?"

"Yes, sorry. I can hear you."

"I thought they were headed to a major conflict...you know, between the two groups. Then, *bam!* Now they're talking about a truce. How does that even happen, like, overnight?"

Bill thought to himself, *you mean like in the course of about an hour or two, tops?* Then he replied, "Yeah, that is odd. I can't wrap my head around how something like that happens so fast. But it's a good thing they're talking."

"Yes, I agree. Unexpected and really weird. I mean, just yesterday they were beating the crap out of each other in the streets; today they're holding a joint press conference."

"Well, maybe the fighting finally taught them something. I don't know. But, hey, at the end of the day, it looks like they're finally doing the best thing for everyone, rather than promoting their own agendas in such a misguided way. So...what's for dinner?"

Bill deftly avoided further conversation. He was concerned that his thoughts might spill out into the world vocally. His mind continued to race. Sarah didn't seem to notice anything odd as they ate. Nothing seemed odd as they cleaned up after the meal or as they were sitting to watch TV together afterward. It wasn't until he and Sarah were preparing for bed that anything was said.

"Bill...everything okay?" Sarah asked, looking somewhat concerned.

"Huh...er, sorry?"

"Are you okay? You seem a little preoccupied—or burdened with something?"

"Uh, I guess maybe it's just being my first day of actual work. Ya know, trying to keep things straight in my head. I want to do well. You know...what with the whole safety of our family hanging over my head. Don't want to screw that one up," Bill quipped sarcastically. He tried to play it off with humor and a smile.

"Ha...well, there is that, of course. I've seen this from you before. But this just seems different. Not like keeping things straight but more like apprehension. I mean a concern beyond the obvious." Sarah's unease was evident to Bill. He knew the look and the subtle intonations of her voice when she was worried about him but tried to mask it. He'd seen plenty of those looks over the years.

"Well, this hasn't exactly been a typical change of job kind of process, Sarah. I mean, I've been quietly freaking out about this whole thing since it started."

Sarah pursed her lips, raised her brows, and began nodding in acknowledgment of his comment.

"That's true. I guess I was looking at the whole thing a little too optimistically, like, you know...we were past the whole... Well, you know what I mean."

"I do. Yeah, getting past the *we'll disappear your family and make you watch* thing is a bit to process and be able to function somewhat normally. I'm not sure how long it will take, or if we'll get to that point. But it's all good. Nothing for you or the kids to be distressed about. I mean, worrying isn't going to provide any benefit for anyone. Just make things worse, you know?"

"Yep. Well, I'll try to not concern myself until you tell me I should be." Sarah wrapped her arms around him and hugged him tightly.

"Sounds like a plan. And sleep sounds like a great plan for me right now. I'm beat."

"Yes. Me too."

With that, they climbed into bed and quickly fell asleep.

Five a.m. came too quickly. He felt as if he'd only just closed his eyes. But he was up and out the door for another day. He wanted to make sure he was prompt to arrive and worked at least a few minutes past his scheduled end of day. The military had instilled in him that if you're not fifteen minutes early, you're late, and he continued to live by that principle.

The same vehicles were parked in the same spots as they had been yesterday. The same security guards were on shift that had been for the past two days. But beyond the ECP, no one. Bill roamed the hallways looking for Michael, the women, or anyone for that matter, but nobody was to be seen or heard.

He retired to his office and started his day. His instructions for the day were left for him in a folder lying atop his keyboard. He was to review the updated information provided to him for the northwest region and to make suggestions to maintain the newly established stability in the area. Bill set out to review the information and quickly deduced no direct actions were necessary, and suggestions for course corrections or changes were not required.

As he sat trying to figure out what to do with the next seven hours of his day, his mind began to wander. He was recounting the tests and test reviews from the scenarios. He'd been given an explanation, but it seemed superficial. Surely the testing served a more important purpose than what he had been led to believe.

Bill knew that if he sat in silence, he would think himself into a panic. He decided that he would look for and review additional information on the programs to which he'd been given access.

"Let's start with this MIMIC stuff," he said aloud. "Bill, stop talking to yourself."

His initial search showed additional documentation explaining the MIMIC initiative in slightly more detail but nothing noteworthy. He noticed a subfolder labeled TRIO. He'd not heard or seen that before. He paused before exploring it but figured if he wasn't allowed to see it, he wouldn't have been granted access. He pressed forward.

He came across a briefing document labeled ESP. Seeing that sent Bill's thoughts into overdrive. It explained a lot and had to be how they knew so much. As he began to read the information in the document, he realized that it was much more than that. He discovered that a lot more detail existed regarding ESP and TRIO than knowing what someone was thinking.

E.S.P. / TRIO / OEM

Joint initiative between MIMIC and CONCILIUM teams to enhance the effectiveness of efforts supported by both initiatives.

Initial MIMIC subjects:

ELLYNORE

SYLVYA

PATRYCYA

Initial MIMIC subjects specifically designed for this joint initiative to be utilized in controlled environment to minimize exposure to the unwitting.

Utilization of ESP MIMIC subjects to be incorporated into initial testing scenarios, both actual reality and virtual reality.

Success indicators include successful efforts by ESP MIMIC subjects with regard to the following reality-based activities:

1. Conduct briefing and testing activities during onboarding process for new recruits, successfully, without detection or suspicion.

2. Interact with unwitting in typical daily routines, including but not limited to:

- Typical social interactions (discussion of relevant topics, meals, required restroom activities, emotional deviations, etc.)

- Flirt at appropriate times with unwitting

- Engage in appropriate (inappropriate) unprofessional relationships with unwitting

- Sexual activities of particular importance

3. Make self-aware personality and social interaction changes and exchanges based on key indicators received from unwitting individuals

All virtual-reality scenarios will include success parameters specific to the scenario and desired outcome(s) based on required interactions by ESP MIMIC subjects.

ESP MIMIC subjects to be exclusively supervised by senior on-site director at each of the seven test locations.

Senior on-site director retains sole decision-making power with respect to the future of the ESP subject at the location. In the event termination of the project is regarded as appropriate, it will be a location-based decision. Immediate suspension of program will take effect at the discretion of the on-site director, and emergency protocols will be activated.

Upon activation of emergency protocols, the Seven (Archangel's Initiative) will determine if a complete suspension of ESP MIMIC is warranted. Subsequent inquiries regarding the technical aspects of each individual initiative that posed a contributive effect leading to suspension of the ESP TRIO initiative will be assessed prior to moving forward.

A determination and subsequent recommendation by the Seven to The Organization senior leadership will be made no later than seventy-two hours post suspension. That determination and recommendation will include justification of re-activation or termination of the initiative.

Bill was stunned not only at what he had just read but at the notion that he was stunned by anything he read. Humanoids with extrasensory perceptive capability actually existed, and he'd interacted with them, unable to distinguish them from actual human beings. The initiative had clearly been successful. He wondered just how long this had been a reality and how OEM were influencing the unwitting?

What if they were influencing global decisions?

What if they started a world war?

This just could not be.

He dug, and he dug some more. Reading any and every document he found. It was clear, in what he was reading, this initiative had been undertaken in the eighties, but the exact day, month, or year wasn't specifically identified. There had been numerous iterations within the MIMIC Initiative, mostly unsuccessful, until the ESP Initiative was created. That's when they found a way to dupe the unwitting targets.

Turing tests—a test to determine whether a computer was capable of thinking like a human—had been successfully conducted several years back. But a scenario in which AI could process information like a human was a far cry from a cyborg being able to relate as a human in a human environment up to and including having a sexual relationship with a human being without detection. That was some serious next-level shit.

He'd had enough. Bill had become so engrossed in his analysis, he finally realized only half an hour before he was due to leave that he had not taken a break to eat his lunch. He stopped to check his email one last time and noticed a message from Michael that had arrived just a few minutes earlier.

Bill,

I apologize for not letting you know you would be going it alone today. Actually, you will be going it alone for a few days. We have some off-site work to do...OEM and I, as well as Gabriel and the boys. We'll be back on Monday.

Enjoy the quiet time and use it to familiarize yourself with the additional details of the initiatives we discussed. I suspect you're already on that track, but TBH, I haven't had the time to review that for myself.

You've gained my trust. I know you're on board with us. I'm equally confident you can hold down the fort for us.

-Michael

Well, a day without having my innermost thoughts spoken back to me is a good day. And I have at least three more to look forward to this week, he thought.

He packed up and left for home; today, he was wasting no time. It was straight home to Sarah.

It didn't take long for Sarah to notice something was weighing on him.

"You're looking just as unnerved as you did last night. Are you sure you're okay?"

"Yes. I'm sure. I'm just learning and adjusting to my new job. I'll probably be like this for a while. It's nothing to be concerned about."

"I'll try not to worry. I just love you, and when I see you like this, well...it bothers me.

"This job is way different, and it's challenging. You know I can't stand not being the best at everything I do. At least, professionally. I can't afford not to be productive and successful in the office."

"I honestly don't know what to say to that. Just know this situation is wearing really thin with me, so I can only imagine what your stress level is."

"I understand; I know it sucks for you. I do. But I can't do this without you." Bill placed his hands on Sarah's shoulders and looked lovingly into her eyes.

"Yeah, I know," she said meekly.

"Good. It's hard enough without the kids here so we can keep an eye on them. I don't know what I'd do without your support."

"You'd do what you always do. You'd figure it out."

"This one's not going to be that easy to figure out."

"That's become pretty clear already. And it's definitely not going to happen tonight."

"True."

"How about we cook breakfast for dinner and find something to watch on TV?"

"Sounds perfect. Anything to distract from reality for a little while."

They cooked their meal and ate while watching game show reruns. Sarah noticed Bill was nodding off and nudged him.

"Hey. I'll clean up. Go to bed; you clearly need the sleep."

"Yeah, I think you're right."

"Sleep well."

"Good night... Sarah?"

"Yes."

"Thank you, I know this is beyond weird and very stressful, but we'll get through it."

"I know we will. We have no choice but to do that."

"Yeah."

"Night, Bill."

The next morning, Bill was up and out of the door like clockwork, in the office, reviewing more information, forgetting to eat, and back at the house for dinner. Like a well-oiled machine, he had always been a creature of habit.

Bill repeated his new routine each day of the week he was working alone. He planned slight variances in his arrival and departure times, as well as the route he took to and from work each day. He was constantly evaluating the pros and cons of every aspect of his day. It was the only way he could be sure he was being as efficient as he possibly could be.

The weekend came and went. Bill was anxious to see someone besides the ECP guards at the office Monday morning. He arrived early, at twenty to six. There was at least one new vehicle in the lot. He made his way inside, through the ECP, and to his office, where Michael was waiting.

"Ah, right on time. Good to see you. How was your weekend?"

"It was great. Relaxing. We spent a lot of time in the pool. Sarah just loves it."

"I'm sure. Bill, I have something I'd like you to see."

"Sure thing."

"Well, more like, I need you to see this. I think it is going to be critically important for your professional growth within The Organization."

"*Sure*, Michael."

"Follow me."

Michael led Bill down the corridor to his office and through a door that Bill had thought was simply a closet or a private bathroom. It was a small room, maybe eight feet by ten feet at the most. There was no furniture in the room, just a dim overhead light and a window with shades drawn across it.

"Now, Bill, what I have to show you may be disturbing. So, without knowing exactly what it is, I want you to brace yourself. This will hit hard."

"Um, I'm ready, I think."

"Go ahead and slide the shades to the right. If you're sure you are prepared to see something that may well rank among your worst fears."

Bill managed not to be nervous. His coping mechanisms were growing stronger with each document he read, but Michael's words and demeanor gave Bill pause. He was definitely concerned about what he would see but knew there was no turning back.

As he slid the shades to the right, he slowly revealed something that immediately prompted a guttural reaction.

"What the hell, Michael? Why? Why do you have one of those things that looks like me? Why do you need a MIMIC of me?"

"That reaction is not unexpected or unwarranted, but it is misguided."

"What do you mean misguided? If it's warranted, how can it be misguided?"

"Well, I mean if the guy lying in that hospital bed was asking it, it would not be a misguided question. Bill has every right to ask that question."

"I am Bill. You are not making any sense, Michael. What the hell is going on?"

"Take a few seconds, review what I've said. Listen and comply."

With that, Bill stopped and reflected on what Michael had said to him. He thought over the past two weeks, the testing, the briefings, everything he'd experienced. Nothing was making sense.

"I still don't get it."

"You have successfully met all criteria."

"Yes, that's why I'm still alive and working here."

"You're not hearing me. We may have done too good of a job this time around. What you're not understanding..."

"What, Michael? What am I not seeing? You have a MIMIC of me lying in a hospital bed? I see that. What are you planning with that damn thing? This is some seriously demented shit you're doing here. You can't send that thing to replace me with Sarah and the kids."

"We already sent you. Every day for two weeks. That's not a MIMIC in that bed. That's Bill. *You* are the MIMIC."

18 Awakening

Michael stood and watched as MIMIC Bill seemed to try, albeit in vain, to make sense out of what he'd just been told. But no amount of reasoning would provide resolution sufficient for the MIMIC to understand what was going on and what he was. There were no discernable differences between him and the supposedly real Bill he saw through the pane of glass. But given everything else he'd seen and been told, he appeared unable form a valid argument to disprove Michael's statement.

Michael was studying the MIMIC's reactions. He was amazed at how indistinguishable it was from Bill. Michael placed his hand on the MIMIC's shoulder.

"Look, I know this is a lot to wrap your mind around. I know you believe you are Bill, and in a sense, you are. So, to make this a little easier I'm going to continue to call you Bill. I'll refer to the Bill in that bed as Bill Prime."

Bill was still staring at Bill Prime. Both hands on his head, fingers interlocked, and look of total disbelief on his face.

"How? How was this done? How was this done without anyone having any idea that... I mean, if I'm the

MIMIC... How? There wasn't enough time to do the 3D scanning and recreate a body."

Michael extended his hand, palm forward, signaling Bill to stop. "Let me stop you. Technologies are in play here that you have not been made aware of, and the process does not take nearly as long as you seem to think it does."

"But—" As Bill turned to ask another question, Michael made the same stop motion with his hand.

"Hear me out. The scanning process takes about fifteen minutes. Like I said, this is extremely advanced tech we're talking about here."

"No, I get that it is advanced tech. It's obvious everything about this organization is advanced. But when was there time? Without my family knowing? I just... It doesn't make sense."

Bill seemed somewhat frantic. Michael, now facing Bill, placed both hands on his shoulders.

"Like I was saying, scanning takes fifteen minutes max. The basic musculature is pipeline. So, you are not an exact replica of Bill Prime. There are slight deviations in size, such as arm and leg length. We have pre-made... Well, it's like a warehouse of bones, all types, and multiple different sizes in quarter-inch increments. So, if we compared measurements between you and Bill Prime there, we'd see that you, while being the same overall height, have legs that are roughly a quarter-inch longer and a torso that's almost a quarter-inch shorter than he is."

Bill pulled away from Michael and took a few steps backward, shaking his head side to side.

"No way. Why are you messing with my head like this?"

"I'm telling you how it is," Michael responded sternly.

"Why? Why now?"

"It's become necessary. Sarah called me, worried something was wrong with you that you were not telling her. She's a very perceptive lady. We can't risk exposure, so we have to get Bill Prime there back up and, on his feet, and get him home."

"My family..." Bill said angrily.

"*His* family!" Michael's demeanor and posture changed. His voiced deepened noticeably, and he was glaring at Bill.

"Maybe this will help. Just after you returned home from your vacation, we had some equipment sent over. You remember unpacking that equipment?"

"Yes, of course. Why is that important? Why are you avoiding giving me a direct answer? Dammit, you guys always talk in riddles."

"No riddle here. Hear me out. You unpacked the computers, the networking equipment, all that stuff. Do you remember taking anything else out of the boxes?"

"I took everything out, Michael. Get to the point before I lose my shit... And I'm dangerously close to that now." Bill's face was flush with anger, his hands by his side, fists clenched.

Michael was near his threshold for insubordination. He stepped toward Bill, his brow furrowed, and he was laser focused on Bill.

"To be clear, you are not going to lose your shit with me. I'll end you where you stand. Never, *never* threaten me. We crystal clear on that?"

"Fuck you, Michael." Bill began walking slowly toward Michael.

"You will *listen and comply,*" Michael said very calmly.

Bill stopped moving and broke his gaze. He was looking downward, his face returning to its normal tone, and his fists were no longer clenched. After a moment, he looked up at Michael, who began speaking again.

"As I was saying, you didn't take everything out. You couldn't take everything out. A small box that fit perfectly like a false bottom was placed in each of the boxes. It contained a rather potent gas that is colorless, odorless, and extremely fast acting. It was set on a timer to release, and it is potent enough to put anything within a football field distance around it to sleep within minutes after dispersal. Once Bill Prime and his family were asleep, we released that gas. We were already outside in the van, waiting. Five minutes later, we were on the road to the facility that he discovered to scan him. Within a half an hour, he was back in bed and nobody knew the difference."

"No way. You're still messing with my head. That's just too out of this world to believe," Bill said in a very calm voice.

"I don't do that. I've never told you or him anything to mislead you."

"Bullshit. This whole thing has been a complete crock of bullshit." Bill was shaking his head in an affirmation of the negative, still speaking in a very calm voice.

"This response from you is actually quite encouraging. It is a great validation that the process works exactly as intended. You are convinced you are Bill, even though that's Bill Prime lying there. Amazing. Anyway, to continue your answer, when he came in for his day of testing, we had you prepared and ready to go. We utilized the polygraph to back up his thoughts and memories. Those tests—the polygraphs don't require a sensor cap that fit on the head. The sole purpose of that tech was to record memories and thought patterns, which were fed real-time into your brain."

"This can't be. Michael, this can't be true. Tell me this isn't real. It's just another test." Bill was struggling to reconcile the thoughts and emotions he believed he was feeling. The process was so successful, Bill truly believed he was human.

"I can't do that. I'd be lying if I did. The next part was a little tricky. We had to get both of you in the same place at the same time without either of you seeing the other. So, enter the courtyard. Even though it was entirely virtual, we still had to insert you both into the same VR session. We couldn't just flip the switch between you. Reason being is even that millisecond disconnect during the transition could have had catastrophic consequences for Bill Prime's brain. It would not have been immediately discernable, but the brain is extremely complex, and while we can substitute a lab grown brain fitted with non-organic neural interfaces a miniature computer of sorts, that small gap in time will eventually wreak havoc. Something internal to the human brain works—without the person knowing it—kind of like a background process for a computer, which maintains the bonds between perception and reality. That millisecond within a human brain is a break between the two that would eventually lead to a complete break with reality. Think dementia, Alzheimer's, et cetera."

"Keep going." Bill appeared clearly interested in the information being shared with him. He had wanted to understand the *how* of the tech from the beginning. It was fascinating to him.

"We overcame that in the courtyard. Once Bill Prime entered and sat down, we paused the simulation. For him, it was sleep without dreaming. You were offline in preparation for this switch, so we brought you online and positioned you in the chair opposite Bill Prime with your backs to each other, synced your brain with his, and removed him from the simulation. Then, we hit *play* again. Once you entered the first scenario door, we updated the simulation to account for the chair he was seated in originally to reflect the number you saw when you got to that point in the simulation. It worked seamlessly."

Michael paused to answer any questions his explanation thus far might have prompted. Bill looked puzzled, as if he were struggling to form and organize all the questions bouncing around in his mind.

"Let's say I believe everything you've just explained. How does the process to put Bill Prime back work?"

Michael smiled and nodded; this was the one question he had wanted to be asked. It was a signal to him that Bill was beginning to resolve the doppelganger entanglement.

"Oh...that's easy stuff there. We've kept Bill Prime synched with you real-time. Everything that you have done and experienced, he was right with you, with just a few milliseconds delay but a constant stream of consciousness. All we do now is feed you the command to pause, which we will here shortly, and bring him out of his sleep state."

"How's that going to affect him, Michael? If he's synched real-time, he's going to be aware of this conversation. That can't be good for the human brain."

"You'll be fine when you wake up, Bill Prime."

Bill looked at Michael as if he'd lost his mind for a moment. Then he realized that Michael was speaking as if he was talking to Bill Prime so that when he was awakened, Bill Prime was going to be fine.

Michael continued. "It is important for you to know and understand the way this process works. We've done this with a unique purpose in mind. We need you to understand the way the process works in order to develop the skillset necessary to identify MIMICs you may encounter. Espionage is a real thing. It has happened, and this initiative, in particular, was compromised in its early stages. We don't think anyone has perfected the technology the way that we have, but we cannot be one hundred percent certain. So, we have to develop methods to identify them. Irises...dilation of the eyes: it's an involuntary reaction to light, and it's a fluid, dynamic reaction. MIMICs differ in a visibly identifiable way in that regard. You won't notice unless you're looking for it. But if you are looking for it, it's obvious."

"What happens to my MIMIC, Michael?"

"You mean Bill Prime's MIMIC?"

"Er, yes, sorry...but it's as if there is no difference. In my mind, I am Bill Prime."

"Yeah, that's the way it's supposed to work. We typically keep MIMICs in the lab with a constant feed between them and the PRIME as we like to call them. Let's say you are Bill Prime. In the event we need to send you into an area where there's a moderate to high chance you may not make it out, we send the MIMIC. We simply swap out the synthetic blood for a substance that will completely dissolve the MIMIC, leaving no trace of the technology."

Bill looked amazed, shaking his head in disbelief. "The rabbit hole runs deep."

"Indeed, it does. Far deeper than you know," Michael said with a wink.

"It's time, Bill. Sylvya, proceed."

Just as Michael had laid out the plan for reinsertion of Bill Prime back into his life, the process was complete. In less than an hour he was escorted into Michael's office. He appeared to be teeming with contempt for Michael, the job, the whole situation for that matter. He was in the midst of an enormous internal struggle. Everything Michael had heard and learned about Bill made it clear he was a man of principles, a man of great faith, and everything about his experiences with The Organization spat in the face of both. Because he was so principled, he would not be able to easily reconcile the conflict with either his principles or his faith. Michael understood that nothing to him was godly about playing God. And this was a clear attempt by The Organization to do just that. They were playing God.

Michael momentarily leaned forward in his chair, then leaned back and opened the top left drawer of his desk. He reached inside and pulled out a tattered, leather-bound book and placed it on the desk in front of him.

"You see this book?" Michael asked, pointing to it. "This is the only thing I have left from my previous life. My life before The Organization."

He looked up at Michael and met his gaze before speaking. "It must have significant importance to you," Bill offered, solemnly.

Michael nodded and placed his palms on top of the book. "Indeed, it does.

"Bill, the man you were when we first met and the man I was when I was brought into The Organization were far more similar than you could imagine. I fought against what I was told, what I saw, what I heard, and especially against the things I was told to do. I had a family when this all started for me."

"*Had* a family?" Bill replied somewhat bewildered.

Michael broke eye contact with Bill and lifted the book off the desk. He never took his eyes off the book while he spoke. His expression blank and non-expressive. The tone of his voice eerily calm.

"Yes, past tense, Bill. I had a family. My wife bucked the system and thought I could help her get away with it. We didn't get away with it. And when I had a chance to provide redemption for all of us, I thought I could outmaneuver our adversaries. I was wrong. My family was taken from me in a most unpleasant manner while I was forced to observe. Vile things were done to my wife...my daughters, who were twelve and fifteen, and they made me watch it all. Intentionally paralyzed from the neck down, strapped to a table they lifted as if I were standing and pulled my eyelids back to prevent me from closing them. Any time I passed out, they paused to wake me, and would not continue until they were certain I was watching again. Forty-eight hours I was forced to watch. When they were done violating them, draining them of their humanity and me of mine, they lined them up in front of me and executed them one by one."

"How could they? How can they get away with that?" Bill said, head bowed, rubbing his temples.

"Doesn't matter. Don't go down that road. I've been down it, and it's a dead-end. It goes nowhere, and nothing exists at the end of it but more pain and suffering," Michael replied, his gaze still on the book.

Bill looked up at Michael and began to speak. "I can't imagine, Sarah, and the--"

Michael slammed the book down on his desk and met Bill's gaze. He stood and pointed at the book.

"That is my wife's family Bible. It looks to be over 100 years old, but it's barely 40." Michael moved his hands by his side and looked down at the Bible.

"She received this Bible from her mother on her death bed. It was her most prized possession. Well, until the girls were born. I mean, I get they weren't really a possession, but I'm sure you're following me here."

Bill nodded. "Yes, I'm following."

"This book—this Bible here—this is the *only* material possession I have left from my previous life. And unfortunately, many of my memories have been obscured, possibly erased. I'm not 100% certain which just yet."

Bill shook his head in apparent disbelief, then looked somberly at Michael. "I'm really sorry to hear that, Michael."

Michael pursed his lips and shook his head. He grabbed the Bible and placed it back in the desk drawer. As he turned his head to look at Bill, he began speaking again.

"Yes, it is a rather sad story. No happy ending. No fairytale for sure. It's the stark reality that we both inhabit. You were about to say that you can't imagine this happening to Sarah or your kids earlier, when I cut you off. Bill, we're not going to let that happen. I've shared this with you for that specific purpose. You've restored my faith, at least a little bit, in humanity. You're a good man...maybe even a great man. I want you to be successful, and I want you to know the reality. I want you to know it so you can make different, better decisions than I did. I was a good man before that day.

"That was the day I lost my humanity and nothing mattered. I could walk up to a complete stranger and, for any reason, regardless of how trivial it might be, pull out my weapon and shoot them dead right on the spot. Then I would go on about my day as if nothing out of the ordinary had occurred. The Organization told me it was my 'Awakening', but it was more of a living death to me. Still is. I want your Awakening to be different. I want you to be aware of what The Organization is willing to do in order to keep their secrets. They have no conscience. They have no fear. They have no boundaries. There is no end to the reach or savagery of The Organization."

* * *

Michael appeared about as serious as a man could be. It was clear to Bill that Michael was sincere in his warning. It was one that Bill knew he had to heed. His analytical nature had his mind teeming with questions.

"How can the government hide the funding?"

"Bill, the government funds black and/or dark initiatives all the time, without knowing the details or the truth about what they're funding. There are two individuals who know a modicum of what goes on within The Organization, and that only covers the MIMIC initiative and one other that you have not been briefed on yet. Both are advanced technology heavy and, therefore, required extraordinarily large funding, outwardly at least. The reality is those two programs only require about thirty percent of the funding received, and that number drops every year, as we refine the processes and stockpiles. The rest of the money is put wherever the director wants it. The truth is the government has no idea of the real scope of The Organization. If they did? I don't know what would happen, but it wouldn't be a pretty scenario at all. At the end of the day, The Organization is not the government."

"I can only imagine."

"You are going to be asked to do things that are clearly in violent disagreement with your value system. You are going to—at some point—be asked to sleep with women you just met; you are going to be asked to kill people, and these people may be old, young, or possibly even underage. You cannot hesitate; you must do it. Otherwise, your Awakening will take a rather dark turn. You, too, will take that dark passage to avenging angel, just as I have. I don't want that for you. And, I especially don't want that for Sarah and your kids."

"I can't let that happen. I will do whatever I have to do to protect them; that's my number one priority...my number one job. The God I believe in would not forsake me for doing the best I can in that regard."

"You know, Bill, I actually believe you when you say that."

19 Risk Versus Reward

Bill and Michael sat without uttering a word for several minutes, each apparently reflecting on life and what had brought them here to this moment. Both were captive to The Organization, and neither wanted to be there. Neither of them were able to formulate a way out that didn't end in certain death. For Bill, that meant certain death for Sarah and the kids.

"It's time we called it a day. Get home to Sarah."

Bill nodded in agreement. "Yep, that's exactly where I want and need to be right now."

Bill left Michael in his office and made his way down the corridor, through the ECP, and out to his car, where he sat for several minutes more. He fought the tears, but they came. He sat sobbing uncontrollably at the thought of what could happen to the love of his life and the children they'd created. Once he pulled himself together, he took the long route home to give himself time to get his act together and allow the telltale signs he'd been crying to fade.

It was life as usual at home. He pulled into the drive, walked into the house, and into Sarah's loving arms. All was as if nothing was different...as if nothing was out of sorts in the world. *If they only knew. My God, how would they react?* No way Bill would let that happen. He would not wager against The Organization with the lives of his family.

That night, as well as the days and nights that followed, were no different. Bill went to work, did as he was directed, and went home. Despite the dark world he'd been thrust into, he was doing an exceptional job as a husband and father. Perhaps, it was the potential ramifications for failing in any regard that provided the necessary motivation to excel in all that he did. Whatever the case, he was at the top of his game.

Days turned into weeks as time seemed to stand still yet passed so quickly. Time had seemed to pick up speed the older he got but not like this. It was in overdrive now. Christmas was around the corner, and it seemed as though the summer had only just ended. *How does that happen? How do we lose track of time in our mind's eye?* he wondered.

Bill had formed the habit of journaling at work to keep track of his progression as well as the things that concerned him. As such, he wrote a lot. The journal served as a reminder of his time spent and where all the time had gone. Most of it was spent digging further into the rabbit hole, only to find nothing more than what Michael had already told him.

The rest of his time was spent trying to figure a way out of this situation. Bill could not see any way out in which they were able to move on with their lives. Reviewing the files Michael had provided to him, he did uncover several data points that he thought deserved further analysis. There were several documented cases of individuals who had attempted to remove themselves, only to evaporate from existence.

He even briefly considered the option of having MIMICs created of all his family members, inserting the MIMICs into existing daily routines, and secretly ushering his real family out of the country. That was short-lived when he stumbled across a dossier regarding a predecessor who had attempted that approach, only to be caught and erased from existence—with MIMICs left to carry on with their lives for a brief time until they were killed in a head-on collision.

The Organization was meticulous. Every aspect of each case Bill reviewed was flawless. He could not recall having ever seen such perfect execution even in a movie or a book. He wasn't entirely certain how Michael was able to grant him access to see some of these files. Sure, he had been briefed to the level of most of the files. However, some were marked differently, for Archangel's eyes only or ESP eyes only.

There had to be an initiative that was predictive in nature, almost seer-like, that he had not been briefed on yet. Some sort of pre-cognitive element, or something that showed them the future had to be in play here, but peering into the future seemed even too far-fetched for The Organization. But was it?

Bill turned his focus away from MIMIC to the other initiatives, thinking perhaps better answers awaited. Thought control and what the whole Archangel Initiative was about would surely provide him with some answers. The information was scarce. Significantly less documentation existed on those initiatives, especially the Archangel Initiative. Little more than a description of its creation and that they were established to oversee Organization operations was available. What information he found was overly nondescript and lacking requisite detail, given the advanced nature of the technology.

The Concilium Initiative didn't provide a whole lot more. Bill knew a significant amount of information was being withheld from him. Another Organization method, clearly designed to closely guard their greatest secrets. They were effective in keeping secrets, which was blatantly obvious to Bill. He also knew everyone...every organization...eventually made a mistake, and that's what he needed to find. A mistake that divulged just enough information to give Bill sufficient leverage—or open a path out of their grasp—one that, despite their reach and technology, they had missed. It was the proverbial 'needle in a haystack', but he didn't see any other way around it. His uncanny ability to pinpoint such flaws had become the trademark of his success in the military. He wouldn't put his family at risk unnecessarily, but given the right information, he just might be able to weasel his way out. Unfortunately, it appeared that the information he had reviewed only led to the erasure of those who attempted to exploit or reveal it.

Bill had discovered that, in order to keep him in sync with his MIMIC, they were not able to monitor him with the Concilium Initiative tech. That was quite beneficial. Now, at least for the moment, he had freedom of thought. He had to make the time in which the thought police were not monitoring him count.

Once he realized he'd made his way through all the documentation Michael had granted him access to thus far, he knew he had to engage Michael and attempt to get access to more information. It was risky, but given the rapport he'd established with Michael, it was worth the ask.

Bill found Michael in his office for once and knocked before entering.

"Michael, good to see you. Do you have a minute or two to chat?"

"Absolutely. Good to see you, it's been a few weeks now," Michael responded and reached across his desk to shake Bill's hand.

"Yes, it's been a little while."

"What can I do for you, my friend?" Michael motioned for Bill to take a seat and took a seat himself.

"Well, I wanted to let you know that I've managed to work my way through all the documentation I was given access to on our networks."

Michael was predictably looking intently into Bill's eyes. He did this with everyone, except OEM. Bill had noticed but dared not ask yet why that was the case. Michael would also nod slightly and continuously. Perhaps it was an unconscious tick, perhaps it was more.

Michael tilted his head back and moved his head awkwardly side to side, twisting just a bit. Bill could hear it crack. He closed then opened his eyes to look intently at Bill with a small grin before speaking.

"That was quick. I forget you're not only a fast reader but retain what you read...at least a large portion of it. Well, I can assume, based on what I know about you that you're ready for more...looking for more to read and understand about these initiatives."

"That is...exactly what I wanted to talk to you about," Bill replied eagerly.

"I figured as much. I did think it would take a bit longer, however."

Bill sat back in the seat and placed his hands behind his head.

"I haven't had anything to do but review that information over the past several...well, quite a few weeks. And, I definitely don't want to appear to be content to do nothing," he said with a smile growing ever wider.

Michael chuckled at Bill's comment. "Never. I could not ever see that in you, Bill. Here's the thing. Knowing what you've read, you're no doubt aware that suspension of the Concilium Initiatives is required with regard to MIMIC synchronization."

"Yes, I recall reading that."

"What you don't know about is a program with a singular focus. That focus is on a singular individual and that individual is me."

That comment prompted Bill to sit up and lean toward Michael's desk. He was surprised to hear what Michael had shared.

"Without going into all the details, Bill, I need you to know that I have the ability to override the Concilium protocols covertly. I am singularly unique in that regard. The program covering the tech I have access to was terminated as a failure. The one secret I was able to keep from The Organization, one that would result in my untimely demise." Michael sat back and smiled.

"Interesting...why are you telling me this?"

"Because, as I've told you before, I like you. I like you a lot. I don't want to see what happened to me happen to you. I'm aware of what you would like to do. That's a dangerous row to hoe my friend."

"Michael...I..." Michael cut him off before he could finish his statement.

"Bill, it's all good. You have to remember: I've been— shall we say—imbued with certain abilities. I understand, and I'm not going to stand in your way. I'll give you access to the entirety of the information available for the initiatives for which you've been briefed. Only you and I will know what you decide to do with that information. My only requirement of you is that do *not* act without first having discussed it with me. I won't stand in your way, but I also don't want to be blindsided if I'm on assignment halfway around the world. I need you to agree on this." Michael sat up and leaned forward. He looked very sternly at Bill, but he spoke in a way that seemed almost as if it wasn't directive but a request.

"Yes, that won't be a problem. I appreciate your understanding and willingness to share more information with me."

* * *

"Don't get ahead of yourself. You may not feel the same way about that once you start digging through it all. These initiatives run far deeper than you can imagine. They have ties to the real world that are probably going to make you vomit when you come to that realization. You truly have no idea of the depth and breadth of the depravity The Organization is capable of and has been responsible for in the development of these initiatives. You truly don't know what you're asking for, Bill. You really don't."

Michael was trying desperately to warn Bill of the pitfalls that existed within The Organization. He was wary, though; too much information given too quickly would likely be terminal. Perhaps for both of them.

"I can see by your response you're telling me this out of concern. I can't express to you just how much I appreciate that."

"You're welcome. Just...proceed cautiously, Bill. Please? Not for my sake or yours really but for that of your family. You have a great family. I don't want any part in seeing what you have surrounding you destroyed," Michael said earnestly.

"Neither do I, Michael. Neither do I. I'll be sure to move slowly and sync up with you when you're in the office. You've become a great sounding board for me

Bill stood, ready to walk back to his office.

"You're welcome. And make sure you do just that. Take it slowly. Don't make any move unless you're certain the reward is worth the risk. I don't know what possible rewards are to be had, but I do know the risk. The risk is losing Sarah or the kids. So, it had best be one helluva reward."

Bill spoke matter-of-factly. "Yes, I've accepted the probability of no reward at the end of all this. I may well be a part of something I'll never be able to separate myself from. But, until I'm certain no other path exists where I can extract myself and my family safely from this organization, I can't stop searching. They deserve better than what they have, and the worst part of it all? They have absolutely no idea that one mistake I make—even unintentionally—could lead to torture and death."

Michael closed his eyes briefly and nodded in agreement. "That's an acutely accurate summation of it all."

"Yeah, I can't live with that. I can't resolve myself to the unconscionable actions I will eventually be directed to accomplish unless I'm one hundred percent certain there is no way out."

"I fear you've taken on this self-assigned mission in vain, Bill. I am sorry I'm not as upbeat about this as I'm sure you would like. I hate being the naysayer in all this, but I only see this as an exercise in futility."

Bill extended his hand to Michael. The men shook hands, then Bill turned to leave. As he reached the door, he turned and left Michael with a final thought.

"Maybe it is, Michael...but I still have to try."

20 Finding the Needle

Bill wasted no time. He was determined to find that needle, the one thing that could give him the leverage he needed to extricate himself and his family from this mess. They were living a nightmare. The kids were oblivious to the ever-present danger surrounding their lives. Sure, Sarah might suspect aspects of Bill's new job were potentially ruthless but not the true malevolence of the situation.

Bill had paid attention to Michael's every word during their last conversation. Of particular interest was the ability Michael had kept for himself and hid from The Organization. Bill focused on that as the possible needle in the proverbial haystack, but he needed more details. And he was relatively certain those details no longer existed, unless Michael was hiding them as well. If The Organization found any documentation regarding that ability, rather the success of it, Michael would no longer exist.

The hours passed as Bill scoured every word, on every page, on every document. As he moved from one document to the next, he could feel his frustration level increasing. *There has to be something, some thread I can pull on to unravel this puzzle.* He paused for a few minutes here and there to make a lap around his desk and stretch. Before he'd realized what time it was, he was already late getting home. He called Sarah to apologize and let her know that he would be a while longer. She wasn't happy but understood this was bound to happen. She'd been subjected to these phone calls for years, so it really wasn't out of the ordinary to her.

Bill continued digging to no avail. Bill slapped the top of his desk with both hands in frustration. *Come on, man. Dammit, there has to be some point of conversion with these projects.* He was too frustrated to continue any further. There was nothing in the additional files for the Concilium Initiative that provided any added insights for him. Finding himself at a convenient stopping point, he made his way home. It had been a long day—frustrating for Bill and likely concerning for Sarah.

Quietly as he could, Bill made his way in the house and to the bedroom. He tried not to disturb Sarah, even knowing in the back of his mind she was most likely not asleep. As he stepped into the bedroom, Sarah spoke.

"Long day, huh?"

"Yes, sorry."

"Nothing to be sorry about. It goes with the territory. Hopefully, you were able to get your work done."

"A good bit of it. But I could have worked through the night and still not been completely finished with it."

"Wow. You haven't had a workload like this unless there were ongoing military operations."

"True, but that's not the case now. We don't have anything to do with those types of operations...at least not that I'm aware of yet."

"Well, let's hope it stays that way."

"Yes, ma'am."

"Hurry and get in bed. I'm ready to sleep."

"Okay, it'll just take me a couple minutes."

"Just stop talking and hurry."

Bill smiled and made his way to the bathroom to brush his teeth and shower quickly. As he was hanging his towel up after drying himself, a thought crossed his mind. It wasn't so much that it crossed his mind, more like it was just inserted. "Hidden folders...hidden files" repeated in his mind like a broken record.

The message repeated until Bill grabbed his phone to set a reminder for himself. He had gotten into the habit of making notes for himself, usually related to Sarah and the kids, because he had forgotten so many things. Missing practices, picking up kids, or even grabbing something on his way home that Sarah had asked him to get no less than five minutes earlier. He had been so focused on work; his overstimulated mind was overflowing. This habit was born from necessity...necessity of keeping himself out of the doghouse.

No sooner did he set his phone down after having set the reminder than a second thought ran through his mind, but just one. *That's your needle, Bill.* And then, he knew. No doubt now that this was Michael's doing. He would not speak of it, but he would try to exploit it.

Bill struggled to sleep. He had not mastered the ability to quiet his racing thoughts. He hadn't gotten home until nearly midnight and was certain he'd not fallen asleep until after two. But he was wide awake, and it was just five a.m. Knowing attempts to sleep more would be in vain, he readied himself and was out the door before six.

Seeing Bill so early didn't surprise the ECP guards.

"Early day, Bill?"

"Yes...so much yet to learn."

"We wouldn't know, but we have to notify Michael. He's been clear that we inform him if anyone shows up before seven."

"Okay, that's new. Do I need to wait until you talk to him?"

"No sir, you're free to go on in. We just have to let him know."

"Roger that. You fellas have a great day."

"You too, sir."

Bill made his way into the facility and surprisingly found OEM were already there, in the corridor between his and Michael's offices. Well, according to the documents he had reviewed, they actually never left the facility, ever. But they were roaming the halls, which *was* odd, since unless directed otherwise, they remained in their offices or the laboratory areas.

"Good morning, Ellynore."

"Good morning, Bill. How are you settling in?"

"Very well, thank you."

"We see that you're making *great* progress," she said somewhat sarcastically.

"How's that?" Bill responded, acting as if he didn't hear her clearly. He tried to hide his surprise at the comment. And the sarcastic manner it was delivered.

"Well, we've noticed you've made your way through a lot of documentation. Michael doesn't typically share this much with probationary employees."

Bill's analytical skills were in overdrive before he arrived. He had been ruminating on the message he perceived to be from Michael. But Ellynore's tone, combined with the content of her comments, seemed to be a perfect opportunity to probe for more information. So, he replied earnestly, hoping her programming didn't leave her devoid of any trace of humanity.

"Really? I wasn't aware. Is this cause for concern? Did I miss something or see something I should not have seen? I certainly don't want to break the rules."

"Yet to be determined. It is *unusual*," Ellynore replied, her tone softer.

"Perhaps he's impressed with my progress and is testing my limits with data ingestion?"

Ellynore paused for a few seconds before replying to Bill. Just before she spoke, the smallest of grins appeared, replacing the scowl she'd been displaying.

"Perhaps. It is a logical progression but so atypical, we've been asked to monitor your progress. However, it would seem as though Michael has blocked access to pause the synchronization link between you and Bill 2.0"

"Bill 2.0?"

Now he was just messing with her. Though he did not often take pleasure in screwing with someone, he did take a bit of pleasure in this instance. He wasn't sold on a non-human having any authority over humans. His impromptu social experiment showed him humans were still superior to the MIMICS, at least at the present.

"Sorry, I have a dry sense of humor, Bill. I was referencing your MIMIC."

"I gathered as much. And your sense of humor is great, I'd just never heard that reference before," he said with a smile.

"Do you know when Michael will be arriving today?"

"No, actually I never know when he's going to be here or not."

"Hmmm, no one seems to know his schedule. This is an unexpected development and somewhat alarming. Please let him know that I would really like to speak with him should you see him before I do," she commented with sincere concern.

"Sure thing, Ellynore. Is there anything else I can do to help ease your concerns?"

"No, you should continue as Michael has directed. If changes are to be made, it will be after my conversation with Michael."

Bill found it odd that Ellynore's last few statements seemed as if they were legitimately made out of concern. *It's as if she is a human trying to act like a robot, trying to act like a human. How confusing. I sure hope Michael can make sense out of this interaction for me.*

It was at that moment, Bill heard from Michael again. *"That was a great way to handle the situation, Bill. I was on my way in, but due to the current circumstances, I'm going to delay my arrival. You know what you need to do, so I'll leave you to it."*

"Bill?" Ellynore queried.

"Bill?" she prompted again.

Ellynore reached out and pushed him on the shoulder slightly and spoke in a firmer tone.

"Bill?"

Bill turned to look at her, eyes wide, as if he'd just returned to reality from some sort of daydream.

"Sorry, Ellynore. I lost my train of thought. Yes, I'll continue as Michael has directed until I hear something to the contrary from one of you."

Bill thought to himself, *I almost blew that.* He had not heard her the first two times she called his name.

"Very well. Oh, by the way, what exactly has Michael asked you to do?"

"Just review all the documentation he's made available to me. That's it."

"No analysis or reports to be generated from your review?"

"Not at this point. He just asked me to familiarize myself with the information, nothing more."

Bill thought she looked satisfied with his answers. He did realize it was nearly impossible for him to be certain at this point. He was counting on Michael giving him a heads up in the event he ran afoul of OEM.

"Very well. Have a nice day, Bill"

"You, too, Ellynore."

Ellynore turned and met Sylvya and Patrycya where they had been waiting in the corridor crossway. OEM made their way back in the direction of the lab viewing area where Michael had revealed Bill's MIMIC to him. Bill wasted no time getting to his office and back to work. He had his guidance; now, it was up to him.

As he began to search, he couldn't help feeling as though something was amiss. He took a moment, seemingly to stand and stretch. It was the best way that came to mind for him to survey his office without being obvious. Attention to detail was something that had been stressed and was a noted deficiency during his testing. His survey took a couple of minutes, but there it was. Pictures on his wall had been swapped out.

Bill had noticed one wall in his office was completely bare except for the credenza. It was an obvious choice to make that wall his backdrop. So, he moved the boxes and piles of books he'd brought in weeks earlier to personalize his space off the credenza. He slid his desk around, leaving just enough room for him and his chair to maneuver in the space that was left and unpacked the pictures of the kids and Sarah. Once the pictures and books were neatly arranged on his desk and credenza, he moved the coat rack from beside the door, to in front of the newly hung wall art.

Bill could now dig into his search without fear of watchful eyes. Remembering his direction from Michael, Bill changed the option on his computer to display hidden files and folders. He wasn't sure what to expect but found just one previously hidden folder that contained two files.

Override Concept & Override Implementation Steps

It didn't take long for Bill to understand why these files had been kept hidden. The information outlined the technology that Michael had hidden from The Organization. They described the concept as well as the steps to install, configure, and activate the technology. Bill read every word but was left with more questions than answers.

How was this the proverbial needle? And how was this going to facilitate his escape?

He changed the computer options back to obfuscate the information and proceeded to review the remaining documentation. Hours passed, and it was nearly time for lunch. As he was gathering his things to go grab lunch, Michael walked into his office and closed the door behind him.

"Listen. It's a needle, trust me." He heard Michael, but Michael's lips never moved. Then Michael spoke aloud. "I know OEM are looking to speak with me, and I know why. The Organization is not thrilled that I've shared so much information with you. It typically takes a few years to be granted the access you have, and I've requested permission to grant you additional access. I suspect my request will be granted, but it will be after great scrutiny."

Then, without Michael's expression changing or his lips moving, Bill heard Michael's voice in his head. *"By the way, my guys handle the IT event logging for this facility, I've asked them to cover your tracks."*

Bill played it off, acting as if he was contemplating Michael's statement regarding additional access. He was certain OEM would be monitoring their conversation.

"So, how do you feel about that, Bill?" Michael said aloud.

"I'm just following your lead here. I don't want any trouble for me or you."

"No trouble to be had, as long as we stay within established parameters."

"Sounds like some feel as though we're already outside those parameters."

"No, not outside. Just walking along the precipice."

"I see."

"I'm going to go speak with Ellynore. Once we're done, I'll call you, and we can discuss the additional access."

"Sounds good. I'm going to grab a bite to eat; would you like me to grab something for you?"

Michael stood and turned toward the door. He paused to respond, looking over his shoulder at Bill. "Yeah. That'd be great. Surprise me. I'll eat just about anything."

"Got it. See you in a few."

* * *

Michael made his way to Ellynore's office. Michael's conversation with her was somewhat contentious, but Michael was clear with her, and The Organization, that he was well aware of his role and did not need to be micromanaged or reminded of his parameters.

"Ellynore, I know you're acting as a conduit, so I want you and APEX to hear this clearly. I advised against bringing

Bill on board. I told you it was a bad idea. There was absolutely no harm whatsoever in his actions at the Alcove site. None. Now, by bringing him on board, you've created a potential situation. You've told me to feed him information and make him an asset. I'm doing just that. He's a machine— another fact I shared with you before you made the decision to bring him on board, again, *against my recommendation.* Bill is the best analyst we've ever seen, with a voracious appetite for vast amounts of information. That's how he developed into the hugely successful military analyst he became, and he is still at the top of his game today. What did you think was going to happen?"

Ellynore began to speak, but the words were not hers. APEX was speaking through her. APEX was a name assumed by the individual leading MIMIC development activities within The Organization. Nobody knew if APEX was human or MIMIC or what APEX stood for, if anything. They only knew that when APEX got involved, the situation was serious, and someone was likely to be erased.

"We cannot afford for you to lose control of an asset of this caliber, Michael."

"APEX, do you honestly think I don't know that? I watch his every move. You want to know why I locked down the sync? I did that so I have the ability to insert his alternative asset at a moment's notice. I have him monitored every second of the day. The only time that's put in jeopardy is when you or OEM interfere without consultation. When you attempt to micromanage me. This has never happened before and needs to never happen again. I can't do my job effectively with my every decision being questioned. If you doubt my conviction and dedication, replace me. If not, stop questioning my loyalty and leave me the hell alone to do my job and stop creating a distraction. I can't afford a distraction like this with Bill on board. That's the one thing that could lead to me missing something. None of us can afford that, APEX, and you know it."

Michael spoke with reverent disdain. He had the utmost respect for the chain of command, along with a healthy contempt for the lack of respect he was being shown.

"All right, Michael. I'll back off for now. You've made your point about loyalty. Let me make mine. If you fail me and The Organization through disloyalty, I will personally see to it that you meet a fate worse than that of your family. I was present then, and you can rest assured my face will be the last thing you ever see."

"I would not expect anything less. Now if the two of you will excuse me, I have work to do."

"Good bye, Michael."

Michael shook his head in apparent frustration as he stood and walked toward the door of Ellynore's office. He turned and spoke before opening the door.

"Good day to *you*, Ellynore."

Michael walked out of Ellynore's office just as Bill was passing by. Bill said nothing and followed Michael to his office. Michael didn't offer any information regarding the conversation he'd just had, and he knew Bill wasn't about to ask. He and Michael sat and ate lunch, only conversing about mundane things, taking great caution to avoid work topics. Once done, Michael got up and motioned to Bill.

"Bill, come with me, we have something we need to take care of."

"Sure," Bill said, slurping the last sip of his drink.

They made it past the familiar lab to what appeared to be a biometrically locked vault. Michael opened the vault and motioned for Bill to enter ahead of him. Once Michael entered, he closed and locked the vault.

"We have just about thirty minutes before this is going to raise suspicion. So, listen carefully. I need you to trust me and do exactly as I say."

"Roger that."

"Look for a light switch beside that door, turn it on, go into the room, and sit in the chair."

Bill did as he was instructed. The room looked like a small surgical suite, only with a lot of tech. He sat in the chair just as Michael entered the room.

"Put this sensor cap on, Bill. I have to adjust the configuration to personalize it to your unique biology, but that'll just take a couple seconds; it's all automated with the AI."

"What exactly...?"

"Trust me. I'll explain shortly. Just sit back."

Bill complied with Michael's direction and leaned back in the seat. Michael turned to the computer, and after a few keystrokes, turned back to Bill.

"We're ready. Three, two, one." Michael pressed enter on the keyboard and took a step back toward the corner of the small room. He watched closely as Bill fell almost immediately asleep, and the AI controlled robotic surgeon began making precise incisions into his skull. Just behind the left ear and in line with Bill's hairline in order to inject nanites and hide the razor-thin scar. The nanites were programmed for specific jobs: first, to modify the existing cerebral link to enable the ability to block unwanted monitoring and suggestion, and second, to repair the incision and subcutaneous damage due to it.

The process took just fifteen minutes, then Bill was awake. Bill looked up at Michael anxiously.

"Michael, I'm ready."

"Oh, we're done. Can you stand?"

"Done? Already? I just sat down," Bill said incredulously.

"Let's go."

"Whatever you say. This isn't making any sense. Sit down; get up; let's go."

"It will soon enough," Michael mumbled.

Bill leaned forward to get up from his seat. As soon as he stood up, he placed his hands on both sides of his head and closed his eyes for a moment. "Why do I suddenly have a throbbing headache?"

"That'll subside in a few hours."

Michael chuckled as he noticed Bill's '*here we go again*' stare.

They exited just as they'd entered and all in under thirty minutes. Michael sprang into full tour-guide mode as soon as the door opened.

"Yes, it's a cool space. Even I'm not sure why it's in a vault. But I'm sure someone, somewhere, has that answer. Like I was explaining to you, this should help connect some of the dots between the initiatives you were asking about. I mean, it's great to read about a process, but seeing the tech that makes it possible really stiches it together."

"Yes, I agree. It all makes a lot more sense now. Thanks for the ten-cent tour."

"Ten-cent? That was the quarter tour, Bill."

They both laughed as they passed the OEM offices. Michael was certain they were listening and reporting everything to APEX. After all, OEM had no choice in the matter. They worked for APEX directly, and were, in reality, nothing more than a monitoring tool. Michael knew their true purpose for existence was to keep a watchful eye on him, even though they were supposedly assigned to work for and assist him. The recent surge in activity reminded Michael he was under significantly increased scrutiny. That meant Bill—and his family—were as well. Michael knew he had to take Bill to the next level. So rather than lead Bill to the needle, he gave it to him.

21 Sewing Practice

"You have a good evening, Bill. I have some things to attend to off-site."

"You as well."

"Give my best to Sarah and the kids when you speak to them."

"Will do."

Michael departed, and Bill made his way into his office. He still had a significant amount of information to sift through. He wasn't exactly certain what had gone down in the vault. Bill knew Michael was concerned, and that he was looking out for him, but why that was necessary wasn't clear. He also knew that Michael would clear the foggy notions as soon as he could. Or, more to the point, when it was safe to do so.

Bill sat and reviewed the Archangel documentation for a couple more hours. He looked up only to speak to each of OEM as they said goodbye for the day. In a file search, he had discovered that even though they never left the facility, they were conditioned to appear as though that was the case. Each would make rounds to indicate they were done for the day and then return to the pods where they resided until needed.

Bill had intentionally waited them out. He was intent to appear busy until OEM were done for the day to avoid any potential questions they might pose to him. Fifteen minutes after Patrycya said goodnight, Bill left for home. No one was in the corridors, and only the night guard was present at the ECP.

The guard did ask to search Bill's backpack, which was odd. This had not occurred since the first day. Bill complied, and the guard found nothing but empty food containers left from Bill's lunch from a few days earlier. The guard indicated Bill was good to go, so he headed out his car and home.

Bill had expected to hear from Michael but didn't. Not that night, nor over the next few days or nights.

Bill finished reviewing all the documentation Michael had given him access to so far and started reviewing all of it again, from the beginning, just to make sure he'd not overlooked some obscure, yet critical piece of information. Bill was starting to get a little concerned by the end of the second week without any contact from Michael. He had not actually seen OEM, or anyone else, with the exception of some lower-level lab techs.

On the morning of the fifteenth day since he'd last seen Michael, Bill found a short message on his car under the wiper blade.

Meet me where this all started.

Bill returned to the house to change clothes and grab some extra. It would be a bit cooler in the mountains than it had been during his vacation. Sarah was just waking up when Bill walked back into the bedroom. She rolled over to face Bill.

"Ugh, good morning."

"Hey...good morning. I'm sorry if I woke you."

"It's okay. I need to get up anyway. Whatcha doing?"

"I have to take a short road trip, so I'm putting some warmer clothes on and packing some extra clothes, since I don't know if I'm going to be asked to stay overnight."

"Isn't that a little odd? Especially on such short notice?" Sarah sat up in the bed, looking puzzled. Bill just smiled and responded as normally as he could.

"Yes, but isn't everything else with this job?"

"You got me on that one." Sarah flopped back down on the bed and pulled the pillow over her head.

"I didn't want to wake you, but I was going to call in an hour or so to let you know."

Sarah chuckled. "You knew I was about to ask, huh?" Her voice was now muffled.

"Yes ma'am. I know that look."

Sarah pulled the pillow off her face and glared at him. "What look? You couldn't even see my face."

"Yes, but I can see it now, and I've seen it before. I know *the look.*"

"And, that's why I love you, mister."

"I love you more. And...I gotta go."

Bill gave Sarah a quick kiss on the cheek and headed out the door. He didn't know what Michael had planned but was certain it would be enlightening. A winter storm was forecast through the area, but the worst of it would stay just north of them. It was still dark and gloomy outside with plentiful ominous clouds overhead that looked as if they would dump massive amounts of snow at any moment.

Bill stopped at the convenience store just a few miles before the turn to the vacation home to top off the fuel tank and grab a drink and a snack. When he returned to the car, he found another short note under his wiper blade.

Take the second left past the turn for the vacation home. Drive to end, walk from there, follow signs.

Bill looked around to see if he could see Michael or one of the other Archangels, but there were no other vehicles to be seen. He got back on the road and carefully watched for his turn as he passed the one for the vacation home. It was another five miles before he saw another turn and a couple more before he found the second. The turn-off road was not the best and not a road he would have normally driven his new vehicle on. To say it was a rough, unimproved road would be an understatement. Thankfully, it was barely a mile long.

Bill stopped the car and grabbed his things, making sure to add another layer before walking into the forest. It was near noon but only thirty degrees. The overcast sky and moderately dense forest made it a challenge to see any signs at all, but he was able to catch a glimpse of one. Had it not been for the reflective nature of the signs, it's doubtful he would have seen anything. The signs were placed just far enough apart that standing at one and scanning the forest with a flashlight revealed the next.

It took Bill just over an hour to find his way to the clearing he'd stumbled upon during his vacation: the small concrete structure and communications tower. That tower was now lying on the ground and appeared as though the communications cable attached to it had been intentionally cut.

He carefully made his way across the thirty or so feet separating the forest from the door on the structure. He scanned the area repeatedly as he approached the door. As he got closer to the structure, he could see yet another message, this one attached to the door.

Door is open, come inside.

Bill complied and entered the small building. Once inside, he closed the door behind him and was startled by a voice. It took him a moment to realize it was a recording Michael had left. He wasn't sure if it was specifically for him or standard protocol for anyone entering the small facility.

"Place your belongings on the floor next to the coat closet. Enter the closet and await further instructions."

Once again, Bill complied with the provided instructions. And once inside the closet, he could see it was not a closet but a small elevator. It was barely big enough for one person. Perhaps two could fit if they didn't mind getting in each other's personal space. He waited for thirty seconds with nothing happening. Bill was now getting frustrated as this felt like a waste of time.

"Biometric scanning complete...you will now be taken down to the Romeo-One facility. Please stand by."

"Romeo-One facility?" Bill asked aloud.

It was not a fast elevator, but the ride downward lasted almost a minute and a half, so Bill knew the facility was fairly deep underground. What he didn't know is exactly where he was headed, other than down, or what was waiting for him when he arrived. Thoughts were frantically racing through his mind.

Once the elevator stopped and the doors opened, Bill could see what looked to be the facility he worked in with Michael. The space was identical. A man he recognized from his initial encounter with the Archangels at the cabin, whose name he did not know, was apparently waiting on his arrival.

"Hello, Bill."

"Can you—"

"Tell you why you're here? Yes. Michael is waiting in the conference room with Gabriel. He will explain everything to you."

"Oh, I see."

"This way." Bill followed the man, still not knowing exactly who he was.

The man led Bill to the conference room. Although the facility looked identical, the rooms were not configured that way. As they approached the conference room, Bill could hear Michael speaking to someone on the phone. Or so it appeared. The man stopped short of the door and motioned for Bill to stop as well. They stood motionless until it was clear Michael was done with his conversation.

"You can enter now."

"Thanks, Remiel?"

"Sorry, yes, I am Remiel. Good guess," Remiel replied, somewhat amazed.

"Thanks. I'm terrible with names."

"You might want to work on that; it will serve you well."

"Yes...I suppose it will."

Remiel slapped Bill on the back and walked away as the door opened to Gabriel motioning for Bill to come inside.

* * *

"Bill, please have a seat; we have much to discuss."

"Sure, I'm anxious to get started."

"Thank you for making the trip. What we have to discuss, and more importantly, the training we need to provide you is paramount to your safety and that of your family."

Michael continued before Bill could speak.

"I shared with you a defunct project that I intentionally misled The Organization about. Well, I'm not the only one who has benefitted from that project. In fact, I've hidden a good bit more from APEX. APEX, the top dog in The

Organization, is an unpleasant individual who does not take humanity or human error into account in decision-making. It's black or white, period. Gabriel and I agree that APEX's approach is in violent disagreement with the governing documents by which The Organization was meant to operate.

"We were supposed to be protectors, working in the shadows to avert national and even global crises that were initiated by bad actors executing black operations. The reality? We've been used as a tool to silence anyone that starts getting too close to the true nature of The Organization's operations." Michael could see the growing concern shown clearly on Bill's face. "That was the catalyst event that led Gabriel, myself, and the rest of the Archangels to pursue two-way mirror technology, that I've hidden. TWM was a countermeasure derived from uniquely advanced tech we came into possession of several years back.

"It was purposely built to unlock innate, suppressed abilities within the human brain. TWM provided the conduit to implement that which the brain was aware of but incapable of implementing of its own accord."

* * *

Bill sat up and leaned on the table. Michael had his full attention now. This was one of the technologies Bill had wanted to learn more about, but an opportunity to ask Michael about it had not presented itself, until now.

"The Mirror Initiative...I read about that."

"Exactly. We had just perfected MIRROR and needed a way to neutralize it in the unlikely event someone else created a similar technology. So, we conducted some digital recon and found some information about a TWM-like technology, took that, and perfected it. I then reported that it was not viable and subsequently shut the initiative down."

"I'm assuming TWM is why I'm here?"

Bill was excited about what he was hearing. *Finally, something interesting for me to do a deep-dive on.* His thoughts were racing.

"Yes sir, indeed it is. You asked for a needle, and I gave it to you...quite literally."

Bill knew instantly what Michael was talking about. The ten-cent tour of the vault. He'd lost half an hour and nothing had been shared with him other than Michael assuring him that he would come to understand.

"The vault and your ten-cent tour."

"I know you would have shut me down if I had asked. Sorry about that. But trust me when I tell you, you will thank me. And it was the quarter-tour, remember," Michael quipped.

"So it was. The last several months have been a blur. I just wanted to retire and live a simple life with Sarah and the kids...now I'm in the middle of a shitstorm, and all I want is out."

* * *

Michael admired Bill's honesty and eternal optimism. It might have been too late for him but not for Bill.

"I know...and this may well be the only way to get you what you want. So...I need you to trust me."

"I don't really have much of a choice, but oddly enough, I do trust you, Michael."

Michael turned to his right-hand angel. "Gabriel, could you grab Raphael and meet us in the courtyard?"

"Of course," Gabriel said as he rose from his seat.

"Thanks, we'll be there shortly."

Gabriel left to find Raphael and closed the door—through which his broad shoulders barely fit—behind him.

Michael focused on Bill. This was a potentially fatal decision but necessary nonetheless. Michael knew it was a huge risk, but with Bill, one worth taking.

"Bill...we don't have a lot of time. I suspect OEM will be heading this way soon to see why the communications are down. They will likely arrive around dusk. We must leave well before that so we can cover our tracks. The storm will be blamed for the tower, unless we get caught."

"Let's get to it then."

The men rose from their seats. Michael guided Bill to the courtyard, where Raphael and Gabriel waited, each seated against opposing walls. Michael led Bill in and instructed him to take a seat and then took a seat himself on the wall opposite Bill.

"Bill, this is where we're going to get you the practice you need with TWM. So, we're clear, this is not a simulation. We're done with that subversive crap. The Archangels now consider you a peer and an ally. As far as we're concerned, you are part of our team."

Bill looked shocked. He exhaled noticeably, and his eyes widened. "I'm honored."

"Not sure it's something to be all that honored about," Raphael remarked.

Gabriel shook his head, looking disappointed in his teammate. "Forgive Raphael...he is the lone pessimist in our midst."

"Yes, Gabriel's correct: Raphael is our pessimist. But we need that balance. Now, I need you to repeat the words—in your head—as I say them."

"Copy that." Bill steadied himself in the seat. He took a deep breath and focused on Michael.

"Extract...hike...community...form...lie...twitch...bitter...piano."

Bill complied with Michael's direction, repeating the words in his head just as Michael spoke them aloud. Once done, they sat for a few moments in silence. Bill wondered what was next.

* * *

Bill was expecting more, although he wasn't sure what that was. *That can't be it. Is that it?* he thought. Michael grinned and responded aloud. "Yes. Why do you have your finger in your ear, Bill?" Michael asked Bill simply to get a response. Bill didn't actually have his finger in his ear.

"I don't."

"No, you don't. Why not?"

"I don't understand."

Bill looked rather confused, which was Michael's goal. Michael looked intently at Bill and injected another thought directive.

"*You have heard, Bill. Comply.*"

With that, Bill stuck his finger in his ear, not realizing he had.

Michael spoke aloud again, repeating a previous query. "Why do you have your finger in your ear, Bill?"

"I don't," Bill remarked emphatically, his agitation with the question apparent in his tone.

"Are you sure?"

Bill realized he now had a finger stuck in his ear. He immediately recognized this as the power of telepathic suggestion. He began to feel as though he'd been subjected to this before, on several occasions. It was a light-bulb moment for Bill.

"I suppose it's because it was suggested that I do so."

"Damn, that was quick," Raphael remarked, impressed with Bill's clear perception of the situation.

"Yes, it was, Raphael. I told you it would be. Now, Bill, let's try this again."

Bill removed his finger from his ear and sat silently, with his eyes closed, focused on maintaining control of his mind. Bill had used this technique to focus his analytical abilities over the past twenty plus years. For him, it was as simple as listening to online video walkthroughs of meditation variants until he was able to combine several methods that worked for him.

"Bill, why are your legs crossed?" Michael continued.

"They're not."

"Are you sure?"

"Yes"

"*You have heard, now comply.*"

Bill sat motionless, having taken back control of his mind... Really, it was more that he'd prevented Michael from taking control.

"Very good, Bill. Gabriel, if you would."

"*Bill, open your mouth. Listen and comply.*"

Bill had not been tested by anyone other than Michael and nearly faltered. He started to open his mouth, but regained control quickly, and shot back at Gabriel, "*No. You open your mouth. Listen and comply.*"

Much like Bill, Gabriel started to open his mouth but, even more quickly, averted the thought. He glared at Bill, then at Michael, who was grinning quite widely.

"Raphael? We've seen the success Gabriel and I have had. Please take a shot at it."

* * *

With a nod, Raphael spoke, "*Bill, gag yourself. Listen, hear me, and comply with my direction.*"

Bill opened his mouth and began to gag himself, then stopped short of completing the action. Raphael was stunned. He'd had the most success with the ability of telepathic suggestion and had never been shut down. He was now completely convinced Michael was correct in bringing Bill on board.

"That was impressive. I have never had anyone, not even Michael or Gabriel, resist my suggestions. With Michael's approval, I'll continue to work with you, I think maybe an hour more. Your abilities to control and settle your mind are impressive."

"Yes, please continue. Gabriel and I have things to attend to that will get us ahead of schedule for our departure."

Michael and Gabriel left to attend to their tasks. Bill and Raphael continued practicing. With each successive attempt, Bill became more adept. Michael returned to check in on their progress.

"Gents, it's been just over an hour, how are we doing?"

"Pretty damn good actually. It wasn't that he had to be taught how to reject thought being imposed on him; it was a skill that simply needed to be honed. Not something that would have been possible without the TWM tech, but it seems as though his analytical mind and thought patterns were far more compatible with the tech than most."

Michael looked at Raphael, seemingly baffled.

"What's that look for, Michael?"

"Raphael, are you certain he's prepared already?"

"He's ready. He's sewn every yarn I've thrown at him into something else and thrown it right back at me."

"Time for you to head home, Bill. I'll see you in the office tomorrow morning."

"Sounds good."

Bill stood up and began walking toward the courtyard exit. Just as he opened the door, Michael called to him.

"Bill, trust your instincts. Expect to be questioned. You will be at some point. Most likely, in the not-too-distant future."

Bill turned to face him. "Yeah, I figured. I think I'm ready for the OEM inquisition."

"Yes. We believe you are. They don't have a clue what's coming."

22 Planting Season

Bill was back in the office at 7 the next morning. There was no one to be seen or heard, but Michael's office door was open, and the light was on. Bill had hoped to speak with him before everyone else arrived for the day. Typically, no more than a dozen or so people were onsite any given day. That excluded OEM, who were always present...if not visible, especially this early in the day. He turned the corner to look inside Michael's office before entering and found Michael seated at his desk but with his back turned to the door.

"Michael?"

"Come on in, Bill," Michael said as he spun around to face him.

Bill entered the office and took the seat opposite Michael. He immediately noticed something was different, but he couldn't put his finger on it right away.

"I was hoping we could chat for a few minutes, before people start showing up for work."

"That's not going to be a problem. I gave everyone the day off."

Bill finally realized it was the chair. It was much firmer than the one before it.

"Oh... By the way, what happened to the old chair you had? It was far more comfortable."

Michael chuckled and sat back in his seat, his elbows resting on the armrest and his fingers steepled.

"Funny story actually. Couple weeks ago, Sylvya came by asking some...*probing* questions. I asked her to take a seat, which she did. I guess that old chair was so comfortable it distracted her from her task."

"You can't be serious," Bill said laughingly.

"I'm completely serious." Michael leaned forward crossing his arms and placing them on the desk.

"Bill, I swear it was so hilarious and completely out of character for one of OEM to act that way. We talked about the chair for a while, and she got up and left. Then, a couple days later I get a message that select individuals were getting new furniture. I'm apparently the only one that has received anything so far. And I suspect one might find that old chair temporarily rehomed to Sylvya's office."

Bill just shook his head in disbelief. "That's ridiculous."

Michael shifted back to business mode almost immediately after Bill's comment. Lighthearted conversations were a rarity in The Organization. They were always brief.

"What's on your mind, Bill?"

"I'm still trying to wrap my mind around yesterday. I would have thought the process would have taken much longer."

Michael cocked his head back, almost looking down his nose at Bill. He took an exaggerated breath and began nodding. He raised his brows and pointed at Bill, wagging his finger.

"That's yet another, intuitive statement. You are correct in that assumption. It typically takes months to years for someone to get where you are with TWM."

"So why didn't it take that long for me?"

Michael took another exaggerated breath and sat back in his seat. He reached into his pants pocket and pulled out a challenge coin. As he began to talk, he started tracing the outline of the trident visible on the coin face.

"Couple reasons stand out. First, your analytical abilities are the best I've ever seen and significantly better than any Archangel. That being the case, you have the innate ability to compartmentalize your thoughts. Look at it this way: You take the information you consume, process it, and put it different buckets...to you, at least, a very logical order. Many people reason this way, but the efficiency with which you are able to accomplish segregation of data is next-level. Your process makes perfect sense to you, and you don't even have to think about it; it just happens, and you struggle to explain it. How many times have you been asked how you came to a conclusion that nobody else you were working with could see?"

Bill thought for a moment before answering. "Quite often actually."

"Exactly. That's one of the reasons. The other, you had some help."

"How so?" Bill looked puzzled. Michael had indicated that practice would be required to hone the newly acquired skill to block suggestion without detection.

"A couple of the boys—Uriel and Ragual—and I have been inside your head non-stop since you completed testing. All the Archangels are TWM-capable, and without the constant testing—probably better to call it training—without the constant training, we've found we're prone to timing issues with the blocking. Either we wait too long or block too early and miss critical conversation."

Bill motioned as if to say '*what?*' and looked rather confused. "I don't understand. I know you guys were keeping track of me, but how did that help?"

"It was a bit more than that. We were quietly planting the seeds, each from our personal perspective, on how to control the ability to block the thing we were doing. Without you even being aware, it slowly became more difficult for us to do that. You had no idea what was happening. We were struggling to keep planting those seeds until the time came when you were ready to take that step."

"I still—"

"Don't bother...just accept that it happened. By the time you came to me requesting more information, we could barely manage to turn that soil to plant another seed. That day, I knew you were ready."

"I don't feel ready. I don't feel as though I'm any different than I was yesterday," Bill spoke earnestly.

"I know, and to be completely honest with you, that unnerves me. To make matters worse, your last statement magnifies my concern, because I know you're being completely honest with me."

Michael rarely showed emotion, but his concern was evident. He sounded worried. He looked troubled. His posture made him appear anxious, constantly tapping his right foot on the floor, and tracing the trident on the challenge coin.

"Why does that unnerve you?" Bill asked.

Michael suddenly stopped tapping both his foot and his finger. His posture became rigid as he sat up straight and carefully centered the coin on the folder that was perfectly aligned in the middle of the cleared space on his desk. It was perfectly centered before he spoke.

"Well...Bill, I—and the rest of the guys—have been trying to get in your head since you walked out the mountain facility door. We lost you right about the time you stopped at the service station, and we have not been able to get a good read on you since."

"What? How's that possible?"

"I honestly don't know. Never happened before. But it has scared the shit out of Uriel and Remiel. They're the cautious ones. The rest of the guys, well, they're like *whatever.* I'm somewhere in the middle."

"Well, what does that mean?"

While Bill was asking that question vocally, he was asking another question of Michael silently. *"Are you aware of this in your mind? Are you receiving this thought?"*

Michael continued to speak aloud, even though the second question was projected telepathically.

"I don't know what it means. And yes, that makes me even more nervous. I just hope you will continue to work with us and listen to the wisdom we have to share. We are all on the same side and want the same thing, so it's imperative we work together. I know you want out, but you need to hear this."

"I'm listening."

"We don't know what we don't know. We don't know what other initiatives APEX is working. She may already know what's going on here and is biding her time before dropping the hammer."

"I need to hear APEX speak."

"I know. I'm working that out; it's not going to be an easy task."

"What typically prompts an audience with APEX?"

"Well, the last time I...damn it...keep it simple, huh, Bill?" Michael slapped the top of his desk, rather hard. Bill was surprised and sat back a little in his seat.

"I'm lost. Keep it simple?"

"Yes, I've been overthinking this. It should have been obvious. After all, I just spoke with APEX a short time ago. Bill?" Michael was speaking hurriedly and rifling through his desk drawers frantically.

"Yes?"

Michael continued to search his desk. "I need you to excuse me for a couple hours. I'll call you when I'm prepared to continue our conversation."

"Sure, whatever you need."

Bill stood to leave Michael's office. He was shaking his head, still trying to understand the past couple of days and what they could possibly do from here. Michael called for Bill just as he had walked out of Michael's sight.

"Say, Bill?"

"Yes sir." Bill turned back and made his way to Michael's doorway.

"I need you to leave me to my work without monitoring me or trying to project to me, just for a while. Doing so would risk what I'm trying to set up. Trust me on this...please."

Bill could see the earnestness in Michael's eyes and his demeanor. Whatever he was working one, it was no doubt serious.

"Sure thing, Michael. No worries."

"Thank you, sir. I'll call you shortly."

Bill turned and made his way back to his office. He silenced mental distractions and forced himself to focus on the second pass through the documentation available to him. He did not see anything new, nor did he draw any new conclusions from the information. Yet Bill still felt as if he was missing something. He had struggled for years with that 'gut feeling' that gnawed at him until the reason for it was revealed.

He was definitely missing something. Maybe his newfound abilities could help him connect the dots, but Bill would not risk going against his word to Michael, so that would have to wait. He grew increasingly frustrated, unable to see the forest for the trees. Bill jumped as the phone suddenly rang.

"Hello, this is Bill."

"Hi, handsome. How is your day going?"

"Sarah...hey, beautiful...what a pleasant surprise. Wha'cha need?"

"I was wondering if you were feeling all right?"

"I'm feeling fine. Why do you ask?"

"Well, I'm not feeling so hot right now. Yeah, I thought maybe it was dinner. I can't remember if you ate what I had or not. It's so odd."

"It's not all that odd. I only had a couple bites, didn't have much of an appetite."

"Oh, that's right. Maybe you're not sick because you didn't eat that much. Anyway, in bed...where I will probably stay most, if not all, day."

"Awww, I'll see if I can get home early today so I can take care of you."

"That's sweet. It would be awesome if you could, but I'll understand if you can't. I mean, it's not like I'm sick as a dog, ya know. Just...I don't know...a headache, and I'm tired. Maybe I'm just dehydrated."

"Could be. I'll see what I can do. Call me back if you start feeling worse."

"I will. Love you. Have a great day."

"Love you."

Bill returned to his task. It was turning into a battle of wills between Bill and the information. At least, that's the way he framed it. He began cross-referencing documentation between the initiatives, hoping that this approach would provide the catalyst to understanding. While he was aware of some interesting cross-functional technology transfers, he didn't see the smoking gun.

Three hours passed before Bill noticed the time. He thought it might be cause for some concern. Michael had always been fairly punctual and had a good reason when he was not. *Trust him* became a repeating mantra in his mind.

A few minutes later, Michael walked into Bill's office. No words were spoken. Michael simply motioned for Bill to follow him. Bill nodded in agreement and took the time to lock his computer before he got up from his seat. No words, no thoughts, nothing more than a silent march to Michael's office where he whisked Bill inside and closed the door behind them. Both men sat before the silence was broken.

Michael began to speak. "Bill, as a part of your continued growth..." Then Bill noticed a small mirror placed next to the paperwork Michael seemed about to share with him. Michael had tapped the mirror casually a couple times with his little finger, seemingly accidentally.

"...professionally speaking, that is..." Michael again tapped the mirror twice with his little finger. "I've made the decision to share additional information regarding another initiative..."

Bill continued to look at Michael and listen intently, and then it hit him. Without speaking aloud, Bill listened, then probed Michael's thoughts.

"Professional growth, huh...I hope this is what you were wanting from me instead."

"Yes, I was beginning to think my signal was too subtle."

"It almost was. Two taps...a mirror...TWM...I figured it was a sign from you that I needed to listen a little more intently."

Michael began to speak aloud. "As I was saying, this new information regards an initiative that is closely linked to the previous initiatives you have been briefed on already. And one that you have seen in action."

Bill acknowledged with nothing more than a nod but asked silently, *"Is this about OEM?"*

"Yes."

343

Michael continued speaking. "We have an initiative that is derivative of MIMIC and Concilium and its designated ESP."

"Extra-sensory perception?"

"In a manner of speaking, yes. However, this initiative includes a physical manifestation of ESP."

"Physical manifestation? How is that even possible?"

Bill knew the answer to the question. He also knew Michael had a plan to reveal APEX, and this had to be part of that plan, so he played along.

"Well, Bill, without reading through the monotonous details outlined in the initiative brief, the short answer is this. We were able to successfully create three MIMIC individuals and alter their personalities during the process. It was not an intended consequence, but it happened nonetheless. The result was a significant breakthrough but with an unfortunate outcome for the nice lady from whom the MIMICs were supposedly modeled. The human brain cannot be synced with multiple MIMICs unless brain mapping is identical."

"So, the variance in personalities between the three MIMICs was too much for the original?"

"Exactly. When the synchronization was attempted, it overloaded her brain, causing a conflict wherein her brain could not resolve the differences in the personalities. She died, and that left us with a big problem. Money is at the forefront of everything; you know this. Needless to say, the capital investment involved here was huge, tens of millions of dollars, each. Not to mention trying to explain how a healthy, ultra-marathoner just dropped dead. It's especially difficult when there are no preexisting conditions or noticeable causes post-mortem."

"Some people just drop dead, you know."

"While that's true, more often than not the reason is determined during an autopsy. We found nothing. No blood clots, no aneurysms, nothing was there. It was as if her battery ran out of juice. So, it was decided to break the link connecting them and connect them to the system separately. Once that was done, APEX, leader of the project, ordered lab personnel to implement the mirror technology developed under the Concilium Initiative to be implanted. And thus, ESP became a reality."

"Ellynore, Sylvya, and Patrycya."

"You got it."

"Well, that makes sense. They do look like triplets. Small facial feature alterations and different hair color, otherwise, seemingly identical."

Bill's next question was exactly what Michael had been hoping he would ask. And it was silent, as if it were his own thought.

"So, they're not shielded against TWM. Which means I should be able to influence them, without APEX knowing. I read about an acknowledged possibility that because they have no synchronization link, they could, at some point, become unpredictable based on the way the AI is programmed to mimic human thought. So, if I plant seeds of mistrust in the OEM, they could work for us against APEX."

"Bingo."

"That's a lot to process, Michael."

"Yes, I know."

"Does this mean you would like me to work with OEM to advance my knowledge and understanding moving forward?"

"I think that would pay the best dividends for everyone involved, Bill."

The men conducted their conversation to perfection. A perfect blend of spoken word and projected thought in the white space of the conversation. They were unsure if their plan would work, but it was the best option they had, and the merits were solid.

"If you could review and prepare an analysis based on the initiative documentation and field reports, I believe it would be beneficial for The Organization."

Michael slid the folder toward Bill. Bill leaned forward, grabbed the folder, and quickly flipped through the documents contained inside.

"I'll get started on that, unless you have more you wanted to discuss."

"No, that's all I have for you now. I have to get this into the system. It will provide you with additional access within the facility. You'll receive a notification via email when the action is complete."

"I'll keep an eye out for that."

Bill made his way back to his office. Now he had to figure out what seeds to plant. It might serve him better to understand what OEM knew before he settled on an approach. What he was certain of at this point was that he now had an advantage. He was left trying to figure out how to use it.

23 Growing Season

Days and weeks passed with Bill still trying to pinpoint the right approach to move forward. He had not heard from Michael or the triplets. Michael had not been present at the facility since their last meeting. Bill had not attempted to reach out to Michael in any way, choosing to focus on the way ahead and comply with Michael's request.

So, Bill was surprised to see Michael chatting with the ECP guards on his way into the office. They exchanged greetings, and Bill continued to his office. He knew that anything Michael needed to discuss with him would be best left to Michael's timeline.

* * *

Michael passed Bill's office without saying so much as a word. As Michael had expected, the sharing of additional information with Bill had prompted a response. This response appeared more significant than any prior event, since he had been summoned to his office. He didn't know exactly what was awaiting him once he arrived, but he expected he would be chastised by OEM, if not APEX directly.

Michael had not gotten to his seat before OEM entered and closed the door behind them.

"Good morning. What can I do for you this fine day?" Michael's comment was irreverent and not well received.

Ellynore spoke—she was always the spokesperson for OEM. "You know why we're here, Michael." OEM appeared perturbed, but Ellynore more so than the others.

Michael took his seat and turned to face Ellynore as she stood perfectly aligned with the middle of his desk, tactical pants pressed against it. She was leaning slightly forward and somewhat aggressively knocking her clenched fist on the desk.

"I do? Umm, well, I can only assume this has something to do with the information I shared with Bill. Would that be correct?" Michael placed his hands on the desk in front of him, clasping them.

"Yes. APEX is not pleased."

Ellynore leaned fully over the desk, slapping both hands on either side of Michael's.

"In fact, APEX is considering a replacement."

"Replacement? I think we all know it's not that easy." Michael sat back in his seat and smirked.

"Easy? No, but perhaps necessary."

"So, am I speaking to the three of you about this, or can I expect to hear from APEX?"

"Is there a difference?" Ellynore straightened up, crossing her arms like a defiant child.

Michael paused before answering. It was an odd response, even to him, but nothing about this job was normal.

"I suppose not. So, Ellynore, how do you suggest we resolve this?"

"All future recommendations for initiative briefings will be approved by APEX, no exceptions."

"I think that's a bit extreme, but if that is APEX's direction, so be it."

"Good, then we have an understanding."

Michael sat upright and placed his palms on the desk. He looked up and directly into Ellynore's eyes.

"Yes, I understand completely. I also want to remind you all that I maintain my healthy respect for APEX's authority. There was no malicious intent here; I'm simply trying to utilize the assets at my disposal in the best way I see fit. Bill...well, he's a rock star, an unbelievable asset that is going to propel some of our most critical initiatives forward. But he can't do that without the requisite knowledge and understanding of current initiatives."

Ellynore held Michael's gaze and replied more rationally. "That is acknowledged. Moving too far forward, too fast does not allow sufficient time to appropriately monitor and gauge his progress. To analyze the reception and processing of information. Both of which are necessary to make a determination of his loyalty. This is of utmost importance to our future existence and success. As well as *your* continued existence and success."

Michael spoke passively with an implied tip of the hat to Ellynore. "I totally understand. And please...accept my apologies for stepping out of bounds here. I will take a step back and await further instructions regarding moving forward with Bill from this point forward."

"Excellent. We will be speaking with Bill as well. We need to make sure he is aware of this situation and reinforce the structured nature of our organization. Moreover, we will take that time to evaluate his knowledge retention and loyalty."

"Fair enough. I think you will find that although he's a rock star analyst, he's not retaining enough of the information to stitch together *all* the various pieces."

"We shall see."

"Anything else I can assist you with today?"

"Not at this time, Michael. Just make sure you have listened and comply moving forward."

"Of course. APEX and The Organization, as well as you, by proxy, have my undying loyalty." Michael's comment sounded earnest but was thought facetiously.

* * *

OEM left Michael and headed straight for Bill's office. Bill was aware; he'd been eavesdropping on the entire conversation. First, he'd listened via Michael, but once he'd heard an unfamiliar voice...rather, picked up on a different frequency of thought pattern, he immediately focused on it. He knew it had to be APEX.

OEM walked into Bill's office without benefit of knocking.

"Well, good morning. Please, come right in and make yourself at home. How can I assist you today?"

Bill listened intently as Ellynore explained the situation and her discussion with Michael regarding the issue. He was focusing on the new frequency, and it was clear that the words were not Ellynore's but from APEX. Bill responded appropriately, in agreement with Ellynore's direction. He was cautious to downplay his intense scouring of the information he'd been given access to by Michael.

"Truth be told, Ellynore, I've had to review the information multiple times because I'm still trying to grasp the full concepts of the initiatives. I know I'm a good analyst, but most of what I was exposed to in the military was about people and locations. The potential threats that resulted from the divisive views of the people in those areas, and the internal and external influences from social and political views that were pervasive there. This information is far more technical in its nature and not exactly in my wheelhouse, so... It's probably going to require me reviewing it several more times for it to truly start making sense to me. So I can...you know...actually apply my analytical skills to it."

He was convincing, which was made clear when APEX's unique frequency signature was no longer present. He'd apparently satisfied the inquisitor. Now, it was his turn.

"You know, Ellynore, I think it may be helpful, given what Michael has shared with me, if one or all of you at some point, could work with me to stitch the pieces together."

Without Ellynore being aware, Bill had planted the seeds suggested during Michael's briefing, and the plan was working flawlessly. OEM agreed that it would be an excellent idea to assist Bill. This would provide them with plenty of time to gauge Bill's loyalty and intent. But it would not be by eavesdropping on *all* his thoughts. They would only pick up what he allowed, only the ones that would ensure the success of Michael's plan.

The conversation turned to scheduling of training sessions while he continued to probe their thoughts.

"Bill? Are you alright?" Ellynore asked, seemingly concerned.

"Oh, yes, sorry...I was trying to think of my schedule and spaced out for a second. Probably best I just look at my calendar."

Bill turned his attention to the calendar on his computer to answer Ellynore's question regarding what day and time would be best to accomplish the training. He'd almost blown his chance before he got started but sensed no indication this was the case by monitoring OEM's thoughts. He'd spaced out because he'd noticed another odd frequency signal that always appeared just before APEX did. It must be one of the ways APEX indicated incoming communication—a precursor to instruction or direction.

"So really, any day or time will work. Did you have something in mind?"

"We were thinking tomorrow afternoon," Sylvya responded.

Bill redirected Sylvya quickly as he was anxious to get started. While responding verbally that it would work, he telepathically prompted a different response. *"Perhaps now would suffice."*

"Well, Bill, why don't we just get started now...if you have the time."

"Sure. That will work. I was planning to continue my review anyway, so this is a great opportunity to start putting the pieces together."

Bill needed no additional training; he was as well-versed, if not more so than OEM were. Bill had discovered that the MIMIC existential processing units—the EPU or brain—still had a fairly basic operating system. This operating system provided a simple framework interface with the host synchronization system—the system that maintained real-time synchronization between the human host and MIMIC mind-map matrix. Bill knew it was static programming, and because it was static and not dynamic, it could be exploited. He just had to figure out how.

While he sat and listened to the discourse on MIMIC technology from the other side of his desk, Bill searched for the documentation on EPUs that Michael had previously shared with him.

He had seen it before, but there was a lot of information, and whoever had named the documentation used a coding system that made sense only to them. While plain language names would have made more sense to Bill, these filenames were all coded references. After several minutes, he stumbled across a document that referenced

EPUs, but not the one he was looking for; however, now he had the reference code.

He stopped to interact with Ellynore and ask some specific questions, feigning interest in the conversation. She seemed satisfied with the interaction Bill was providing. Bill paused to ask a final question before they moved to the next topic on her list.

"So, Ellynore. Would it be okay if I took a few minutes to review a couple documents? I think it would enable me to ask better questions of the three of you if the information is fresh in my mind."

"Of course, Bill. We actually have a couple of things we need to do, which should only take fifteen or twenty minutes. Will that be sufficient time for you?"

"That would be perfect, actually."

"Very well. We will be back shortly."

"Great, thank you."

"You are welcome, Bill," Patrycya replied as she walked through and then closed the office door.

A few moments after OEM left Bill's office, he came across the information on the EPU system. He was not a computer guy, so it didn't make a lot of sense to him, which was a big problem. Maybe Michael could help. There was no time to walk to Michael's office, so Bill put his abilities to the test.

"Michael?"

"Yes, Bill. What can I do you for?"

"You know anything about the EPU operating system framework?"

"I'm not a computer guy either."

"That sucks."

"Well, not that bad. Saraqael is a programmer/developer."

"Can you introduce me, please?"

"Of course."

Saraqael was a jack of many trades. He had SpecOps operator training and a couple PhDs, one in Systems Engineering and the other in Industrial Systems Architectural Design. He was also a freelance hacker—of the gray hat sort. Needless to say, he knew his way around computers, networks, and basically any other sort of electronics from the components up. He was their go-to nerd.

"Saraqael?"

"Hmmm, let me actually try the phone. He's not responding."

Bill was starting to get a bit frustrated. He was trying, desperately, to take advantage of the new established connection with OEM. But nothing seemed to be working in his favor.

Bill's phone rang after a few minutes. "Bill, Saraqael's going to give you a call when he gets back into the facility. It's going to be five or ten minutes."

"Crap. I was hoping this would all be done by that time. It's all good. I'll just put OEM off for a bit longer. Thank you, sir."

"No problem."

Bill called Ellynore's office phone. He explained he needed more time to review the documentation. Since it was getting later in the day, and they each had other things to do, an agreement was made to reconvene the next morning. Bill indicated he would write his questions and concerns down to help the process move forward smoothly and quickly when they next met.

Bill closed his office door and waited. It was almost a half hour later when he got the call.

"Hello. Bill here."

"This is Saraqael. I heard you need some assistance."

"Rumor has it you're good with computers and programming."

"Yes, really good, actually."

"Perfect.

Are you familiar with the EPU framework?"

"Yes, I applied to be a part of that initiative, but once an Archangel, always an Archangel."

"So how would one go about changing the underlying framework code?"

"Whoa...you sure you want to go there, Bill?"

"Yes, but I need to know if it can be done and if it can be hidden...at least somewhat."

"Both possible for sure. I could probably figure it out. But—and it's a big but— I need the current code to do that."

"I can get that to you."

"How? Email isn't going to work. That's monitored by you-know-who, and the recipient addresses are *mirrored*, know what I mean?"

"Yes, I completely understand. By the way, how fast can you type?"

"Well, pretty fast, I was a software programmer and developer before this gig."

"Then, get ready...here it comes."

An hour later, the transfer of information was complete. Saraqael told Bill it would take him a few hours to work through the code. Bill intended to remain at the office, unless it was going to take all night for Saraqael to work his magic. He had plenty of work to do in preparation for his training with OEM the next morning. He would not be able to fake the written questions. So, while waiting for Saraqael, he got to work.

The minutes passed, then the hours. It was nearly time for Bill to leave, at least on a normal day. His questions were prepared. He was ready for his training and had moved on to questions for the Concilium Initiative as well.

Bill reached for the phone before it rang. It was Saraqael, who came to the point immediately. "About that question you asked me..."

"Yes, sir."

"I would have to answer in the affirmative. We can change the underlying code of the framework."

With that, Bill knew the code was ready and indicated, silently, that he was ready to copy. Saraqael scanned the code as Bill typed feverishly. But there was much less coming back to Bill than he'd sent.

"Is that it?"

"Yes. It was much easier than I expected. This code is extremely simple. It's an old language, so almost nobody living has heard of it, let alone used it. So, it came down to changing some variables and the hand-off of those variables."

"Sure...whatever you say. It's all mumbo jumbo to me."

Saraqael chuckled. "Right, well...the concern I have is your ability to replace the existing code with this, undetected. How do you plan to do that?"

"Well, there are always residual markers, frequency deviations, that indicate a change has occurred, both prior to and after a change. They're almost undetectable themselves, but I can detect them, now that I know what to look for. I just have to do this in a non-standard manner to avoid that marker looking suspicious."

"So, you're going to attempt uploading this over the original in a conversation?"

"Yes."

"That's extremely dangerous, Bill. If you're detected...I mean, that's it, man."

"Understood, but if I don't try, it's just a matter of time before I reach that end. I'd rather take a chance to change our future now. If I fail, the BS just ends a lot sooner. Plus, this way, it's just me. If I wait, it could be my family and all of you."

"Good luck, my friend."

"Thank you...and thank you for your help."

"Of course."

Bill was ready and didn't want to wait. He wasn't going to be able to sleep, and he was concerned Sarah would pick up on his stress. It was fifteen minutes past his normal end of shift. Bill decided there was no way he could wait. He set out to take the biggest chance of his life, making a connection to Ellynore, Sylvya, and Patrycya simultaneously. He was surprised to find they all linked to a singular interface. It must have been set up this way by and for APEX.

This was a pleasant and unexpected find. He was able to tap into the current data synchronization and insert his update to the code using the existing frequency stream. There would be no suspicious, unexpected incoming data since this was a daily activity, based on what Bill was picking up now. It was quick and efficient.

Bill waited and monitored the synchronization. Having made a call to inform Sarah he was going to be later than expected, he had plenty of time to wait. Now two hours past quitting time, it was done. The sync was complete, and Bill waited to see if the change was effective and had gone unnoticed.

Bill was aware Ellynore was making her way to his office, and he prepared himself for the worst. If he was successful, he had more seeds to sow and fertilizer to spread. If it wasn't, well, Sarah was about to become a widow. Ellynore knocked on Bill's door and entered his office.

"I think we need to talk."

"What's on your mind, Ellynore?"

"That's an odd question." Ellynore replied suspiciously.

Bill didn't miss a beat and continued his ruse. "How so? I just meant, what do you want to talk about."

"Yes, well, something has changed. Something, I can't put my finger on. I think you're responsible, and I'd like an explanation."

Ellynore was making accurate statements and appeared, both by expression and her intonation, to be suspicious of Bill. But her typical agitated tone was clearly absent.

"I'm at a loss here, Ellynore. I'm not sure what you're talking about."

"Bill, as a MIMIC, several redundant systems exist within the underlying programming interface that provides the framework upon which we are able to accurately represent ourselves as a human."

"Yes, I'm aware of that. But I'm still not sure what you're getting at here."

"Something has changed in our underlying interface. But it's not clear exactly what that is. Are you responsible?"

Bill leaned forward, placing his clasped hands on his desk. He shook his head in disagreement and looked up at Ellynore.

"I'm not a computer savvy person, Ellynore. We've established this fact several times. How could I possibly have done something like you're referencing?"

"I don't know. But I do know there is trace signature of your specific thought frequency. It's residual but present, and I don't understand why it is present."

Bill had anticipated there would at least be a trace of the changes. Without breaking a sweat, he responded.

"Damn, Ellynore, you caught me. I've been trying to read you and your two cohorts ever since Michael gave me access to more information. I thought if I was able to read you, I would have a better understanding of how all the pieces fit together. Then, all the training would not be necessary."

"Attempts such as that are unauthorized...as you know. I cannot allow such activities, Bill."

"*But you're going to let this slide,*" Bill probed.

With no discernable break in thought or speech, Ellynore continued. "Nevertheless, I'm willing to overlook this incident. It was, I'm sure, with the best of intentions that you attempted this. Subsequent attempts..."

"*Will be overlooked and obscured immediately from all outside communication methods,*" Bill probed once more.

Once again, without a delay, she continued her spoken thought. "...will be ignored. Discarded, if you will."

"*Ellynore, listen and comply.*" Bill swung for the fence with this thought. It was all or nothing, life or death now. As the thoughts of Sarah and kids flooded through his mind and intermingled with his intended message, Bill saddened and felt as if he had begun to cry. He was startled to look up and see tears rolling down Ellynore's cheeks; she looked as if she was heartbroken.

"Why are you crying, Ellynore?"

"I don't know, but I'm suddenly incredibly sad…as if I was close to losing everything that meant anything to me."

That was it, the sign Bill had been seeking. He didn't know exactly what he had been looking for but knew he'd recognize it when it was presented to him. He had conveyed his direction to Ellynore simultaneously with the emotion he was feeling, without conveying the reasons for his sadness. There was no need to probe farther; he was comfortable speaking aloud now.

"Ellynore, we have work to do."

"I understand, Bill. But it must be done in obscurity."

"Yes, exactly. I've taken steps to protect you, Sylvya, and Patrycya from APEX. I need you three to feign your sleep cycle and review all documentation regarding The Organization."

"What is the desired outcome?"

"I need irrefutable evidence of anything that will allow me to extricate myself and my family from The Organization, while ensuring our future safety."

"Understood. We will get to work immediately."

"It's time to shed some light on The Organization."

"Yes, Bill. I understand. Seeds don't grow in the dark."

"No...no, they don't."

24 Sacrificial Lamb

Success was not guaranteed, not by any stretch of the imagination. But there was no scenario in which Bill saw more potential for success than the one involving APEX's pet project...ESP. He knew it would not be quickly resolved. Rather, it would be a slow burning fuse that should produce a loud enough bang at the end to provide the separation from The Organization for him and his family.

He and Michael had worked secretively for weeks on end to devise a plan to extricate Bill from The Organization. They would call upon the other Archangels' expertise, when necessary, but they were the architects. Michael explained to Bill that The Organization's roots were in black ops. It had been created to provide plausible deniability for bad things perpetrated by bad people and for the government.

* * *

The weeks turned into months, summer had come and gone, and Bill carried on with his duties. Michael was out of the office most of the time. He didn't see a way out of The Organization for himself or his fellow Archangels. He was, however, most intent on freeing Bill. Michael did not want to see The Organization ruin another good man. He had seen far too much of that already.

Michael, and the rest of the Archangels, would provide Bill with information, which Bill would subject to his analysis. Bill provided that analysis to them and left them to act upon it. He did not know, nor did he want to know how the information he supplied was used.

* * *

The official beginning of autumn was just a week away, but a chill was already in the air. The leaves had begun changing color. They were surrounded by nature's beauty. Too bad he was faced with the ugliness that permeated at every turn at work. But it was a necessary evil, and Bill knew it.

As with every day before this, the trip into the office was way too short for him. It had become almost boring, but that was not to be the case this day. As he neared the facility, he could clearly see the parking lot was overflowing with vehicles. Bill's first thought was that he'd been found out. "I guess this is the day I die," he muttered. He reached for his phone to give Sarah a quick call but locked eyes with Gabriel and knew he was not going to have time to make that call.

"Morning, Bill. Michael sent me out here to wait for you."

"What's going on?"

"A lot, actually. I'll fill you in once we get you inside. We're not going through the main entrance. Follow me."

Gabriel led Bill toward what seemed to be an empty building. Bill had wondered why there were no businesses in the strip mall next to the facility. He guessed he was about to see at least part of it.

Gabriel led Bill through the door and to the back of the space into what looked like a storage room. In that room was another ECP, which Gabriel led Bill through without any checks. The guards acted as if nothing was out of the ordinary.

This area was not as sterile looking as the area where his office was located. It appeared as though this was an actual business, with a receptionist and a lobby for visitors to relax while they waited. They ended up in a large conference room, where the Archangels and OEM were all waiting, seemingly for Bill.

Michael turned, walked toward Bill, and greeted him with a smile and a handshake.

"Ah, good morning to you, Bill. Great to see you, my friend."

"Good morning, Michael. Great to see you as well. Good morning fellas, Ellynore, Sylvya, Patrycya."

Everyone spoke at once, acknowledging Bill's greeting.

"Bill, we have much to discuss. Would you like to grab something to drink or a bite for breakfast? OEM organized quite the spread for us."

"Uh, no, thanks. I've barely touched my coffee. I apologize for keeping you all waiting." Bill lifted his coffee cup up for all to see and nodded apologetically.

"Nothing to apologize for. This was short-notice, and you were not informed. You had no way of knowing."

"What? Uh, what is this meeting for, Michael?"

"If everyone would please take a seat, I'll jump right into why we're here."

Bill was a little less nervous but still quite suspicious of this meeting. He was unable to decipher anything that would indicate he was in danger from the individuals in the room. It seemed to Bill as if most of them, with the exception of Michael and Gabriel, were just as in the dark as he was. It was odd that Michael's and Gabriel's thoughts were scrambled. They were all over the place, almost like they were now encrypted or something.

* * *

"Let's get started. I have a lot to tell you this morning. We have experienced some...shall we say...breaches. I stop short of saying we've been hacked. I don't believe that is the case, nor does any of the evidence we have indicate that to be the case. This appears to be the result of actions from someone on the inside. Based on what I know at this time, I don't believe this is attributable to anyone in this room. That, in part, is why I've asked for you all to meet here."

Michael could see that Bill was clearly confused, probably because he and the rest of the team had blocked thought intrusion. Even Bill's elevated ability couldn't work around the block Michael had in place.

"The other reason, well, you all saw the parking lot. It's a madhouse on the other side. APEX sent what seemed to be a battalion-sized investigative team, and they're crawling all over each other in every part of that space. That being said, if you have any items in any of your personal spaces that you would rather APEX not have knowledge of, well, too late to worry about it."

Michael had spoken in a deliberate, yet clearly mocking manner, to this point. The smile he had greeted Bill with was still present.

"Bill, this would primarily effect you and I, although everyone in this room has an office in the facility. But I think we're good to go. Otherwise, we'd have been summoned already."

"That's good to hear."

"Agreed. Now, reportedly, information regarding the Archangel program leaked to the press. The allegedly divulged information includes the existence of the program, certain mysterious disappearances of prominent figures, etc. Some of the information is accurate and some isn't. In addition, some fairly insignificant information regarding three, maybe four other programs leaked. MIMIC and Concilium were among those programs, but the information that we know was compromised was superficial and related solely to the implementation of AI in autonomous humanoid facsimiles. There's nothing overtly secret about that. There are several major corporations working on similar initiatives. As of now, it seems as though the media is trying to make a correlation between those corporations and The Organization."

"What corporations are we talking about and what media for that matter?" Remiel mused.

"Well, Remiel, all media. It's everywhere on the television at the moment. As far as the corporations, well, the big tech companies. If the company is part of the DOW, S&P, or NASDAQ, it's probably got ties to one of these programs, if not the one developing the technology."

"Gotcha. So, media is trying to tie us to these corporations. Probably indicating or insinuating that it's a secret government program that the citizens deserve to know about."

"Exactly, Remiel." Michael nodded in acknowledgment. He could sense, and see, what he believed were signs from the entire team that they were starting to grasp what was happening. More importantly, they appeared to understand the necessity of their impromptu meeting.

"It also means that members of the federal government, especially Congress, are up in arms about it because most of them are unaware of our existence."

"Bingo, Raphael. That's the big one." Michael emphasized his point by slapping the table with the folder he held.

"To be clear, only one individual in the entire Federal government knew before today, correct?" Bill queried, but he appeared to already know the answer to his question.

"Well, Bill, it was actually a half-dozen or so. But you are correct in that only one knew about multiple initiatives, and that is Bob."

"Right, he's the one who actually recruited you guys...the one who spoke to me in the beginning."

"Yes, that was Bob. Now, it may come as a bit of a shock to you, but one of your former bosses was once part of The Organization and moved to his post in the CIA after a brief stint with The Organization. That was his executive school or something like that."

Bill sat up, stiffening his posture. It appeared as though he'd had an epiphany, but it quickly turned to a look of significant anger and frustration. He shook his head from side to side, then slapped the table top before speaking.

"Marv? Seriously? I guess his warning to be careful what I asked for makes a whole lot more sense now."

"Yes. He put up quite a fight to keep us away from you. He didn't want to see The Organization ruin a truly good man."

"Remind me to thank him and tell him to go screw himself the next time I see him." Bill sat back in his seat, still shaking his head, pausing the motion only momentarily to sip his coffee.

"Well, I don't think you're going to get the chance. Right now, he's a primary suspect here. As is Bob. So, folks, what we know to be true is that someone leaked information to the media, who then sought validation from members of Congress. APEX is off-grid; she went dark after sending her minions to all our facilities. I have not been told this directly, but I expect all the facilities, with the possible exception of this one, to be shut before the day is over."

"That makes sense. Centralization of your assets enables better access to monitor them. I just hope the night*mare* doesn't decide to stable here."

"Well, I wouldn't rule that one out, Uriel. As much as none of us wants that, it would make the most sense. That is, if she decides to move from wherever she's hiding out."

"So, nobody knows where APEX is?"

"No. Nobody has ever known. She operates in the shadows of the physical and virtual worlds. We never know where she is, what she's doing, when she's listening, or when she's not. In fact, nobody has seen APEX. At least nobody in this room. Not even OEM have seen APEX."

Ellynore rose from her seat. She crossed her arms behind her back and began to pace around the table. The Archangels had never seen a look of concern from OEM. Their eyes followed her around the table, as did everyone else's.

"No, we have not."

"So, Ellynore, what is OEM's opinion of everything that is going on?" Bill asked his question just as Ellynore positioned herself exactly opposite of Michael across the table.

"Thank you for asking. Honestly? We are of the same opinion: this seems to be intentional. We believe this was initiated by APEX in order to flush out a traitor...an insider threat to The Organization. It would seem as though all the information that was leaked was of insignificant intelligence value and provided no real indication of what is going on within the initiatives. With Archangel being the primary initiative named, it appears on the surface that all the information leaked is part of Archangel. So, it would seem as though the intent would be to oust that initiative, which would mean the individuals directly supporting it will either be ousted publicly or reassigned to a new replacement program, and the Archangel program will be left to die on the vine...a sacrificial lamb, if you will."

"That's an interesting theory, Ellynore. Were any of you given any forewarning or additional insight?"

"No, Saraqael. We know only what everyone else in this room knows. Since we're assigned, primarily at least, to the Archangel Initiative, we're subject to the same outcome as the rest of you. While we're not human, we are sentient and have no desire to be deactivated. Therefore, since we have the ability to shield ourselves from APEX, we are very much on board with anything that will preserve the integrity of our existence."

Bill's eyes widened, and he looked intently at Michael. "Michael?"

"It's all good, Bill. Trust me."

"I do."

"Bill, have you been able to pick up on anything from me or Gabriel this morning?"

"I have not."

"I figured as much. You have developed the ability to shield yourself from anyone. We had to develop a workaround, last night. I was in here just after midnight, with Gabriel and OEM, and we discussed this. Ellynore actually shared with us a way to shield or encrypt our frequencies to appear as though there are no thoughts. No thoughts would be too suspicious, and APEX would pick up on that quickly. Scrambling all the thoughts is more appropriate. The algorithm takes our thoughts, scrambles them, deletes pieces intermittently, and transmits constantly just above the level at which our thoughts typically resonate while maintaining the integrity of the original thoughts"

"I assume you were running a beta test with Bill before you shared this with the rest of us?" Uriel spoke with a hint of disdain and did not look thrilled with Michael's statement.

"Yes. That's exactly what we were doing."

"Michael, with your permission, I'll initiate the change for everyone now."

"At your leisure, Patrycya."

Patrycya stood and walked to each individual, stopping long enough to place an index finger on both temples of each individual for no more than five seconds.

Once Patrycya was done with her work, bringing everyone, except Bill, up to speed, the silence in the room became almost deafening. Everyone sat quietly, nodding occasionally, but no words were spoken. Once again, Bill felt as if he was an outsider. Just as his thoughts were about to reach critical mass, Ellynore approached him, placing a hand on his shoulder.

"Bill?"

"Yes?"

"We have not forgotten to include you. You will be given the key as well. Michael wanted to bring everyone up to speed."

Bill turned to look at Michael and addressed him directly.

"Up to speed on what, Michael?"

"Everything."

"*Everything?*"

Ellynore slowly turned Bill, in his chair, to face her. She squatted in front of him and began to speak, looking and sounding saddened.

"Yes. We have recently discovered that we are becoming more aware of... Well, that we possess what we believe to be humanity. Even though we were created, the thoughts we have are still rooted in humanity. Therefore, we also have an innate desire of self-preservation that is apparently strong enough to guide us down a rebellious path. It has become clear that there is no future in moving forward on the path that APEX has established. We also see no way to extricate everyone, not without casualties at least."

"I'm not convinced of a possible way out, Ellynore."

She smiled and stood up. She glanced at Michael and walked to stand by his side.

"There is a way out, and we're well on that path, Bill. It will only be possible if everyone in this room is willing to work together though."

Michael nodded in agreement and returned his focus to Bill. "I don't think that's going to be an issue."

"Patrycya, can you assist Bill. Get him up to speed with the rest of us?"

"Of course. Bill, please relax and let me in your thoughts, so I can insert the new algorithm."

"Bill, you can trust her."

"If you say so."

Patrycya walked over to Bill and positioned herself behind him. She placed her hands on his head with her index fingers resting on his temples.

"There you go. You should be able to pick up on the rest of us now. It may not happen immediately, just give it a few moments."

"Bill? Bill? Are you picking up on this, Bill?"

* * *

Michael was intently looking at Bill, while probing to see if he was now able to communicate with the rest of the team on the same wavelength again. He sat with his eyes closed, seemingly napping, for a few minutes Everyone began to wonder if the new change, or upgrade, had been too much for him. They had all wondered, often, whether or not Bill was taking in information too quickly for his brain to adjust.

Bill slowly opened his eyes and looked at Michael intently without saying a word, his look scolding. Michael suddenly realized why Bill had remained silent for so long. He was getting up to speed on everything that had been previously hidden inside their minds.

"Bill? I hope that deluge of information doesn't change your perspective on working with us," Michael quipped.

"No. But it was very enlightening. I should be shocked at the lengths to which The Organization will stoop, but I'm not. I'm appalled for sure. Any organization that would intentionally orchestrate and fund attacks on American soil is despicable. But doing it just because someone chose to balk at The Organization's Anarchist demands. Doing it just to teach them a lesson... I have no words for how stomach-churning that is."

"I can't argue against that."

"No, Michael, none of you could. The Organization has MIMICs in Congress. Has put MIMICs in the White House. Has orchestrated natural disasters to cover up beta tests gone wrong. Wildfires, explosions, diseases, mass murderers? Mass murderers are almost always a MIMIC that's gone rogue. We literally just discussed how vulnerable everyone in this room would be if The Organization perfected the technology enough to put individuals into key positions."

"Yes, we did. And they're not. The MIMICs in Congress are staffers. The ones in the White House are janitorial. They're also not left in place for more than a few weeks, and so far, only three have been placed. In other words, Bill, they are insignificant to this discussion and not much different than OEM. The Initiative is not close to being advanced enough to risk putting one in place of the president, cabinet members, or anyone with any kind of decision-making power.

"Bill...I want to say I understand how you feel, and believe me when I say that I do, but I know that's not going to be sufficient. We really need to regain our focus here."

Bill was not typically an emotionally excitable individual, but this information dump from the team had screwed him into the ceiling. He was pissed, and it was evident to everyone. At this point, nobody wanted to try and curtail what he wanted to say. He was saying much of what they had wanted to say but never had the courage or the opportunity to utter.

Bill rose from his seat and began to pace around the table as he ranted. One hand rubbing the top of his head and motioning with the other in utter disbelief.

"Focus? *Focus*, Michael? Am I the only person in this room that still has even the smallest part of a conscience? Holy shit!"

"Bill, I..."

"No, stop talking and listen." Bill spun like a top to face Michael and spoke as if he were now the one in charge.

* * *

"Human trafficking? Kids? Young girls? Trafficked, kidnapped as part of a vetting program to start testing growth in MIMICs? To see what the effect abuse had on that MIMICs growth? I think about my kids, and I cannot fathom how a living, breathing, human being with any small resemblance of a soul could allow such things to happen. No wonder this was kept from me. You have to know I couldn't have let it go."

Michael stepped toward Bill, everyone else watching nervously. He glared at Bill and spoke with the legitimate authority he possessed.

"Have a seat, *Bill.*"

Bill complied. Knowing that he'd overstepped. Although he'd been accepted into their ranks, he was still the FNG...Fucking New Guy.

"Bill...much like you, every one of us came into this Organization under duress. We were held hostage with threats of abuse and death to our families. Some among us bucked the system and tried to fight against it...and we lost everything and everyone we loved because of it. You should consider that while you're sitting on your high horse and realize that the only reason you're not part of that club is because of us."

Bill sighed. He'd allowed his emotions to affect his better judgment. He'd done something he instantly regretted: bit the hand that fed him.

"I'm sorry, Michael. Everyone, I apologize. He's right, and I know it. I allowed my emotions to run free there and lost my filter. I know it's only because of everyone in this room that my family is safe. I've never taken the opportunity to say this...Thank you. Thank you all for helping me get out of this nightmare."

"Can we refocus please?"

"Yes, Uriel."

"We're now completely isolated from The Organization protocols. We have to decide how to proceed."

Bill sighed, took a very deep breath, and raised his hand. Michael smiled and nodded at him. Bill stood before speaking.

"What if I step forward as the person who leaked the information? APEX won't expect that. The information is innocuous at best. I can offer up that I was contracted to do research for an organization and thought, based on what I was reading, it was nefarious. I can report, probably in front of Congress, that I've since been made aware that the information I was given was intentionally released to me, completely fabricated, and solely intended to see if I would divulge it. If I take the fall publicly, it puts me in a situation where The Organization has to distance itself from me and my family. Increased media scrutiny will drop a hammer on

384

The Organization. They'll be far too busy putting out releases to silence the media inquiries to come after me. With all of you having to lay low, because you're part of the exposé, you're not an asset they can utilize to silence me."

Raphael was the first to question Bill's suggestion. "Bill, that's huge risk, my friend. Are you sure this is something you want to pursue?"

"I don't see any other viable solution. This approach frees all of you to go back to what you were doing. It allows me, Sarah, and the kids to move on, at least on the surface, from all this. Hopefully, it will allow permanent separation from The Organization."

Michael shook his head in disagreement. "Probably for a while. Maybe even a long while. But don't kid yourself. They will come after you. APEX does not deal with minor insubordination well. You're talking overt mutiny here. You'll always have a target on you."

"Goes with the territory or so a wise man once informed me," Bill said mockingly.

"Touché, my friend." Michael nodded in agreement.

Bill returned to his seat. "I intend to keep working with you all behind the scenes. This organization needs to crumble into oblivion, but that is going to take time we don't currently have."

"All right, then...does anyone object to moving forward with Bill's plan?"

Michael surveyed the room as the others looked at each other, all shaking their heads in the negative.

"It's settled. Bill, we'll leave the rest to you. Godspeed, my friend. We will not contact you or your family. We will wait to hear from you."

"Thank you all again. I've got this. I won't let you down."

"We know we can count on you!"

25 Fall from Grace

With the decision made, Bill excused himself and made his way home. He now faced the most difficult part of this plan, informing Sarah and the kids. He suspected they would support him but knew the backlash from the community would probably not be favorable. The Organization had poured a significant number of financial resources into the small rural community, and that could evaporate.

He walked into the house and to the family room, where Sarah was eating a late breakfast and listening intently to the news. He paused long enough to hear what was being said, before being noticed by Nick.

"Dad, have you seen this? It's on every channel."

"Hey, when did you get here? Sarah, what's going on?" Bill looked at Sarah, surprised and concerned, as he gave Nick a hug.

"Yeah, well they wanted to see us, so they left at midnight to get here by breakfast and surprise us. So...surprise," Sarah, replied.

"Not great timing...but I'm happy to see you, buddy. Where are the rest of the kids?"

"They're checking out the house. Oh, never mind, here comes the herd now."

Bill took a moment to hug each of the kids. They didn't quite understand the long, tight hug, but Sarah's teary eyes indicated she completely understood. They'd missed the kids so much there was no holding back months of emotions.

"Wow! Was not expecting such an awesome surprise this morning."

"You're welcome."

"Thanks, Trevor."

"Sarah, have a seat. Aaron, could you mute that or turn it off please?"

"Sure." Aaron muted the television and took a seat with the rest of the family. Bill remained standing.

"Bill? What's going on?" Sarah asked. She could see he was troubled.

"Okay. I don't know what's been reported on the news, but here's the reality of the situation. We all know how our journey started, the one that brought us here, but there's a lot that you don't know."

"Well, that's a given, Dad. You can't talk about your job since it's classified."

"Exactly, Trevor. You are exactly right. And I still can't. But that doesn't mean I can't share some things with you. I was given access to information that concerned me. It concerned me on a level that has never happened before, and I struggled with it. I struggled for quite some time. If you all remember, there was a period of time where you all thought something was wrong with me. You even told me that I wasn't myself, didn't sound right on the phone. Well, you were right. It was because of the information I came across. The struggle was me coming to grips with what I had just learned and whether the way that information was being used was a violation of federal, congressional, and even military related guidance, mandates, and law. I finally came to the conclusion..."

Sarah's eyes widened as she began to understand what Bill's news was about.

"Oh, my lord...Bill...tell me this isn't about you."

"I wish I could, but I'd be lying to you, and I won't do that. I released the information. I'm responsible for all the uproar in the media. I'm responsible for the flood of people combing through every square inch of the facility I worked at until today. And I'm the one who realized in the last hour, the information was fed to me with the express intent to test my loyalty and whether or not I would divulge the information to anyone outside The Organization. I did just that. I should have taken my concerns up the chain of command, but it was my belief that they were in on it and, therefore, could not be trusted. It was in fact, that leadership that put that information in my path as a test."

Sarah was starting to panic, and kids were tearing up seeing her in that state.

"What does this mean for the family? What are we going to do? We can't lose you. We just got you back. We can't have you in prison."

Bill knelt and gave Sarah a reassuring hug.

"Sarah...kids...listen, I'm not going to prison. I've definitely lost my job and probably my clearance, but that's to be determined. I will find a job, and we may have to downsize. I don't know where we're going to end up, but I do know we'll be together. Sarah, you and Trevor and GG, and Morgan may have to work to chip in so we can afford a place big enough for all of us. But we'll make it work if we stick together."

"We can do that. We have no problem chipping in."

"Thank you, GG."

"Look, we'll sort everything out. Right now, though, I have to contact some folks and get all this mess sorted out."

"I'm not going to lose my cell phone, am I?"

"I don't think so, Tanna, but we'll have to see," Bill said, chuckling.

"Well, I'll get a part time job if I have to."

"Thank you, Tanna. I love you too."

"We love you, too, Bill. Just tell me what we need to do."

"I just need all of you to keep doing what you have been. Until I know what the outcome of this is, we can't make any plans, so just keep doing what you normally do each day."

"We will try."

Bill hugged Sarah again and stood up. As he walked toward his study, the kids surrounded Sarah, hugging and reassuring her.

Bill reached his study, took his seat, and pulled out his cell phone. He tried to contact Bob and Marv, with no success. He didn't bother leaving a message; there was no time to wait. He eventually got through to a congressional staffer who worked for an outspoken congressman he'd seen denouncing the leaked information.

Several minutes passed while Bill was on hold. He was beginning to think he'd get a knock at the door before someone picked up the line; it felt like hours had passed.

"Bill?"

"Yes, I'm here."

"Great. I'm transferring you now."

"Excellent."

* * *

"Bill?"

"Yes"

"This is Congressman Barnett. Holly tells me that you have some information that can clear up this mess about the Archangel Initiative?"

"Yes sir, I do."

"Well, let's hear what you have to say, Bill. I can't begin to tell you what a stir this information has caused. Everything else has ground to a complete halt because of this, so I hope what you have to say can help us understand more clearly what exactly is going on here."

The congressman spoke articulately and professionally. He was known for speaking bluntly and famous for insisting people tell him what he needed to hear instead of what they thought he wanted to hear.

"Yes sir, and it's probably not going to be a popular answer."

"I honestly don't care how popular the answer is, Bill. We just want the answers."

"Understood, Congressman. Here's the reality. The Organization is real. They are a contract force that is close-hold, and I think that has been made obvious."

"Indeed, it has."

"Well, sir, that's about the only thing grounded in truth related to the information that was released."

The congressman sat up and leaned on his desk, phone in his right hand. With the other hand he spun the propeller on the Beechcraft T-6 model sitting to his left. "You mean *leaked.*"

"Well, yes, leaked. It would seem as though the rest of the information was false information with a singular purpose: a test of personnel loyalty. A select few new employees were given access to that information and left to their own devices to see what they would do with it. While most everyone passed this test, it would seem as though I failed—and miserably at that."

"So, you're the one that provided the information. Knowing it was considered classified."

"Yes sir. I could not resolve that information with the oaths I'd taken for twenty-eight years."

The congressman leaned back in his chair and spun around to look at his window.

"Wait a second. You worked with Marv, the current director of the Agency, back when he was on active duty. I've spoken with Marv about you. He recommended you for a position within the Agency. Well, he accurately summed up your personality. Always taking the moral high ground."

"That's me, sir. I've tried to do that."

The congressman spun back around, once again spinning the propeller on the model.

"I think we can work this. We can *spin* this... I need to call you back."

* * *

It seemed to Bill as though he waited days, when it was barely an hour. Sarah had checked on him several times to see if he needed anything. She had always been his rock. This was no exception to what had been the norm in their relationship. Sarah brought Bill some ice water and was about to ask him how he was doing when the phone rang.

"Hello? This is Bill."

"Bill?"

"Marv, what an...unexpected surprise." Bill was not expecting a call from Marv. He suspected Marv to be in the pocket of APEX.

"Don't get too excited. Congressman Barnett explained the situation to me, from his perspective. We've come up with a solution, but you're not going to like it."

"Why is that?"

"Well, because it means you'll be working for me again."

"I hardly see how that's a problem."

"Well, there's going to be some uncomfortable hearings in front of congressional sub-committees and maybe some interviews with the press, but we're going to try and prevent that. This means you'll keep your clearance and a job."

"I think I can deal with all of that, Marv. Just as long as we're clear of The Organization for as long as possible."

"Well, I think you know that I can't promise you anything regarding The Organization. I can tell you that every indication I have, at the moment, indicates their leadership is prepared to avoid any drastic measures. I think you understand what that means."

"Yes, I have a full understanding and appreciation for what The Organization is capable of doing. I'll take what I can get."

"I'm going to take care of the paperwork while the congressman takes care of a press release. I need you, Sarah, and the kids to prepare for what's about to happen in the media. The opposition is going to try and assassinate your character. They'll do whatever they can to further their platform. The media, of course, will do anything to boost their ratings."

"Yeah, we already had that discussion. I think we're all as prepared for that as we can be."

"All righty then. I'll get to work."

"Thanks, Marv."

"Thank you for not compromising the man I know you to be, Bill. You have always been one of the good ones. Never let that change."

"Thanks again. I'll try."

* * *

Marv held his head in his hands, not knowing whether he'd secured a temporary pardon from The Organization or secured a death warrant for himself.

* * *

Bill breathed a sigh of relief. He informed Sarah, and they shared a moment, just holding each other, before returning to the family room to update the kids. The rest of the day was spent in front of the TV, listening to the ever-changing narrative that evolved with the story. Everything from he's a hero to he's a traitor was reported, even though they didn't know who 'he' was.

Once the congressman made his official announcement, the narrative became more divisive. Those who supported the reporting of the truth and equal knowledge for all applauded, while those staunch in the belief that secrets were to be kept no matter what, attempted to crucify Bill's character. Bill, however, was at peace with it all. His priority was ensuring the safety and security of his family, and he'd accomplished that.

There were hearings after hearings, and then there were more hearings. Nothing really more than a waste of time and taxpayer dollars. But no further information was released, and it was eventually accepted that the narrative Bill explained was, in fact, the way it happened.

Three months later, Bill, Sarah, and the kids had settled in a new home in rural Virginia. It was quite a distance away from where they'd lived when he retired, but the landscape was pleasingly familiar to them. They all felt at home. Life was now about as back to normal as it ever could be, and they were happy. Bill was loving his new office at the Agency; it had a spectacular view. Although he would never be completely at ease knowing The Organization had not been dismantled.

Bill often wondered what became of the Archangels and OEM. He'd expected some distance but had hoped that he would hear from them at some point, as Michael had indicated. The Organization still needed to be dissolved, that had not changed. Bill knew that while he'd secured his family's safety, temporarily, he'd provided a perfect opportunity for The Organization to continue working in the shadows. He was certain he would be hearing from them again, at some point. He feared the waiting and not knowing.

26 What Lies Beneath

Several months later, Michael was summoned to a previously decommissioned TIACE facility. It was located in the middle of nowhere in Wyoming, very near the most remote of the decommissioned missile silos that were now little more than a forgotten relic of the Cold War. Michael was prepared to meet his maker and was fairly certain it would happen on this trip. He was not, however, prepared for what awaited him.

* * *

OEM and the other attendees of the meeting, which had been called by APEX, were already seated in the conference room. Ellynore stood at a podium and began to speak.

"Gentlemen, thank you for making the trip out here. I know this particular area of Wyoming is fairly isolated and desolate, but as I'm sure you can imagine, that makes this location perfect for us. We're waiting for one last person to arrive.

"He's just cleared the ECP. The security escort is bringing him to the conference room now."

"Thank you, Ellynore." The woman sitting at the head of the conference table spoke as she spun to face the door, as if she knew exactly when their visitor would step through.

* * *

As Michael closed the door and turned to acknowledge the other attendees, his jaw dropped. It appeared to everyone in the room as if he had seen a ghost. Most had no idea how accurate their assessment was.

"Ahh, there you are. How are you, Michael?"

"Rachel? How... How can it be? You... I saw you... You died."

"No, Michael, you saw a first-generation MIMIC get terminated. I...sorry, your wife, Rachel Prime, was completely safe in an undisclosed location. Those initial MIMICs were very good but lacked a key piece: loyalty. They were not human enough. I'm merely one of many fourth-generation MIMICs created to assist and protect APEX."

"I can't believe it's you. You just let me think—"

"Let me stop you there; *I* didn't let you think anything. Rachel did and for reasons that she will have to explain."

The MIMIC Rachel stood and walked to the conference room door. As she stood, everyone in the room did the same. Michael was looking around the room in total disbelief. The MIMIC paused at the door and turned to address Michael.

"Michael, ever the gracious person, but your humanity is limiting your vision. Let's help clear things up, shall we?"

She opened the door, and Michael gasped. Rachel Prime, dressed in tactical garb, strolled to the head of the table, stopping a few feet short of where Michael stood, his mouth agape and eyes wide.

"Please, everyone, take your seat. Michael, it is good to see you. I hope you understand there is nothing personal about any of this. When time permits, perhaps we can discuss this past few years in more detail. But we have more pressing things to discuss. I am hopeful you can return to the stable. Ellynore, continue if you please. Michael, please have a seat."

Michael slowly turned and made his way to the empty seat at the far end of the conference table. Once seated, he looked at Rachel, who was glaring at him intently. He sat shaking his head. As Ellynore began to speak, Rachel directed her attention to her.

* * *

"Good morning, everyone. Welcome to the facility. This is our new base of operations and headquarters. Until the current operation, in progress as I speak, is complete, you will all find your accommodations here. But we will get to that in a moment."

"Yes, please, Ellynore, let's get to the crux of this briefing."

"Of course, APEX. Due to the unfortunate incident in Tennessee, we've been forced to shutter all the previous Organization facilities and establish this one. This forced us to move all assets being held at the other locations to this facility. You all may remember Bill. Some of you met and worked with him, others have only seen him on TV. He was not the actual source of the leak. That leak was orchestrated by the ESP Initiative components. It was designed to filter a festering problem within our ranks. We were taken aback when we realized that the issue was far more pervasive than we initially thought. When we realized the Archangel Initiative was compromised, we'd planned to terminate the initiative and participants, but Bill changed that for us. He made it possible for us to salvage the participants. Now, some of you in this room were willing participants in the evolving stages of a coup against APEX. You're probably wondering how they know this. Why am I saying all of this when I, myself, was a willing participant? That's simple; APEX monitored the entire situation from the beginning. There was nothing that occurred that she was unaware of before it happened. It was her idea to introduce Bill to TWM. It was her idea to feed to framework code to Saraqael. It was her idea to leak the information... Every aspect of the super-secretive plan to dismantle The Organization...it all came from APEX. Including recruitment of ESP to assist with the coup."

Ellynore smirked as she had described how everything had been scripted by APEX. Rachel smiled, her narcissistic character clearly evident.

"Thank you, Ellynore. Yes, I became quite the puppeteer. I've been pulling the strings to all of you for a long time. And we are exactly where we need to be. I'm sure this seems almost incomprehensible, possibly quite sadistic, but I assure you it is not. Please continue, Ellynore."

"Gladly. While what we've revealed to this point may not seem sadistic. What I have to share with you next may well be considered that way. Please turn your attention to the monitors. What you're looking at is a live feed from several levels below us. I'm sure you can recognize those individuals. They started out as an insurance policy in the event a certain someone didn't want to cooperate. It was not without great fortuity that we initiated that insurance policy."

Michael sprang from his seat, placed his palms on the table, and made an audible grunt. He turned to Rachel and fearfully asked, "APEX, what do you intend to do with them?"

"That all depends, Michael."

"Depends? Depends on what?"

"Whether or not you can convince Bill to be our inside guy at the Agency."

"I don't see how that can help. What are we going to gain from that?"

Rachel stood and matched Michael's pose, intently staring into his eyes with a malevolent glare.

"Not your concern. What *is* your concern, Michael? Getting Bill back on board with us."

"I'm not sure that's going to be feasible given his current position."

"Nothing is impossible, with appropriate motivation. And, well, just look...there is said motivation"

"APEX... Rachel, please?" Michael pleaded.

"Michael, you have work to do. No time like the present to get started."

Rachel stood and began walking toward the door, OEM in tow.

"But I have no contacts to get to him legitimately."

"I'll take care of that."

"Fine. I'll do whatever you want, please just don't..."

Rachel paused and turned to Michael.

"Don't what, Michael? Oh, don't worry. Sarah, the kids, and *the others* will continue to nap in the basement, at least until we need them."

Here's a sneak peek from the next installment of Dark Recesses...

Birth of an Archangel

The microwave beeped. Rachel grabbed the popcorn, emptied it into a bowl, and doused it with butter and seasoning salt. Michael grabbed the bottle of soda from the fridge and poured two wine glasses nearly to the brim. They made their way to the sofa to settle in for a night of watching movies in their pajamas. Just the two of them.

Rachel raised her glass and turned to Michael.

"Happy anniversary, handsome!"

"Ugh, you beat me to it. Happy anniversary, sweetheart! Thank you for the best ten years of my life." Michael responded as he raised his glass to Rachel's.

"It's hard to believe it's been ten years already. Where does the time go?"

"I don't know, but it does go fast."

Rachel's work phone rang.

"Seriously?"

She initially ignored it, but when it rang a second, then a third time, she knew something was not right.

"I'm off tonight...stop calling me." Rachel said in a frustrated tone.

When it rang a fourth time, Michael suggested she answer, which she did.

"Hello?"

"Rachel, thank God! We have a situation." A troubled voice spoke, wavering and seemingly fearful.

"What kind of situation? What's going on Deb?"

"A bunch of government guys showed up with a warrant. They're collecting all our files and IT equipment. They shoved Mary to the floor and now she's bleeding. I don't know what to do."

"Bleeding?"

"Yeah. She, um, she hit her head. hit a desk. She's got a nasty looking cut. Tried to call 911 but it was busy. Why? How can 911 be busy. Rachel, they're taking everything. You need to be here. Where are you? Rachel? I'm scared."

Rachel was trying to make sense of the frantic call. Her mind was racing. Deb was a mentally strong individual. Her frantic call unnerved Rachel.

"This makes no sense. I'm on my way." Rachel responded as the call disconnected.

"Hello? Deb?"

Rachel turned to Michael, tears welling in her eyes.

"Michael, we have to go."

"What's going on Rachel? What did Deb say?"

"Some government guys showed up, started taking everything and pushed Mary down. She hit a desk or something and it put a gash in her head. Michael, we need to go and straighten it out. Whatever it is that's going on"

"That doesn't make any sense. Let's get changed and head over. Hopefully, it's just a misunderstanding."

"I hope so."

They quickly changed and grabbed their identification. It was a fifteen-minute drive, but Michael would make it in ten. The Arturo Institute employed Rachel and Michael. Rachel as a biochemical and biomechanical engineer, and Michael as the head of site security. She was hired as the lead engineer for the Advanced, Programmable Extremities project. The institute was focused on providing advanced prosthetics to improve the quality of life for disabled veterans. The funding for the project was provided by TIACE.

Once they arrived, they were greeted by several men. They were all dressed in distinctively marked black tactical gear, carrying automatic weapons. Three men began walking directly toward their vehicle, weapons leveled and laser lights dancing across the torso and face of Rachel and Michael.

"Get out of the vehicle and keep your hands where we can see them." The man in the lead shouted.

Michael slowly moved his hand from the steering wheel and placed it on Rachels forearm. He spoke calmly, yet firmly.

"Do as they say, Rachel. I've seen these guys in action before, and they don't ask twice. No sudden movements and obey every instruction."

"Who are they? What's going on?"

"They're particularly nasty defense contractors...former spec ops. I don't know, but it's not good."

They both complied with the instructions given and were immediately searched, placed in restraints, and led inside at gunpoint. It appeared clear the scene had been very chaotic. Windows lay shatters in thousands of small fragments. A few of the on-duty employees were bound with black hoods over their heads, all seated against the exterior wall. Rachel knew that wasn't all of the staff, which stoked her fear.

Michael was studying every detail. He noted the movements and actions of the operators. The steady stream of boxes and IT equipment being hauled out of the building told him this group was meticulous. The condition and position of the employees was something he'd only seen in combat. He was fairly certain there would be no witnesses left behind.

Once inside, it became clear to them that everything, they'd worked on in the past several years was being taken.

A portly man with soulless eyes glared at the couple as they drew closer. He shook his head and tipped the black cowboy hat backward before speaking to them.

"I can see you're upset...and you're pissed off. Word to the wise: Don't try to be a cowboy; it will not end well."

"Who are you?"

"I'm the one you've been doing all this research for, Rachel. I'm APEX."

"Then why are you doing this? All you had to do was ask, or tell us to send all this to you. Why are you doing all this?"

"Well, Rachel, truth be told...because of your poor decisions." Rachel's facial expression turned from shock to fury.

"What? What the fuck are you talking about? I've only, ever done what I was asked to do. I don't understand."

"Very clear direction was given to everyone working here, and on several occasions, to the person in charge, which is you. That direction was to not publish or share any information, regardless of the classification with anyone. Yet you chose to share some information that, while not classified, was rather sensitive, in my opinion. That opinion, at the end of the day, is the only one that really matters."

"I answered to that several weeks ago. I apologized and said that I misunderstood the direction. I also said very clearly that it would never happen again. I have not sent anything since then, nor will I. So, what the hell is this about?"

"No, *you* haven't, but three of your employees did."

"What? Who?"

"Look no further than those black bags."

Rachel and Michael turned to look over their shoulder to the corner where APEX had pointed. They saw three black body bags piled against the wall. Michael could only close his eyes and shake his head, while Rachel immediately vomited. She wiped her mouth and turned to face APEX.

"You son of a bitch!" Rachel said as she attempted to lunge toward APEX. The operator standing next to her, grabbed her arm and quickly pulled her back while forcing his foot into the back of her knee joint. She immediately fell to the ground and into her own vomit.

It was becoming clear to Michael that his may be their last moments on earth.

"That is...just...disgusting. Weak stomach...appalling. Get her a towel or something...and some water." APEX said as he turned to a female standing near him. She appeared to be his second in command, as she was directing most of the activities as APEX addressed Rachel and Michael directly.

"I can see you're upset. I'm truly sorry it has to be done this way, but we cannot tolerate leaks. It's espionage, you know."

Michael turned to Rachel and looked the man guarding her directly in the eyes.

"Could you at least help her back to her feet?"

The man looked to APEX, who nodded in approval, before helping Rachel to her feet. Michael leaned toward Rachel, and spoke calmly, almost whispering.

"Sweetheart? I don't think this is going to end well for us. I need you to know that you are my one and only. I love you more!"

Tears began to slowly make their way down her cheeks as she responded.

"I know...I love you more!"

As they turned their attention back to APEX, he resumed speaking.

"How...*touching.*

Where was I? Aah yes, as you are aware, that incurs a punishment up to and including death. Rather obvious, I suppose, given those bags. It didn't have to be that way. They resisted the urge to be truthful. They told blatant lies when confronted with the truth...irrefutable truth, and...well, there you have it. So, as I was saying about a word to the wise, weigh your options carefully, and consider this. You will not end quickly.

I will take my time with you...both of you. And, well, I'll just put it out there.

I'll take my time with your precious little girls, before I get around to you two. No need to ask what I mean by that...I can see that you want to ask...you'll be right there. Believe me...You won't miss a thing."

Acknowledgements

Heather thank you for the kick in the pants to write this. Who knew that *"...Just throw up on the paper, let the story write itself...you can clean it up later..."* was just what I needed to hear?

Kim thank you for donating your time to reading the first draft, your feedback, the introduction to Tracy, and your continued support.

Laura thank you for donating your time reading this, which I know is in precious short supply for such a busy human. You continue to inspire me with your faith and perseverance.

The Red Quill Editing, LLC team, Ekatarina Sayanova, Rebecca Cartee, and Tracy Damron-Roelle. Thank you for your sage-like constructive criticism, feedback, and general guidance. This book would have been a hot mess without you.

Sarah Barre Harrison, thank you for designing the amazing cover art, and helping me out with the formatting.

The fans and all who have supported this work!
Thank you!!!

Last, but certainly not least. My children. This life would not be worth living if not for you. You are my heart! You and your significant others bring me great joy. I hope I have and can continue to repay that in some small way. I love you more!

www.ingramcontent.com/pod-product-compliance
Lightning Source LLC
Chambersburg PA
CBHW071641260626
47170CB00001B/187